ARNAV BHARDWAJ

The Bird That Ruled Bombay

First edition

ISBN: 978-1-7381394-0-8

This book was professionally typeset on Reedsy.
Find out more at reedsy.com

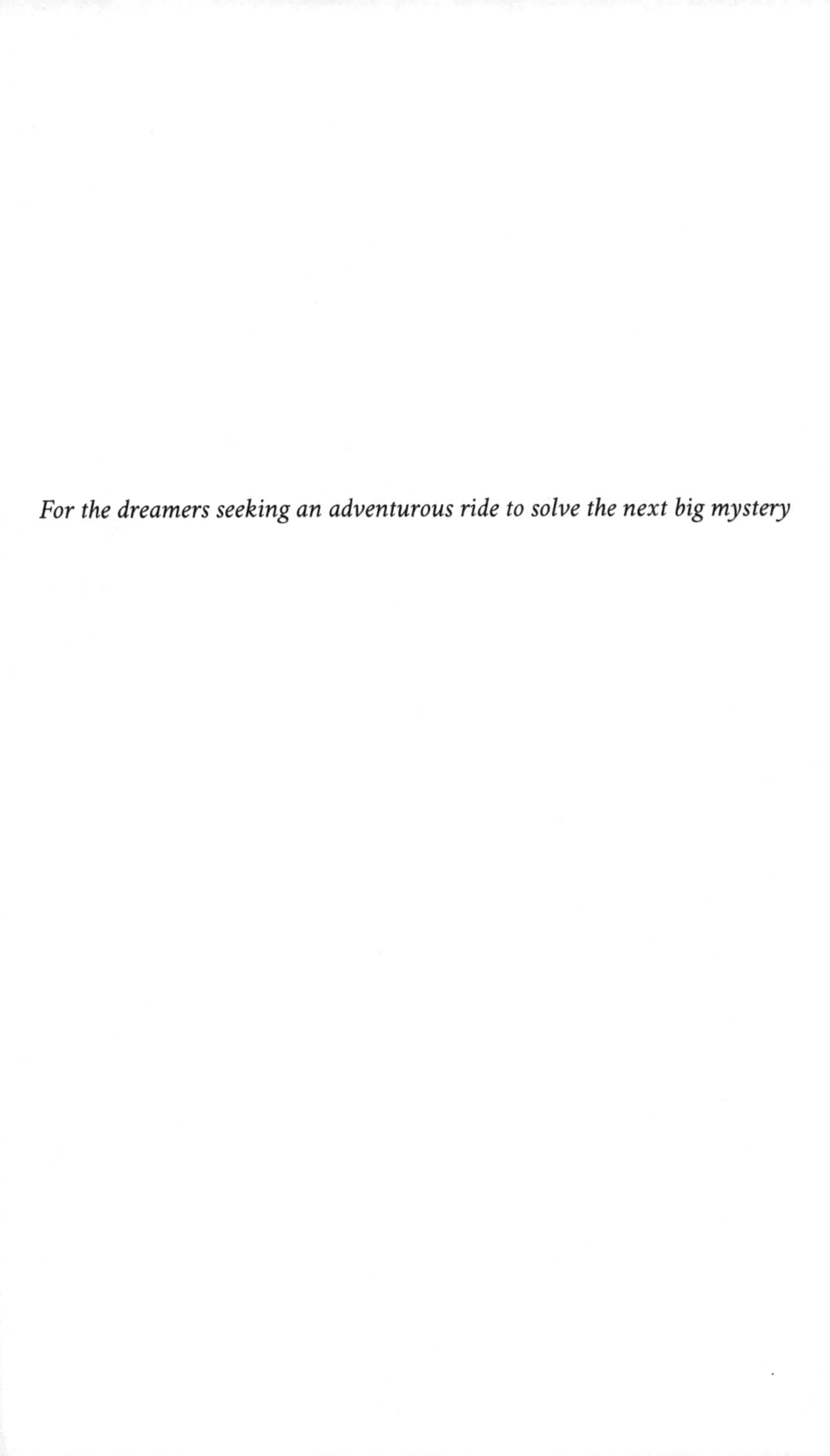

For the dreamers seeking an adventurous ride to solve the next big mystery

"If you cry in the forest,
nobody hears your wails"

- INDIAN PROVERB

Contents

CHAPTER 1

THE MAGNANIMOUS MONKEYS OF MUMBAI

The motivation to stay healthy might have been sufficient to prompt the dozens of young joggers, sporting trendy headgear and tracksuits, as they sped past Samantha on the walking trail in Mumbai's Sanjay Gandhi National Park. However, that wasn't the case with Samantha, whose biggest streak of attending the gym hadn't lasted more than three days with the best of commitments. This was probably because she felt betrayed by the vagaries of life, which had taught her how the most unfortunate circumstances could occur even in perfect health.

One of her neighbours, Karan, was a professor of behavioural economics at the University of Mumbai. On hearing about her condition, he had advised her,

"Nudge is a common concept used in behavioural economics to subconsciously entice people to act in specific desired ways. Some Swedish cities use stairs installed with giant piano keys to encourage people to climb stairs instead of using the escalator. Beer yoga is a newly developed hybrid form of yoga, during which people drink beer glasses after every hour of yoga practice. People, who are fond of dancing, attend ballet or kathak classes to keep themselves fit. In all these cases, people are linking their fitness regimes to something that they are fond of like dancing, drinking or music in order to compel themselves to stay healthy. If the gym doesn't look enticing enough, you should seek fitness activities elsewhere."

So here she was as she sped in her newly bought white track shoes on the long dusty Gaumukh trail. The trail led to the historical Kanheri caves, which possessed paintings and inscriptions dating back as far as to 100 AD. As a history buff, who spent most of her childhood around magnificent historical forts and palaces in the Indian state of Rajasthan, the opportunity to revisit a bygone era inspired her. The occasional gust of wind blew her long brown hair, which swayed from side to side as she struggled to tie them. The morning sun was glowing brighter with time, causing the summer heat to become more unbearable. She took off her jacket to wipe her dust-laden glasses before tying it around her waist and resuming the uphill climb.

As she strutted past the dense cluster of banyan trees with dangling aerial roots, she spotted a peacock nestled amongst the intertwined branches of the canopy. Its green feathery tail almost camouflaged it but its bright blue body stood out prominently amidst the slender green leaves. On a rainy day, one could have observed the peacock in full colour while it spread out its bronze and green tail plumage in an arc over its head. However, on that day, the peacock was only interested in seeking recluse amongst the spooky dangling roots of the tree, which hung from the leafy treetop like a giant octopus's tentacles. The extreme heat and strenuous jogging had begun to wear her out and she wondered if there was a bench nearby. As she scrambled for the water bottle on her back, she realized that she had forgotten it at her home. Disappointed, she decided to walk until she could meet another person to ask for water or arrive at a resting spot.

After another half a mile of walking, she heard the gurgling sound of water. A scent of wet soil wafted through the air. She was about to reach out for the map in the pocket of her bag when the whistling thrush, perched atop the wooden signboard, grabbed her attention with its piercing sound. The signboard read in bold letters - ' MINI WATERFALL 200 m AHEAD '.

After walking a few steps ahead, she spotted the distinct logo of a canteen as the forested region gave way to a grassy clearing. She could hear voices of loud chatter as she approached the canteen and was surprised when she noticed only a handful of people sitting inside. Apparently, some interesting turn of events had taken place and a group of excited teenagers didn't mind airing their gossip aloud for everyone to hear.

"Did you hear about the supernatural expert, who claimed to have seen a dead man's spirit in the park?"

"Yes. I am sure that he will claim to have a magical trinket to ward it off next, which he will sell at exorbitant prices"

The last comment was met by roaring laughter. Samantha sat down to have her ordered cold coffee in peace at the bench outside the canteen. The elevated hill offered a glimpse of Mumbai's skyscrapers in the background, which were partially shrouded by the dense vegetation on the hill.

"Samantha, is that you? I wasn't expecting you here!"

Samantha turned back to see the tall and burly silhouette of her neighbour, Karan Ghosh, who was descending the deodar tree-laden slope of the hill and waving to her. As he emerged from the shadows of the trees, the glaring sun brightened up his gleaming face with long and wavy hair hung till the shoulders. Even though he was currently a professor of behavioural economics, he had been initially drawn to the entertainment hubs of Mumbai and not its academic circles. According to popular narratives, regular rejections in acting auditions had forced him to think otherwise but he still surreptitiously sneaked away to act in stage plays on the weekends with the hope that his costumes would conceal his second identity to a possible colleague or student in the audience.

"Quite a coincidence running into you here! Actually, it was your advice, which prompted me on this arduous trek," exclaimed Samantha with tones of shock and pleasant surprise.

"I see. So, is the passionate history teacher chasing her fascination with the past?"

"Yes, I am. The Kanheri caves have some really intriguing inscriptions and elaborate carvings. As a history buff, I am not sure why I never visited this place earlier in all the years that I have been living in Mumbai. In retrospect, it might have been family duties, which kept me busy."

"I am so sorry for your loss. I think…"

"John and Rick may still be alive but the world cannot stop offering condolences. I am sick of people making convenient assumptions for themselves and stifling my hopes. Nobody has the right to…"

John and Rick were Samantha's husband and fifteen-year-old son respectively. While embarking on their vacation trip to South Africa two months back, their flight had been hijacked by terrorists. According to testimonies, the hijackers had been eventually overpowered by the onboard passengers but not before the hijackers killed the pilot. The crew had managed to help some of the passengers escape in parachutes and life jackets as the aeroplane began to crash into the Arabian sea. After an hour of failed communication with the aircraft, these few drifting lucky survivors had been flown back by rescue aircraft to the nearest shore of an island in the Lakshadweep archipelago. However, there was no sign of John and Rick even though search parties repeatedly scoured the area for dead bodies or survivors. Most people believed that they had sunk to the bottom of the ocean like the aircraft, which was also nowhere to be found.

Karan had not anticipated such an unnerving outburst and he gathered himself to make amends immediately.

"I sincerely apologize. I didn't intend to hurt you. It was wrong of me to assume the worst. I am sure both of them are in a safe place and will contact you shortly. The rest of the passengers went on to survive and there is no reason to believe that your husband and son could not have escaped."

The wrathful expression on Samantha's face instantly changed to a sombre one. After a moment of contemplation, she asked as a gleam of hope flashed in her eyes,

"Do you actually believe that?"

Even though Karan's initial statement had made it clear that he didn't, Samantha didn't mind some external validation to her optimism, which was weakening with every passing day.

"Wasn't John a pilot before he opened his restaurant chain in Mumbai? The aircraft is also missing."

"Are you suggesting that he piloted the aircraft and flew away? I was pondering over that possibility too. It seems strange that we haven't received any communication if that's true."

Their conversation was interrupted by a loud shriek from one of the loudly gossiping boys near the food stall. As they turned their eyes towards the scene, they noticed that one of the boys had slipped on the ground. A soft drink can, apparently slipped from the boy's hands, rolled on the stone-paved ground towards them. As Samantha walked towards it to fetch it for the boys, she heard a series of screeches. They seemed to be coming from the branches of the deodar tree.

"Samantha, look out!" yelled Karan as he ran towards her.

As Samantha looked around in confusion, a noisy monkey descended from the tree and swiftly leaped towards her. She let out a scream and stepped back but the fear had almost frozen her. She remembered something John had told her once -

"Monkeys can see through a person's vulnerability. If you display signs of weakness like running away or screaming, they are more likely to attack you. Never try to run away from a monkey unless you want to be bitten

and get rabies"

As the monkey gnashed its teeth as it sped towards her, she tried to justify her inability to move with this advice even though she knew that she was subconsciously shifting the blame in case her first fitness endeavour culminated in stitches at the hospital.

The rolling can slowed to a halt at Samantha's feet, who was shivering in fear. The curious monkey promptly picked up the can and sniffed it before running back to the tree.

"It was after the can. Why didn't you move away though?"

Samantha recuperated from the shock and turned back to see Karan running frantically towards her with a broom in his hands.

"Were you planning to fight the entire troop of monkeys with that broom?" she chuckled as she pointed to more monkeys, which had descended to share the spoils of war. There seemed to be a whole family congregation - the mother with an infant clung to her back, the plump grandfather with a grey tuft on his head, agile and noisy youngsters and the grumpy uncle, who disapproved of its taste and tossed away the can in a fit of rage, bringing the exciting turn of events to an end.

"John had advised me once about not running away from a monkey, due to which I stopped in my tracks. He used to believe in some rather peculiar and unscientific beliefs," she continued in a tone, marked by strong disapproval.

Karan was stunned. A few minutes earlier, he had been the subject of intense lashing because he merely suggested the possibility of John's death. Now, Samantha was openly criticizing her husband, who was most likely deceased. On realizing how her impulsive outburst had led to an awkward situation, she hastily added,

"He was quite funny in that sense. When a black cat crossed the path in front of us one day, he picked up a rock and flung it across so that the bad luck befell the rock and not us. I and Rick laughed all day about it."

"To be fair, I think that he was actually right about monkeys. Monkeys are actually known to adhere to a strong social hierarchy. They see the act of running away as one of submission, which makes them more aggressive and violent."

Samantha felt the need to divert the topic to avoid any more awkwardness. She remembered the signboard mentioning a mini-waterfall, which had directed her there in the first place.

"Karan, I heard that there is a mini-waterfall nearby. I even heard a mild gushing of water when I was approaching this place. Where is it?"

"It is actually visible from the elevated mound over there. In fact, I was observing the waterfall from there when I spotted you around the canteen below. Do you want to catch a glimpse of it? We can head to the Kanheri caves together after it."

"That sounds like a great plan," replied Samantha with a broad smile.

Even though she usually appreciated the calmness of nature, the silence of the forest was beginning to freak her out. Her urban lifestyle in metropolitan Mumbai caused her to be habitually exposed to the sounds of cars and humans, due to which the silent environment appeared alien and almost eerie. Having a companion on the remaining part of the trek was an effective way to alleviate the disturbance caused by the creepy silence.

"I think I chose to be deluded by the mini tag for a moment and actually conjured up a breathtaking waterfall falling over a cliff.," remarked Samantha as she peered down at the gurgling water, which spilled from the trough into a larger circular pool.

"Well, it is an artificial installment, which is meant to act as a drinking pool for the local birds and enliven tourists with their sights and sounds."

"You are right. It doesn't look that disappointing now.," she said, pointing to the newly-arrived bright green parrot, which intermittently wobbled and dipped its red beak into the water.

"Do you know where I have witnessed the most magnificent waterfall in my life?" said Karan. "It is in South Africa's Royal Natal National Park. Tugela falls is the second largest waterfall in the world and there have even been significant recent claims that it is actually the world's tallest."

"I wanted to visit South Africa with John and Rick too but..."

"But what, Samantha?"

"I think that I should tell you. It doesn't seem right to hide it from a close friend like you, who has generously helped me in the most turbulent of times. I and John were planning to get divorced before he embarked to South Africa with Rick. We had mutually agreed that I would get custody of Rick since John's business required him to travel across the country, which would have disrupted Rick's school education. Yet, I didn't want Rick to think that he would be eternally separated from his father and get very emotionally disturbed. So, I had proposed to both of them to spend a vacation together to lighten up the issue."

"This comes as a shock since I never felt that you and John didn't get along. Of course, both of you must have had your reasons. I am quite impressed by the way in which both of you strove to handle this delicate issue maturely."

"I thought so too until that unfortunate day."

The heat had ebbed as the afternoon approached. The remaining walk didn't seem that dreary as the chirping sounds of nightingales and sparrows reverberated throughout the forest. Most importantly, Karan and Samantha had found solace in companionship as they trampled the fallen autumn leaves, occasionally scaring the squirrels crossing the road. As they approached the canteen area, they saw the playful monkeys again, which were still prancing around the tree.

Karan said, "Samantha, I have a speculation, which I sincerely hope is not true but it makes reasonable sense to believe it."

"What would that be?"

"Do you look at that monkey, which has the infant clung to her, swiftly climbing the tree as if it is escaping?"

"What are you implying?"

"Could it be possible that John escaped from the accident but isn't contacting you because he doesn't want to give up Rick?"

There was a moment of stunned silence. Both looked at each other expressionlessly, hoping that the other would initiate an effort to break the silence. A group of cuckoos flew in unison from the tree, creating a loud fluttering sound.

"That would be a very treacherous and inhumane act. I was planning to separate from him because of certain issues but I still think that he was a nice man. I would rather believe that he is dead than believe that he abducted my son."

"I am really sorry to have crossed the line on this one. I hope you understand that I didn't mean to offend you but rather…"

"I get what you were trying to do, Karan. You have been a great friend and I do not doubt your intentions. Can we avoid this topic for today though and resume our walk to the Kanheri caves? It has been a great day. Let us not ruin it with disturbing conversations."

"Sure, we can. Let us forget whatever just transpired and resume this merry trip."

Samantha smiled and gestured to him to walk by pointing her hand towards the exit gate from the canteen area.

"Wait a minute!" said Karan. "I left my bag near the waterfall. Let me fetch it and return in a jiffy." As he sped off towards the grassy mound, his shirt fluttered due to the strong wind. The mother monkey on the tree branch began to howl loudly, causing a few of the playful monkeys below to stand on their toes and peer around as if in confusion. The mother monkey made another high-pitched shriek, which was louder than the last. The final call immediately caught the attention of all the monkeys, which immediately took notice and hurriedly scrambled up the tree.

Meanwhile, Samantha stood on the concrete path, which looked increasingly desolate as the strong dust-laden winds caused humans and animals alike to seek refuge beneath trees and ceilings. The bright sunshine had given way to shadiness as the sun got obscured from view. It had been ten minutes since Karan had left and Samantha grew increasingly uneasy with the shady loneliness, which had returned to haunt her. All sorts of wild thoughts crossed her mind.

Have I offended him? Has he abandoned me and fled somewhere? I should seriously think before I speak. Seems like I have lost another well-meaning friend of mine with my senseless and apathetic conversation.

As the growing insecurity gripped her, she imagined the worst scenarios and blamed herself for them. She raised her hand and glanced at her watch again. Fifteen minutes had passed since Karan had left. As the wind began to recede, revealing the sun again, she had a sudden epiphany.

She stood beside the only exit gate from the canteen area. Karan couldn't have possibly crossed the surrounding high walls or climbed the rocky hills to get away from her.

Samantha ran swiftly towards the grassy mound. Sweat trickled down her forehead but the weariness didn't slow her down. The gushing sound grew louder as she approached the waterfall. As she looked down from the elevated mound, she observed that the erstwhile clear water in the pool had acquired a reddish tinge. When she moved her head towards the edge of the pool, she noticed Karan's head, which had been dunked into the water. He laid flat with his head and hands immersed in the water while the rest of his body outside the pool supported him. Bloody ripples and bubbles emanated from the water around his head as Samantha quickly pulled it out from under the water. Samantha's hands trembled as she brought them closer to Karan's nose to check for signs of breath.

CHAPTER 2

HISTORY LECTURE AT MONTE HIGH SCHOOL

The half-eaten vada pav stood out in the backdrop of the framed family photograph. The apparent stress on Samantha's face had been manipulatively concealed from the observant eyes of her fellow teachers. The pile of uniformly-sized student notebooks on the left intermittently declined in height as a notebook was pulled from the top, checked and tossed to the right. Her grief in the past months had driven her to develop the motto - *If your mind isn't productive, put it to mundane tasks instead of wasting time.* The mundane task at that moment was checking examination quizzes. Meanwhile, the neatly-stacked encyclopaedias and research papers on the shelf waited in anticipation. This routine was interrupted by the occasional SMS notification, which immediately caught Samantha's attention for a second or two.

In stark contrast to the gloomy scenes on Samantha's desk, the regular lunchtime gossip sessions were in full swing as evident from the loud chatter of teachers and the distinctive smell of vegetables in the staff room. The staff room was a chamber of secrets in its own right as teachers unlocked more personal angles to their lives.

"Samantha, why don't you relax and eat with us for a while? You have been working since morning.," beckoned her friend, Ms. Madhvi

Sharma, from the dining table in the center of the staff room.

"Of course, Madhvi. I could take a break from this mundane examination checking," she replied as she swerved back in her chair.

The jolliness and concern in Madhvi's invitation was too rude to refuse, even in those distressing times.

"Samantha, you seem rather stressed from the checking. On the other hand, your face lights up whenever I see you researching papers and encyclopaedias to prepare for your next lecture. Have you ever considered becoming a professor at a university? You will be able to devote much more time to research in that role."

"As a matter of fact, I was indeed considering a career switch a few months ago. However, most professorship positions require more advanced qualifications. Considering the time investment in higher studies, I was postponing it for a few more years until Rick grew up. Now, I don't know."

The conversation was abruptly broken as the Principal, Dr. Matthew, entered the staff room and announced in a deep voice,

"I am sorry to announce this but the school will have to reschedule the student-teacher excursion to Sanjay Gandhi National Park. Considering how everyone was so genuinely excited about the trip,

I know that this comes across as a disappointing decision. Unfortunately, the park administration has closed the park temporarily, owing to the recent accident of a man within the premises."

"What kind of an accident would prompt the park administration to take such a drastic measure?" asked Mr. Patar, the teacher of fine arts.

"The victim is a professor of behavioural economics at the University of Mumbai. He was found severely injured near a waterfall installation with his head drowned in the pool. The injuries have raised suspicion that a leopard might be roaming freely, waiting to attack its next victim. Therefore, the entire park is being scoured for leopards or any other possible predators to ensure the safety of the park visitors."

Samantha felt clearly awkward as she saw her attempts at distracting her mind from the tragic incident ending in vain.

"I have visited the Sanjay Gandhi National Park at least five times now," commented one of the teachers. "I haven't seen a leopard there even once. Occasionally, the safari guide will try to bring in some excitement by pointing to howling monkeys and claiming that the howls are alerts of a predator in the vicinity. You expect to see a leopard spring up from the bushes but nothing ever actually happens."

Samantha remembered the constant howling and subsequent flight of scared monkeys on her walk earlier. The chain of events made more sense now.

"I don't understand. Why would a leopard attack a human but not eat it?" chimed another visibly disappointed teacher.

Samantha felt the urge to reveal her relationship to the incident and the victim but the thought of being bombarded by incessant queries quietened her.

"I am sure the park administration has its own reasons for closing the park.," said Dr. Mathews. "We can't really risk the safety of our students or convince the park administration. Why don't we settle on another place for our excursion?"

"Let us visit the Byculla zoo instead. We will still get to observe wild animals," suggested a teacher.

"I think we should give up our obsession with animals and, instead, visit a historical monument like the Gateway of India. What do you say, Samantha?" said Madhvi.

Samantha was too happily absorbed in her own world to respond to Madhvi. She softly read the message to herself again-

"While he is still unconscious, Karan is responding well to treatments and is out of danger now."

* * *

"Do you think that Akbar would have stood any chance against Hemu at the First Battle of Panipat if his artillery hadn't been stolen from him just before the battle?", chirped in a voice from the back of the class.

They were almost at the end of the history lecture and Samantha was pleasantly surprised to hear a question. While she used to expect such inquisitiveness from a broader audience earlier, the enthusiasm of that single student seemed enough to justify her decision to teach history to a bunch of uninterested school students those days. She answered,

"As students of history, we don't generally look at it through a speculative lens since one can practically conjure up any chain of events to subvert what actually happened. While there are speculations that Hemu could have emerged victorious if he had been able to deploy artillery during the battle, we have no actual way of knowing what could have transpired if a few events in the whole chain were tweaked. Therefore, we derive conclusions from what actually happened and not what could have happened due to the unreliability of the latter."

As a teacher of history at Monte High School, Samantha wasn't particularly used to enthusiastic students in her class. History wasn't a popular subject amongst the students, who were keener on studying subjects like mathematics and computer science to grab lucrative high-paying jobs in the technological hubs of Bangalore or Mumbai. The promises of the technological revolution had ushered in new hopes and aspirations of a better future. The technological boom was rewarding for economic growth but detrimental for teachers like Samantha, who found it increasingly difficult to entice students into lively class discussions or even simply paying attention to what was being taught.

The bell rang to announce the end of the day. The students, many of whom had spent the entire lecture twiddling with pens, began to pack their bags. Aman Gill was different though. The lecture had piqued his interest in medieval Indian history and almost led him to an epiphany. Had it not been for his almost royal upbringing, which had endowed him with all the courtesies and social graces of the perfect gentleman, he would have yelled out 'Eureka' loud in the middle of the lecture.

"Ma'am, I just had an interesting idea. Do you mind discussing it now?"

As she collected her register from the drawer, Samantha peered up to see Aman shining his sparkling white teeth as he broke into an enthusiastic smile. Aman was a lanky boy, whose every attempt to gain weight through dietary changes and exercise had ended in vain. Unlike Samantha, who had given up on the idea of a healthy lifestyle, he was still persistent in his efforts to gain a few pounds before meeting his family during the summer break. As the thinnest boy among three generations of a plump and affluent family, he was a subject of surprise and even mild disappointment for his family, who otherwise were very proud of his academic brilliance.

Samantha was exhausted but the prospect of another stimulating discussion was too invigorating to refuse. She smiled back at Aman and said, "Yes, I would like to. But I am famished at the moment. I am headed to the canteen. Let us discuss this over lunch."

The canteen, a recent addition to the school, consisted of a small seating space alongside an open kitchen with a counter. The space was decked with colourful chairs and tables, which stood out prominently in the backdrop of the makeshift gray partitioning walls. The potpourri of vibrant colours in the furniture could be attributed to their past origins in the kindergarten classrooms, which had recently been discontinued to divert more focus towards higher classes.

The newfound craze for engineering had opened great economic opportunities for private high schools, which now fiercely jostled to get the brightest names adorned on their achievement billboards.

Monte High School was no different as evident from the countless flashy posters for programming workshops on the notice board besides the counter.

As Samantha and Aman entered the canteen, a fragrance of steamed vegetables infused with the smell of fresh paint wafted through the air.

"What will you have, Aman?" Samantha asked as she scrambled for cash in her wallet.

"Thank you, Ma'am but I am not hungry"

"Stop shying, Aman. I have told you often and am reiterating that I am like your mother away from home. It is similar to how you youngsters refer to your friends as 'brothers or sisters from other mothers'," she winked.

"Well, I guess that I will have my regular samosas and lemon soda in that case."

"Now that's my boy!"

Considering that the students had left for the day, the canteen was occupied mostly by teachers staying after school hours to perform extra duties like checking examinations or discussing upcoming events.

"So, what grand unified theory of computer science and history are we talking about today?" grinned Samantha as she crossed her fingers in anticipation at the table.

Aman said, "When you were talking about the factors that would have to be tweaked in order to bring about any change in an historical outcome, this led me to think of an idea."

"What would that idea be?" said Samantha.

At that moment, the waiter arrived and placed the glasses of lemon soda cautiously on the table. After taking only a sip, Aman continued before he forgot his idea,

"We often rely on old artifacts and manuscripts to understand what happened in the past. Unfortunately, such hard physical evidence isn't always available, leaving missing pieces in the puzzle of historical events. That's where artificial intelligence can play a major role by filling those information gaps with reasonable estimates."

"Data science and artificial intelligence are certainly the future. I am intrigued. Tell me more."

"We could create a model that looks at the data of historical events for which complete information is available. The model can find patterns within this data and calculate reasonable estimates for incomplete details about other lesser understood historical events."

"If I understand you correctly, the model can try to explain why something happened in history based on the factors that shaped its outcome. The model can probably learn how much an army's size or type of weapons influences the victory outcome of a battle. By learning these patterns, it can predict the outcome of a battle whose victor is unknown."

"Precisely," said Aman with a mix of admiration and disbelief at how quickly she grasped his idea.

Samantha had a sort of Pavlovian aversion to technology, which had been induced by the constant disinterest of aspiring engineers and scientists in her history classes. She wasn't too keen on adopting the technological ways of the modern world and still preferred the idea of skimming through piles of textbooks for an answer instead of searching for it online. Despite that, discussions with Aman were gradually opening her eyes to the opportunities offered by marrying science and technology to history. Her distrust and skepticism of technology was fading slowly step by step. The remnant distrust was probably the reason that the idea of searching for the contact number of a nearby hospital online struck the canteen owner earlier than Samantha, who got overcome by panic and cluelessness upon seeing Karan's unconscious body.

"I couldn't have explained it better myself," remarked Aman.

"Of course, you couldn't have, dear! I have devoted more years to teaching than your entire life.", she chuckled teasingly.

"Come on! I am not that young. I hope you remember that I am actually not studying in high school anymore.," replied Aman with a cheeky smile.

An ecstatic call was heard from behind.

"Of course, you are not. Aren't you the boy who graduated from high school last year with the highest marks in computer science?"

Aman turned around to see his high school computer science teacher, Ms. Madhvi Sharma.

"I guess that is me. Why don't you join us for lunch?" beckoned Aman as he pulled out a chair for her.

After joining the table, she said, "I remember that you went on to study computer science at the Indian Institute of Technology Bombay. What brings you back to school?"

"I have been taking history lessons from Samantha Ma'am. Since the commencement of my first year last week, I have been rethinking my whole decision to pursue a career in software development. Reading some non-fiction books piqued my interest in history. I wanted to explore it in an academic setting before making a final decision. She had taught one of my friends, who graduated with a minor in history from Delhi University. My friend recommended me to take a few lessons from her. The school has been gracious in allowing me to attend her classes."

"That's great. Dropping out would be a drastic move indeed and should be taken only with due consideration. So, how do you find my favourite student, Samantha?"

"He is a wonderful student indeed. He has a great eye for detail and analysis. He looks at history through a novel perspective, which is only possible because of his technical background. I don't think his passion for history has to be at loggerheads with his proficiency in programming. The answer perhaps lies somewhere in the middle. He could use his technical proficiency to pioneer a new kind of history research."

"I couldn't agree more. 'Interdisciplinary' is the new buzzword these days. You can combine the expertise and knowledge of various disciplines to develop comprehensive and effective solutions," chimed in Ms. Sharma.

"Seems like you are in luck," said Samantha. "Look at the poster being posted on the notice board." She pointed her index finger at the board.

As Aman and Madhvi turned their eyes in that direction, they saw the clerk pinning a bright red notice with white and black text. The heading in the center read in capital bold letters - "NATIONAL TECHNOLOGY FOR HISTORY COMPETITION". Beneath it were three subtitles, which read - "Open for high school and college students", "Organized by the History Society of India", "Internship offer for winner".

"That seems like an excellent opportunity. I will definitely partici-pate," said Aman enthusiastically.

Samantha and Madhvi wished him simultaneously,

"Best of luck!"

"Thank you. Let me brainstorm some ideas and come up with a proper pitch for the competition. If you are free, please come to witness it on Monday. I promise that you won't be disappointed!"

The euphoria in Aman's voice was abruptly cut off by the loud request of a teacher on another table,

"Sonu, can you please turn on the TV and open the sports channel? The India-Australia Test Match has started."

Sonu, the owner of the canteen, switched on the TV but forgot to lower the volume. As the TV blared and reverberated at full volume, he rushed to the reception area to fetch the remote.

The news channel would have generally invited rebelling voices from the dining sports enthusiasts but the reported headline was too attention-catching to be hushed up. As the headline at the top of the screen flashed - "No CCTV footage of leopard found in suspected animal attack.", a disturbing video streamed below the headline.

The video displayed a trembling Karan taking backward steps, oblivious to the pool behind him. It seemed that he was being approached by some danger, which the gleeful water-spouting marble frog and the calm lotuses couldn't convey. A strong gust of wind momentarily lashed against the camera screen and whipped up a mountain of dust. The settling of dust revealed Karan's terrified face again as he stumbled on the pool boundary behind him and fell with a splash. The surroundings seemed indifferent to his still and unconscious body until the time his rescuer arrived. While the faces were blurred for the spectators, Samantha clearly recognized herself as she approached her unconscious friend on the glaring screen.

CHAPTER 3

WHEN THE SEAS SPOKE ON MARINE DRIVE

The wide and large audience, comprising of historians, archaeologists, academicians and technologists, murmured excitedly in the packed auditorium as Aman began his presentation as the first participant -

"Our efforts towards getting glimpses of the past have traditionally been focused on gathering and interpreting eye-opening physical evidence. The most accurate understandings of the past have come from texts in interpretable languages, buried treasures or long-standing architectural marvels. We haven't always been lucky though. The course of time takes its toll on physical relics by scarring and degrading them as they lie buried deep in the soil for several centuries or even millennia. Many languages, in which historical texts are written, have simply vanished without leaving a way to understand them. In such limiting cases, where the evidence is only partial, we can only hope to make logical guesses about why a historical event had a certain outcome. I have developed a model to specifically explain the reasons for the victory of a certain side in historical battles."

The audience looked at Aman with mixed feelings of awe and curiosity as the young boy eloquently proposed to resolve a problem statement, which had been confounding historians since time immemorial.

"The model looked at various factors that determine which side won a particular battle in history - the army size, battle formation, number of horses etc. By analysing existing data,

it was able to learn which of these factors were more important than the others in determining the victor of any battle."

On observing the perplexed faces in the audience, Aman could see that his proposed model had only been half-understood.

He bent down towards his laptop, clicked a few buttons and the presentation screen gave way to the painting of a battle scene. On the left side of the vivid painting, there was a conventional army with swordsmen, archers etc. The other side had these typical soldiers too but their army was also joined by war elephants and dogs. A woman wearing an armour could be seen atop one of those elephants. A blue sea with rising waves could be seen behind the army on the left.

Aman said, "I can demonstrate my model using an example. This is a famous painting, depicting a battle in which Queen Loma successfully defended her kingdom of Vidika from the numerically superior invading forces of a neighbouring kingdom called Magadush. She is said to be the first ruler who used elephants and dogs in a battle together. Queen Loma's victory in this battle has been historically attributed to the shock of an unprecedented encounter with war elephants and dogs, which apparently completely demoralised the Magadushian troops. As we will see soon, my model suggests that there were more factors at play here."

The audience looked at Aman with a childlike curiosity. Aman turned his face towards the screen and asked in a loud voice,

"Dear model, who would win the battle shown on the screen?"

A reply was heard from the screen in a robotic voice,

"The army on the left will win this battle."

A green circle appeared around the army of Magadush.

The robotic voice stunned the audience as evident from their widened eyes and loud chatters. Aman smiled, making no attempts to hide his smug satisfaction upon grabbing the audience's attention.

He continued, "We know that Queen Loma's side actually won this battle. Let us check why the model predicted otherwise.

Dear model, why do you think the left side will win?"

Another robotic reply was heard from the screen, "The army on the left has a much higher number of soldiers. Dogs cannot effectively fight armed soldiers in combat. The number of elephants on the right is not high enough to trample the much bigger army on the left."

Aman said, "Let us see if the model can come up with an explanation for the actual victory of Queen Loma."

He faced the screen and asked, "Dear model, this battle was actually won by Queen Loma on the right. Can you come up with a potential explanation for this?"

A spinning circle appeared on the huge screen, indicating that the model was doing some calculations to come up with an answer. After a minute, the robotic voice was heard again,

"While the dogs could not have been effective killers, they could have acted as effective spreaders of the rabies virus through their injurious bites. One of the defining symptoms of rabies is hydrophobia - the fear of water. This would make the soldiers scared to retreat towards the sea behind them when the elephants move forward to trample them. The ensuing panic from a supposed attack on both sides could demoralise them. This could have caused the army on the right to win."

The model's hypothesis led to even louder mutters across the packed audience. One of the judges swerved his head back towards the audience and gestured them to hush up. Upon noticing the dying noises, Aman concluded his presentation,

"As you can see, the model can learn patterns observed in historical battles and highlight critical missing pieces in other incompletely understood battles. In this case, it points to the possibility of the dog's rabid infection being responsible for turning the tide of the battle."

There was a loud round of applause as Aman finished his presentation. The loudest claps came from none other than his history teacher, Samantha, who beamed at him with admiration and pride. His mannerisms and intellect reminded her of the virtues she envisioned to imbibe in her son as he grew up. Unknowingly, Aman was helping Samantha get over her grief by giving her hope that she could still make a positive influence on young lives.

While most people in the audience seemed impressed, the judges weren't completely sure. The idea of an undergraduate student coming up with a wild theory, which had never been heard of before, was difficult to digest.

"This theory seems far-fetched.," said a judge. "We have never heard of such a battle strategy being ever deployed in history."

Aman replied, "I did some background research which makes this theory sound more reasonable. The tradition of raising elephants has been prevalent in the modern-day city of Vidika, the capital of Queen Loma's empire, for several centuries. However, as documented by Queen Loma herself in her memoirs, forcing the nobles of her kingdom to adopt elephants was an unpopular decision. Elephants required enormous amounts of food and therefore, proved to be expensive upkeeps. Fearing overthrow by an internal rebellion, she permitted the nobles to switch to raising dogs while continuing to raise elephants herself. Barring a few affluent families, most of them returned their elephants to the royal palace and adopted dogs instead.

While a select few families kept the tradition of raising elephants alive through the centuries, the tradition of raising dogs got arbitrarily discontinued around the 18th century without any apparent reason. The tradition was rekindled only in 1970 to boost tourism as well as honour Queen Loma on the 300th anniversary of her famous battle victory. Keeping in mind the lower costs of raising dogs, the selective discontinuation of the tradition of raising dogs back then did not seem coherent. The launch of a rabies vaccine, only in the past few decades, seems to have made the difference in ensuring safe and sustainable human upbringing of dogs."

The questions were still going on when Samantha's mobile rang in an ear-piercing tone -

Tring. Tring.

It was from her friend and fellow school teacher, Madhvi. She lived in the same neighbourhood as her and Karan's and the word had got around. Anticipating some news about Karan, Samantha picked up the phone despite the disapproving glares of the people sitting next to her. Madhvi said,

"Samantha, Karan has finally gained consciousness. Let us visit him and know the exact details to put an end to all these obscure supernatural theories surrounding his accident."

"That sounds great. Should I pick you up on the way?"

"I am not at my apartment. We are finishing the final leg of our school trip at Marine Drive. I will join you at the hospital itself."

Aman's questioning round almost seemed to be on the verge of ending. As much as Samantha wished to see the entire presentation of her favourite student, she was too curious and impatient to wait any longer. She took out the car keys from her purse and hurried out of the crowded hall.

* * *

"Dear friends, they also call it the 'Queen's Necklace'. The reason for that is apparent in the dark sky. These glittering buildings dotting the seaside arc resemble a string of gems in a necklace. Can you see it?" the guide pointed to the brightly shining skyline on Mumbai's Marine

Drive.

"Can you see it?" said a middle-aged woman, who was one of the tourists being shown around by the guide. She looked at a kid standing next to her and pointed towards the buildings visible on the other end of the arc. The boy frowned and replied,

"I can, Mom. Can we please head back to our hotel? The buffet ends in thirty minutes and I don't want to skip the tempting delicacies that I saw on the menu."

"We wouldn't miss it, dear. This is the last segment of the tour. We will head directly to the hotel after this. Also, you can relish food anywhere. But you will not get a chance to witness these amazing historical sights again soon. So, let us divert our focus to where it is required."

"But what about the mango lassi and…"

The boy's words were cut short by the yell of the guide, who had walked ahead but rambled on,

"The area that you are currently standing on has been entirely reclaimed from the sea since 1940. In order to accomplish the reclamation, a huge amount of debris was poured into the shallow seafront that once existed here. This place is called the Nariman Point."

While the sea had been pushed back, it had definitely not vanished. As if to show its might on hearing the guide's mockery, the sea's waves rose to a great height and crashed against the concrete rocks lining the beach, creating a thunderous splashing sound. A family of three strolling around the rocks screamed and immediately scrambled to climb up the elevated embankment.

Having been hushed by the sea waves, the guide tried to get the tour group's attention back by yelling,

"As you may know, the moon exerts a gravitational force on the sea waves, which causes the phenomenon of moon tides.

This explains such unusually high waves during the night."

"I am sorry to interrupt but we need to get out of here. Even moon tides do not lead to such high waves," the kid's mother said as she pointed to the gigantic wave coming towards them, almost as high as the skyscraper behind them. A strong gust of misty wind lashed against their faces.

The road was filled with screeches and shrieks as speeding cars halted with scores of panicked people rushing fearfully past them. Confused drivers, who were used to ruling the traffic-packed streets of Mumbai, were shocked to find people stumbling and falling on their wind shields. Some of the drivers fled from their cars to join the retreating crowd while others just froze in horror as the wave approached them at lightning speed.

The colossal buildings shuddered as the enormous gurgling wave crashed against them, shattering the glass windows to smithereens. However, none of them perished unlike the sea wave, which fell and retreated as quickly as it had arrived.

The warning had apparently been received on time as most people dealt with nothing worse than drenched clothes and a salty taste in their mouths. Some of the adventurous people scrambled out of their building shelters to feel the fresh dewy air in the open. The relief turned out to be short-lived.

A flapping sound reverberated through the air. This was followed by a shrill call. The diners on the rooftop restaurant balcony saw it first. A pair of wings emerged from the dark clouds, casting a huge shadow on the brightly lit-up road below.

A slender beak protruded from the stormy grey clouds. As the clouds cleared, the face of a giant bird with its shiny black eyes emerged. If the bird had been the size of a regular house sparrow, those innocuous eyes would have been perceived as endearing and cute. However, in that gigantic form, they invoked terror in the eyes of the diners, who immediately deserted the restaurant as the candlelights and exquisitely decorated meals stayed on.

"Since the aircraft is headed here from the sea, this must be an international flight," the boy on the street said to his friend.

"The wings of an aircraft stay still and do not flap. Aircrafts aren't adorned with feathers. And most importantly, they don't eat humans. Run!" the other boy screamed.

The bird began to gradually descend towards the ground as the drenched pedestrians and drivers ran helter-skelter. One of the most bustling roads of Mumbai was left with closely packed empty cars, stuck in the middle of a mile-long traffic jam.

The drivers knew that they could escape faster on foot than by driving their cars.

A sleeping passenger in the backseat of a taxi apparently did not. His formal tie-decked coat and laptop bag hinted at a recent professional endeavour. The noises had disturbed his slumber but he was accustomed to taking naps amidst the chaotic car horns of Mumbai. The thud, followed by a creaking metal-scraping sound, awoke him though. His eyes went wide in shock as a talon pierced through the car roof. As the bird perched atop the car roof, it let out a deafening and piercingly shrill cry.

Madhvi muffled the shriek of her ten-year old student by capping his mouth with her hands as they trembled under one of the cars. That car was only three cars away from the one on which the bird stood. None of them had expected a supposedly enjoyable school trip to turn out that way as they panted for breath in the dusty air. The eerie calm was shattered by Madhvi's mobile phone, which abruptly started ringing. The bird moved its frighteningly shiny eyes in their direction.

* * *

As Samantha entered, Karan sat up and propped himself against the white pillow in his blue hospital overalls. There was a bandage on his forehead and a drip attached to one of his hands.

Samantha said, "Thank heavens that you recovered. I would never have been able to forgive myself if anything had happened to you. How are you feeling now?"

"I am getting better. My accident was not your fault at all. You have no reason to blame yourself," replied Karan.

"Perhaps not. But I am guilty of insulting you even though you gave that suggestion about John only out of pure intentions. I owe you an apology."

"Not a big deal. You seem tired. Why don't you sit down and have some tea?"

"Definitely. Should I call the nurse?"

"No need. I had just ordered tea when you called to tell me that you are coming with Madhvi. Can you please pour it from the thermos kettle on the table?"

Samantha picked up the thermos from the table beside Karan's bed and poured it into the two disposable glasses kept on top of the thermos. She handed one of them to Karan as he carefully moved his hand, which had been tied to the drip.

"So why didn't Madhvi come? I thought she was coming with you," asked Karan.

"She told me that she would arrive on her own. I called her a few minutes back but she didn't pick up. I assumed that she must be driving on the way here. She should be here any minute."

Karan nodded. Samantha felt unsure about the way she should address the elephant in the room as she sipped the tea. She felt that reliving the accident might be traumatic for Karan but her impatience and curiosity got the better of her.

"If you are comfortable discussing the circumstances which led to this accident, can you tell me what exactly happened that day?"

"I am more than comfortable. Since the time I have woken up, I have heard all sorts of crazy rumours surrounding the nature of my accident. My brother from London called me to advise me to buy some anti-supernatural trinket. Apparently, a major news channel telecast a CCTV camera recording of the accident and attributed the accident to a resident ghost of Sanjay Gandhi National Park. That just sounds crazy."

"I know. I don't believe in supernatural superstitions. I was hoping for a saner explanation for the whole incident from you to quell all these crazy rumours."

"I doubt that my explanation would sound saner. When I told my brother about what actually happened, he requested that I consult a psychiatrist."

"I doubt it would be that crazy. So, what is it?"

"When I bent down to pick my bag, which lay beside the pool, I heard a rustle of leaves from the trees behind me. I presumed that the monkeys had followed me to the waterfall but then, I heard a shrill call. I turned back to see a huge black bird plucking leaves from the tree. I would say that it resembled a seagull but it was gigantic by the standards of any bird on this planet, even those of an ostrich. It could completely fill a small bedroom in both breadth and height. It had shiny yellow eyes, each of which were almost as big as globes. When it saw me, it spread out its feathers and started flying towards me. I got scared out of my wits and stepped back, forgetting for a moment that the pool was just behind me."

"The idea of a mammoth bird sounds unbelievable indeed. However, I remember the commotion among the monkeys just before I witnessed your accident. Monkeys are known to make warning calls when there is a predator around."

"I doubt this bird was a predator though. If it had been, it would have appeared in the video recording and you would have seen bare bones near the pool instead of my bruised body."

"I could have done without that gross explanation," Samantha said as she teasingly smiled at him.

"If you think about it though, I saw the bird flying towards me before I passed out. However, it isn't visible in the recording."

"Maybe it wasn't coming towards you. It probably flew into the sky."

"I am actually surprised that you believe me. Most of my friends and relatives have refused to believe me and have simply expressed sympathy for the unfortunate turn of events."

"I don't see any reason why you would make up a story, which makes you look like a fool. There are a lot of new animal species that are discovered every year. Another discovery shouldn't be a surprise."

"But it isn't a tiny frog or insect that can go unnoticed and undiscovered for years. You could see a giant bird like that from a mile away."

"Don't you want me to believe you?" said Samantha as she broke into a laugh.

The laughter was interrupted by the ring on Samantha's mobile phone. When she noticed the contact name, she said,

"It is Dr. Mathews, the school principal. He will probably reprimand me for leaving behind the students in the auditorium. They are grown up high school students, who told me that they would manage to go back to their homes on their own. I wasn't expecting word to go around but it seems like someone complained about me."

Samantha picked up the mobile with a frantic expression on her face.

"Samantha, it is Dr. Matthews. If you have watched any news in the past hour, you would know that a giant bird just went on a rampage around Marine Drive. The bird has kidnapped one of our students and Madhvi got injured while trying to rescue him. We can't reach her family. Do you happen to have the contact number of any of her family members?"

CHAPTER 4

THE GIRL OF THE MOUNTAINS

She was barely ten years old when Tisha first met a fully drenched and whimpering dog on the mountains. It was a rainy day when Benji's rope-thin legs and rib-protruding belly had moved her immensely, initiating a chain of rescue operations for street dogs across the hilly town of Lonavala. As the years went by, the residents of Petsville, as Tisha fondly referred to her home, grew even more diverse as abandoned cats, hamsters and cattle entered the scene.

As her first pet, Benji was the most special though. Having received intense care and training from Tisha, he had transformed into an unrecognizably healthy and fluffy version of his former self. Even though dogs have been traditionally recognized as intelligent pets, Benji's presence of mind was unusually remarkable. When Tisha forgot to take her lunch box to school one day, Benji grabbed the sandwich between his teeth and sped off to her school. He searched classroom after classroom, creating a ruckus among the teachers and students wherever he went. He stopped only when he finally found Tisha on her usual spot at the first bench in her class. Since then, Benji followed Tisha everywhere - the school, supermarkets and even her undergraduate university in Delhi. The repeated hassles of traveling with a pet failed to dissuade her over the years as she successfully negotiated with hostel wardens, flight administration and train ticket checkers. However, luck didn't seem to be on her side that day.

"Come on! He weighs only 10 grams more. You can surely accommodate such a minor deviation.," she said to the woman on the flight counter.

"Madam, I am very sorry but the rules are very clear. No pet over the weight of 10 kg can be allowed to board the plane."

"I know that but animals can grow healthier and gain weight. Are we really penalizing them for that?"

"Believe me. I have no personal say in this. I cannot tweak flight policies on any grounds whatsoever."

Benji was a growing dog and Tisha hadn't anticipated a sudden increase in his weight since when she had booked the flight tickets to Mumbai a month ago. While she was still mulling over possible alternatives to make it to Mumbai in time, Benji seemed to have found a solution. He let out a series of barks to catch the attention of Tisha and started tugging at the leash on his neck as she looked down. Tisha immediately removed the leash and placed her pet on the weighing balance again.

9.998 kilograms - the balance read. The flight assistant nodded in approval as Tisha smiled and hurried Benji into the pet carrier. While she felt her routine guilt about locking up Benji in a restricted place, the dog seemed to have adapted to his traveling schedule. He fell asleep within the carrier by the time that she wheeled her heavy luggage through the noisy airport gates and boarded the aircraft.

As she slid the carrier into the leg space in front of her seat, she saw an old lady on the seat beside hers. She smiled as Tisha slid past her towards her window-facing seat. She remarked,

"Your pet looks endearingly cute. He appears so calm and smug while sleeping."

"He is definitely beautiful. If only we could remove our prejudices about street dogs, we would observe that there are many such beautiful dogs roaming on our streets. They just need the right love, care and attention to become like Benji."

"You are absolutely right. Providing a conducive environment for growth can propel not just dogs, but even humans, to evolve into better versions of themselves. The world would certainly be a much better place if we could discard our preconceived notions and help each other fulfil their potential."

The air hostess entered the corridor and beckoned everyone to fasten their seat belts. The old lady joined her hands in prayer as the aircraft lunged forward on the strip and lifted off into the air with a whistling sound. Tisha said,

"It is interesting to see how praying before a flight seems like a universal practice among the previous generations. As a child, I remember how my parents used to make me pray before flight take-offs too."

"In our generation, you watched aeroplanes only in movies or from your rooftop terrace. You could just imagine and dream about actually flying in one in a distant future. However, the economic boom of the past decade made flying a less exclusive experience and brought us earlier to the dream than we had envisaged."

"So, do you pray to thank God for giving you the opportunity?"

"Yes, indeed! We also pray for safety since flying is a novel experience for us. While novel experiences bring in excitement, the uncertainties induce feelings of risk too."

As Tisha looked out of her window, she could see the clear blue sky with the fluffy white clouds below them. The sun appeared to be setting and glowed with a bright orange colour.

"I forgot to ask. What is your name? Do you live in Mumbai?" said Tisha.

"My name is Maya. I live in Vidika. My grandson is studying in Mumbai. I am going to visit him. What brings you to Mumbai?" asked the old lady.

"I will be attending an international conference on evolutionary biology in Mumbai. I work as a graduate researcher at a zoology research institute in Lonavala. Attending such international conferences allows me to present the research being done at my institute to a wider audience as well as learn from the research being pursued by others."

"That's impressive to hear. I am curious though. Most people prefer to work in the cities. Why did you choose the serenity of the mountains?"

"The mountains have been an inspiration for nature poets and writers since eternity. However, they can also be inspiring for scientists like me. The calmness often leads to thought-provoking ideas for my research as I feel the forces of nature at play - the trees swerving amidst the misty wind as the nightingale sings its melodious tunes. Also, I have a huge shelter for abused animals near my home, whom I have personally raised while closely studying their behaviour. Neither can I abandon them nor can I afford a similarly spacious residence for them in a city."

Benji let out a low yelp in his carrier. He opened his eyes, looked around curiously at Tisha and her co-passenger. After a brief observation, he fell asleep again. Upon noticing this, Maya said,

"Your pet seems like a smart fellow. It doesn't seem that he will wake up till the time we land."

"He is smart indeed but I am yet to ascertain the true extent of his smartness. Sometimes, I feel that his displays of intelligence might be pure coincidence. However, he makes a better case for himself on every subsequent occasion."

"I don't understand. How exactly?" Maya replied with raised and twisted eyebrows.

"For instance, the flight attendant refused to board him on the flight today because he was exceeding the weight limit. While I was still figuring out what to do, he started tugging at his leash. It might have been the heat and itchiness but the timing seems to be too much of a coincidence."

Maya continued her puzzled expression for a moment. It was difficult to guess if she was surprised, impressed or suspicious. She bent down to peer closely at Benji in his cage. His eyes were closed and his tail lay curled up beside his back.

"Smart fellow indeed," she remarked as her puzzled face gave way to her former jolly smiling expression.

Tisha and Maya must have subsequently dozed off for an hour because they awoke to the announcement of the air hostess, asking the passengers to fasten their seat belts. The aircraft was apparently beginning to land. There was a moment of silent listening, which was followed by noises of excitement and chaos. The teenage students high-fived each other. Some anxious parents gave up on teaching their kids how to fasten a belt to do the job for them eventually. There were a series of whistling sounds as the aircraft tilted downwards and swiftly whirred through the air, only to slow and speed up again. As the elderly lady closed her eyes and joined her hands in prayer, Tisha felt that it would be rude to interrupt her by continuing the conversation.

Within a few minutes, the aircraft landed and sped on the runway as the flickering colourful lights on its wings stood out in the dark evening. The air hostess announced the prevailing temperature of 35° C outside, prompting Tisha to take off her jacket and pack it in her bag. Maya opened her eyes when the aircraft finally came to a halt.

"Do you have any luggage in the cabin that I can take out for you?" Tisha asked her as she stared down while struggling to unload her own heavy luggage from the cabin.

"Thank you, dear! I don't have any luggage there. You can't carry heavy bags at my age, so you pack only a bare minimum to begin with."

Benji woke up and let out a few mellow barks to startle the frantic passengers, who were earlier jostling with each other to get out. While there were contrasting signs of endearment and glaring disapproval among them, everyone calmly proceeded in unison to form a queue in unison at Benji's call-out.

The departure section at the airport was abuzz with gleaming stores, selling a variety of stuff from books to fine wine.

One of the chocolate shops caught Tisha's eye as she realized that she hadn't bought any gifts for her aunt, whom Tisha had planned to meet in Mumbai. She looked at Benji intently, who was on his feet and prancing about in the carrier that she was trolleying around with her luggage. Benji would only invite panic and disapproval if she took him inside the shop. She didn't want the stares of unwelcoming and fussy shopkeepers to ruin her shopping experience. She was still contemplating what to do when her mobile started ringing.

"Tisha. Aunt Mona this side. I called your mother to ask about your flight arrival time. I and Chintu have come to the airport to receive you. Come to Gate No.3."

Chintu was Tisha's five year old cousin. The idea of denying chocolates to a kid almost seemed cruel. His unexpected arrival at the airport itself left no choice.

"Benji, you stay here. I will just go, buy that almond chocolate and be right back in a jiffy. Please stay quiet and don't create a commotion," she said while bending down and making hand gestures in front of the dog, who almost seemed to be listening obediently.

She rushed inside and picked up the almond chocolate, which had been encased beautifully in a tin case and placed prominently on the front shelf. As she moved towards the counter, a few people sped past her and formed a queue in the front of the counter, which had been devoid of customers till that time. She almost thought of giving up but the cashier allayed her concerns. He billed the handed items, took the payment and handed back the change with remarkable dexterity and swiftness. It didn't take long for the queue in front of Tisha to clear. She thanked the cashier and went out towards the left entrance of the shop, where she had left Benji.

However, there was no trolley to be spotted anywhere. Benji was gone along with her luggage! She wanted to shriek but then she reconsidered her impulse. She recalled that there was a lost and found section on the airport. She ran frantically towards the airport gate to ask the security guard for directions to the section. Her attention was suddenly caught by a mellow bark.

It wasn't an imagined sound that arose from optimism. The bark grew louder as she approached the exit gate. As she picked up her pace in anticipation, she bumped into a burly man and fell over. Her spectacles landed a few feet away from her. Her vision was blurred but she clearly saw the outline of Maya, who was pushing her trolley through the gates as Benji barked in dismay. She lay frozen in disbelief at the betrayal of a supposedly friendly co-passenger until a few people rushed to help her get back on her feet. As the barks began to drown out, it became clear that some cries of help were less discernible than the others.

CHAPTER 5

THAT IS MY BENJI

The road gleamed with a clear black colour, having been cleansed of dust by the pouring shower of rain. There were still some puddles of water, forcing the occasional pedestrian to frown and pull up their pants or skirts. Wading through the water in an almost perennially rainy city was hardly out of the norm though. Aman partially opened the window of his car to allow the nostalgic smell of wet soil to waft in along with the soothing cool monsoon breeze. Nothing like a pleasant scent to calm the stress of a heated conversation.

"It was clear as day that he was no regular dog," said his grandmother, Maya Gill, as she wiped the dew drops on the window with her sari. "He was our Raja. He had a golden furry coat. He displayed his idiosyncratic intelligence. And to top it all, when I picked him up, he also had a white spot behind his ear.

That is his birthmark."

"There are practically millions of dogs that would fit that description, Grandma. What would have happened if you had been convicted for theft?" said Aman while steering the wheel and trying his best to stay focused on the busy road.

"I realized that after a few minutes. So, I left him near the airport gate and just plucked out a hair from his furry skin. We are going to get the DNA test and confirm that it is Raja."

"Even if you are able to verify that it is Raja, how will you even find him in this megacity of 20 million people? And even if you find him, how can you claim him when someone else raised him all these years?"

"When your parents died, I promised them that I would take care of you and Raja. I still feel guilty that I couldn't hold on to the second part of that promise."

The disappointment conveyed through her upside-down lips contrasted with the optimism of her gleaming eyes.

Aman seemed unfazed. He said, "I don't understand. What is so special about a pet dog?"

Maya rolled her eyes.

"You understand, son. You just choose to feign ignorance. Raja was a part of the lineage of royal dogs that our family has been raising for many generations. We are the only family in Vidika that didn't abandon Queen Loma's tradition of raising intelligent dogs. The new families that jumped on the bandwagon after 1970 have been raising dogs only to make money in a booming animal tourism economy. For us, Raja isn't a source of revenue. In our eyes, he is a part of our culture, our values and most importantly, our family."

There was a pin drop silence in the car. This was symptomatic of discussions where the grandmother-grandson duo disagreed with each other but didn't pursue it further to avoid conflict.

"Turn to the left. The Kutram pet clinic is over there," said Maya.

"Are you sure that you will be able to call a taxi and get home?" said Aman.

"Yes, don't worry about me. Wish your friend a happy birthday on my behalf and have fun."

"Call me when you reach home."

Aman whizzed off in his red car, leaving behind a puff of smoke as his grandmother stood on the pavement in the bustling evening marketplace.

The restaurant was only a five-minute drive from the market.

Its entrance was bedecked with a mosaic of cat and dog photos. The restaurant name prominently shone in a glimmering yellow light amidst the dewy evening sky - "Pets-o-mania Cafe". There was a green billboard with the subtitle mentioned below the name - "India's most pet friendly restaurant". A giant chandelier, visible through the revolving entrance glass door, seemed to be screaming for the attention of affluent diners.

When Aman entered, he saw that the hall divided itself into two separate dining chambers on each side. In the middle of the hall, a woman was handing out bright red leashes bearing embroidered restaurant logos to pet owners. The long queue of guests with cats and dogs of all colours and sizes made Aman feel out of place without a pet. The lady seemed to be directing guests to either one of the two dining chambers on each side. As the queue began to clear, Aman realized that the chambers were being assigned based on the accompanying pet.

"Which section are we supposed to go to if I own a cat but my friend owns a dog?" asked the teenager in front of him.

"I think a cat and a dog won't get along with each other. Why don't you let our specialist caretakers for cats and dogs take care of them while you enjoy a scrumptious meal?" the receptionist replied with a broad smile.

Aman heard a whisper from his back. He turned around to see a girl, who was dressed in a black gown. A panting dog pranced around her in circles.

"Happy birthday, Tisha! It is so nice to meet you after almost two years."

After they embraced each other with a quick hug, Tisha drew his attention to a winding staircase on the left that had escaped his eyes.

She said, "We don't need to stand here. Come upstairs with me. I have booked a table on the second floor."

The table adjoined a window, which offered a view of a cluster of tall bamboo trees. The larger than usual full moon shone with a reddish-ochre tinge through the gaps between the trees.

"How are you finding the back-to-school classes by Samantha Ma'am?" said Tisha.

"They are amazing," said Aman. "She has a unique storytelling approach to teaching history. Thanks for recommending me to take a few of her classes."

"You are welcome. I knew that you would enjoy her classes. Attending her classes in high school greatly motivated me to pursue a minor in history apart from my biology major at Delhi University."

"I am so grateful for having joined the Science Club during my high school. Otherwise, I would have never got the opportunity to meet senior students, who were equally enthusiastic about pursuing careers in science and technology. The perspectives of senior students like you shaped my decision to pursue a computer science major at the Indian Institute of Technology Bombay."

"That's great. Thankfully, you didn't take an uninformed and hasty decision about dropping out and contacted me again for advice after all these years."

"Yes, thanks for your suggestion! Knowing how you were able to choose a minor in history has reduced some of my concerns indeed.

I can now think about pursuing a career at the intersection of technology and history without having to commit solely to just one field."

"Exactly. As you know, I arrived in Mumbai for a short seminar.

The seminar gave me the chance to present my research findings on a collaborative project with a prominent organization. The project has historical as well as biological aspects to it."

"That sounds interesting. What is it about?"

"Sorry, I can't divulge details about it at the moment."

Aman nodded. Their conversation was interrupted by the arrival of Tisha's friends, Priya and Sam. There was a round of introductions followed by a series of icebreakers to get the conversation flowing.

"Mumbai is truly one of the most fast-paced cities in the world," said Tisha. "There is always an atmosphere of vibrancy and enthusiasm here, which never ceases to a stop. A gigantic terrifying bird attacked the city's core barely a week ago but the Marine Drive is as crowded as ever with unfazed tourists, partygoers and picnickers. The city knows how to bounce back from a disaster."

"The resilience is commendable indeed," added Sam. "The way the bird was euthanized and captured by the animal control department within an hour of its arrival is actually quite commendable."

Aman said, "I read in the newspaper that the bird will be shifted to the city zoo after preliminary studies. That would draw in a lot of tourists to Mumbai from all parts of the world."

Priya remarked, "Controlling it within zoo premises might be tough though. I heard that it whipped up a storm in the Arabian sea simply by flapping its aircraft-sized wings."

Aman nodded and added, "I was watching an interview with a prominent ornithologist on TV. His analysis of the bird's DNA concludes that the bird belongs to a species called Pelagornis Sandersi. This species became extinct around 25 million years ago. What makes it even more surprising is the fact that this bird has never been known to be endemic to India."

Sam gasped at the revelation and said, "It couldn't have been hiding. Its enormous size would make it too conspicuous in any Indian jungle for it to stay in oblivion all this while."

Aman revealed further details, noticing the enthusiastic expressions of his companions,

"The interview has gone quite viral these days. It is omnipresent on every television screen in the country. Apparently, the only fossil of this bird ever discovered was unearthed halfway across the world in South Carolina. However, the fossil sitting in the Charleston Museum in the US is much smaller than the size of the captured live bird. So, scientists are now hypothesising that the fossil probably belonged to a baby and actual adult birds might have been much larger than previously thought."

Priya said, "So, that is the actual name. Everyone is just calling the bird the 'Bollywood bird' since a reporter commented that the bird's appearance seems straight out of a Bollywood movie."

Tisha said, "I am glad that the bird didn't kill anybody despite its enormous size and strength."

Aman didn't share the optimistic sentiment. He sighed,

"It might not have killed anyone but it definitely injured many people. It grabbed a fifth grader from my school with its talons and kicked the computer science teacher, who tried to rescue him. It couldn't hold the kid for a long time though and dropped him after a few seconds. Thankfully, after three days of intense medical treatment at the hospital, both have mostly recovered from their injuries. The kid is traumatized though and still undergoing therapeutic sessions to recover from the mental shock of the event."

"Poor kid!" said Tisha with her palm covering her mouth.

A waitress entered the cabin with a chocolate truffle cake. There was a smaller dog biscuit cake beside the larger one.

Aman reached out for the birthday gift besides his chair. He could only feel the wooden armrest, which had become ice-cold due to the air conditioning. He knew where the gift was.

"Grandma, did you accidentally keep the gift with you?" Aman asked his grandmother on the mobile.

After a brief silence, the reply came, "Yes, I have it. I guess that I mistook it for my shopping bag."

"Can you tell me your location? I will come and fetch the gift."

"I am outside the Millenium mall."

"Perfect. It is just on the opposite side of the road. Cross the underground bridge and you will emerge on the other side. I will meet you there."

Aman excused himself from the group and ran down the flight of stairs. He spotted his grandmother near the door of the restaurant. She seemed confused as she kept looking around in all directions until her eyes met Aman's.

"Are the DNA test results out?" he asked as he caught up with her.

"Not yet. They usually take a few hours."

Maya took out the gift from her leather purse and handed a small glittery paper bag to her grandson. He thanked her and had almost booked a cab for her on his mobile to take her home. Until Tisha came out the restaurant door looking for Aman and unexpectedly yelled,

"You are the one who kidnapped my dog!"

As Aman recovered from the sudden disclosure, he muttered nervously to himself,

"Holy cow. So, that dog was actually Benji."

He rushed forward to explain but Maya gestured to him to stop and wait. As Tisha approached them, Maya recognized the familiar face and said, "Dear, I know that my behaviour was erratic and I apologize for the same. I am sure you would be able to relate to my situation once you know the complete facts."

"She is my grandmother," said Aman with an awkward smile baring his teeth.

Tisha's curled lips gave way to a slight smile. She said,

"I am more intrigued than furious by your actions. I would certainly want to know the reason for what you did. Meanwhile, why don't you join us for my birthday celebration?"

"As long as you keep your hands off Benji…," she added with a pinch of sternness to remind her that all had not been forgotten.

A bit reluctant at first, Maya agreed to join them. It was a short birthday celebration, involving the ceremonial cake cutting followed by a hearty meal of dog bone-shaped fries and burgers, which was served in miniature dog houses. Once all of Tisha's guests had left except for Aman and Maya, they sat down to discuss the matter at hand. Maya narrated,

"Let me start with a story. Vidika, my hometown, served as the seat of power for Queen Loma's empire during the 18th century. According to folklore, her uncle attempted to murder her as a child on a family hunting expedition in the forests so that he could ascend the throne after her father's death. In those times, the royal contingent used to be accompanied by hunting dogs, which helped in tracking down prey with their keen sense of smell. When one of these dogs heard the princess's shrieks as her uncle approached her with a dagger, it leapt forward at the uncle and severely bit him. This incident prompted the princess to recognize the intelligence of dogs.

Her father, King Surma, had pioneered the taming of elephants to aid large scale construction of fortresses and palaces in his kingdom.

Upon ascending the throne, the princess took it a step further by launching a military training program for those elephants as well as the hunting dogs. Bolstered by her initial success in using them in battles, she mandated every noble family to raise elephants or dogs and prepare them for warfare. Our family has participated in this tradition of raising dogs for the last hundred years. The last dog of this lineage, whom we called Raja, went missing when Aman was a young kid."

"And do you suspect that Raja is Benji?" asked Tisha.

"Precisely."

"What characteristics of Benji make you think that he was a part of this lineage of military dogs?"

"First of all, obviously the looks. Benji is physically bigger but retains the basic physical characteristics of Raja - light brown fur, white spot behind left ear etc. However, what especially stands out is his exceptional perception of situations. For instance, when he realized that he was on a flight and might not be able to step out of the cage for a few hours, he decided to pass time by going to sleep. The military dogs of Vidika were especially trained for action based on a precise understanding of their surroundings. This allowed them to defend themselves and attack in chaotic battle grounds, where they could face a variety of weapons from all quarters."

"If the fact that Benji belongs to you is true, how did he end up on the streets?"

"I went on a holiday trip to Lonavala several years ago and took Raja with me since he was too young to be left alone. Unfortunately, on one of the days during my trip, I left him in the hotel room but forgot to keep the door locked. By the time I returned, he had already sneaked out. I tried my best to find him everywhere but my endless efforts bore no fruit."

"Benji or Raja must have tried really hard to look for you. When I was a kid, Benji used to follow me all the way to my school whenever I left my lunch box. When he got lost in Lonavala, he probably couldn't retrace his steps because of the new surroundings and got lost."

"That makes sense. Did you still live in Lonavala around ten years ago? When you told me on the flight that you live in Lonavala, that further heightened my suspicion."

"Yes, I did and as you know, I reside there to this day. It seems highly plausible that Benji is the grown-up puppy that you lost in those hills. However, I have raised him all these years and we both have grown very close. He would be distraught and unhappy if he was separated from me. If you are actually his original owner, I am sure that you would wish the best for him."

"You are right, Tisha. At this point, we don't need a DNA test to claim Benji. We are just hoping that the mistake that I made several years ago didn't prove too costly for our beloved puppy. If he landed in your caring hands, I would guess not."

The three people on the table smiled in unison at each other as Benji let out a bark of approval. Maya's mobile phone rang.

She went outside for a few minutes to take the call. On coming back, Aman asked her, "Did the DNA test results come out?"

"Do they even matter anymore?" smiled Maya.

"I guess not but I am still curious."

"My guess was wrong. Benji isn't Raja. Benji is Raja's puppy."

* * *

A huge number of police personnel in khaki uniforms stepped out through the gate and drove away on a jeep as Samantha entered the police station. There was a small queue in front of each of the three parallelly-placed desks inside the room. On seeing a constable, she gestured to him and asked, "I just got a call to collect one of my belongings, which had been withheld by the police for investigation. The case has been closed now. Can you tell me where I should go?"

"Please stand in the third queue. Mr. Shukla will help you with the same," he replied while pointing to the desk.

Samantha thanked him and stood in the queue. When her turn came, she explained her situation and after a few document signatures, the policeman pulled out a small necklace from a tightly packed plastic bag. He asked while holding it up,

"This is the necklace that we retrieved from the site of Mr. Karan Ghosh's accident. Is this yours, Ma'am?"

She opened the locket on the necklace while the policeman held it in his hands. The golden circular locket revealed a photograph of her family behind its lid - Rick in the middle with John and Samantha standing on each side. Everyone was wearing a beach hat in the picture. She inspected it for a few seconds with tense frown lines appearing on her forehead.

"Yes, this is mine. Thank you for finding it," she sternly replied and sped out of the police station upon receiving the necklace.

As she sat in the yellow taxi on the way home, she remembered Rick's eighth birthday. It was the first weekend of the year 2000. She was at the jewellery shop, which was brimming with customers optimistic about investing in gold at the turn of the millennium. She had wanted to buy a typical heart-shaped golden locket but John had persuaded her to buy the less conspicuous circular one instead. He had said,

"Rick is growing older. He might feel embarrassed of overtly explicit symbols of affection."

She remembered Rick's joyous smile when he had received his gift. He had wanted to get a golden necklace since the age of five but Samantha hadn't been able to trust a kid with valuables. So, he had been asked to wait until that momentous day.

She thought to herself, "I clearly remember tying the necklace around Rick's neck before his flight at the airport. Why did Karan possess my son's necklace? I can only think of one explanation. He is the one who kidnapped my son. Maybe that's why he was trying so hard to make me believe that John kidnapped him. Conveniently shifting the blame indeed!"

She muttered under her breath, "I don't know and care why Karan kidnapped both of them and why he was roaming around with my son's necklace in the national park. All I care about is rescuing them from his clutches at any cost."

CHAPTER 6

THE BOLLYWOOD WAY

She tossed around in her bed but each toss made it harder for her to sleep. She tried to concentrate and keep her eyes closed with the hope of inducing sleep. However, the realisation that she would have to wake up early tomorrow caused counterproductive sleep-depriving stress. She regretted going to the park in her residential society for a night walk. The unexpected encounter with her garrulous neighbour near the tennis court had led to hours of chatting on seemingly every topic under the sun. The past week had seen the municipality impose a curfew to assess the danger from the bird. No wonder that there had been a lot to gossip about. However, the prospect of not being able to wake up on time frightened her because it would cause her to wait for another week. Tuesday early mornings were the only time when Karan went out for movie auditions and left the keys under the earthen pot outside his house. The cook usually picked up the hidden key and prepared a delicious breakfast for him in the meantime. As she lay in her bed while staring at the ceiling, she thought,

"My husband and son have been held as hostages in his house for more than a month. I can't let them linger with another week of suffering for a few hours of sleep."

The morning sun rays streamed through the translucent blue

window curtains. Samantha rubbed her eyes as she attempted to wake up. The gentle nudge by the sun rays soon gave way to a blaring alarm and Samantha knew that the time had come. She peered out of her window to see the desolated park surrounded by buildings on all sides. Nobody could be spotted even on the balconies. It was too early, even for the most enthusiastic of morning risers.

She found the keys as expected and entered Karan's apartment. She scoured the entire living room for any clues that might lead her to her family. She even peeped beneath the grandiloquent velvet sofas but found nothing more than a forgotten rupee coin in a heap of dust. The temptation to yell out for her son and husband was strong. But the fear of alerting one of Karan's nosy neighbours was stronger. So, she resorted to a meek call,

"Rick. John. Are you there?"

There was no response. She knew that the task ahead wouldn't be easy. Karan would have had to be very discreet in order to conceal two smart and physically strong hostages in one of the most bustling residential societies of Mumbai. The dining table in front of her was unusually long, especially considering that Karan lived alone. She wondered if it had any secret hollow chambers underneath it.

She tapped the wooden table-top with the knuckles of her hands for any signs. She heard a minor echo. With greater anticipation building up, she tapped the table-top again with greater strength. The loud reverberating sound made the hollowness of the table apparent. She felt her hand around the table for any signs of a knob or handle without success. She knew that it would be impossible to house an alive human within a chamber without offering any sort of opening to breathe.

She circled around the table as she slightly bent to check for any visible opening. On the corner facing the kitchen, she found a tiny slit. She tried to force her hand inside but it was too narrow. She squinted her eyes to take a peek but the inside was completely shrouded in darkness. She let out a hiss with the hope of eliciting a response from within the chamber. This attempt also ended in failure. Her eyes fell on a pencil kept on the table. The size of the pencil seemed small enough to pass through the slit. Samantha picked it up and pushed it inside. The pencil hit a hard surface close to the outer wall. A circular object immediately began glowing with a bright red light inside the dark chamber. Apparently, it was a button. Samantha stepped back in fear as the rectangular portion in the middle of the table-top popped up. After waiting for a few minutes, she realized that it was just a harmless lid over a secret storage facility within the dining table.

She carefully bent forward to check the contents of the table inside it. There was a dark blue leaflet brochure with the letters "NTFHO" written boldly in white colours on the front page. There was a small caption highlighting the full form of the acronym beneath it - "National Technology for History Organization".

She rummaged inside the facility to find more NTFHO brochures and spiral-bound documents with 'Classified Information' stamps.

"This is the same organization, which held the competition last week. How and why is Karan involved with this organization?" she wondered.

As she searched through the documents for any answers, she came across a dusty newspaper. One of the front page headlines had been circled with a black marker. She muttered the headline slowly while reading it - "Engineering student stirs controversy by hinting at biological warfare in medieval Vidika".

Sweat trickled from Samantha's forehead as she contemplated possible repercussions of this strange highlight on Aman.

"Was he meant to be the next victim?" she thought.

She had barely started to digest the bizarre scenario when she heard a sneeze. It was coming from the kitchen. Adrenaline rushed in through her veins. In anticipation, she ran towards the kitchen. However, there was nobody to be spotted. She checked the kitchen compartments, drawers and even the fridge for the source of the sneeze but only found onions and tomatoes.

She had almost given up on her search when she heard a tiptoe of steps on her back. She turned around to see a middle-aged man trying to sneak out through the entrance. Caught by surprise as they looked face-to-face, he let out a loud yell.

"Aren't you Karan's cook?" she said.

"Yes, I am. Please take away whatever you want but spare my life. I have two young kids who need…"

"I am not a robber. I am Samantha, Karan's neighbour. I came to meet him."

That was the best excuse that she could conjure up on such a short notice.

"Thank God! I thought you were a robber. I had been hiding in the flour compartment since the time I saw you in the dining room. When you started checking the compartments and drawers, I decided to step out and quietly escape."

"I am sorry. It is my fault. I should have knocked or rang the doorbell before coming in."

"It is fine. Let me call Karan and put him out of stress. I had called him frantically about a possible theft. He is on his way home from the audition."

Samantha sighed. The sense of disappointment was palpable on her face. The impatience annoyed her. She had just begun to visualize her son in front of her eyes. Now, it seemed like a hallucination. Tears of frustration welled up in her eyes. In order to prevent the tears from getting noticed, she made her way towards the entrance door.

As she held the handle to close the door as she stepped out, she heard a voice. She turned around to see Karan, who was wearing eye shades and a breezy summer shirt.

"Sorry for the mess up. Did you receive your locket necklace?" he said.

"Yes, I did. How do you know?" replied Samantha.

"The police found it in the waterfall pool at Sanjay Gandhi National Park. When they asked me if I recognized it, I opened the locket and immediately got to know that it was yours. I gave them your address for delivery."

"So, you were the one, who…"

She paused and contemplated the sudden change of expectations as she mulled over an appropriate response.

"Does it not belong to you?" quizzed Karan.

"What makes you think it does not?"

"Never mind. I was just confused about your expression of apparent disbelief. Do you want to join me for a cup of tea? I will tell you all about the strange Bollywood movie role that I auditioned for today."

"Thank you for the offer but I am getting late for school.

I must go."

As she walked away, her curiosity increased with each step. The turn of events had given her more questions than answers.

A part of her wanted to turn back and demand an explanation from Karan as her friend of many years. However, her cynical distrust suppressed this impulse as she decided to wait again for another week.

* * *

Karan sat beside the ornamental fireplace with his hands crossed. The fireplace was purposeless in the dining hall during most of the year. The proximity of Mumbai to the sea ensured that the weather stayed warm with very little seasonal fluctuation. Even when the weather grew mildly cold occasionally, a small electric heater saved the mammoth effort of hauling, chopping and burning wooden logs.

As Karan looked at the empty fireplace, he felt that the authenticity of his friendship was dying like a ceremonial fireplace, which had outlived its purpose. He had sensed that Samantha was clearly upset about something. Yet, he hadn't been able to win her trust enough for her to reveal the cause of her distress. The sombre expression on Karan's face prompted the cook, Ashu, to ask, "Sir, Is the food not good?"

Karan regained his senses and remembered the fried idlis that he had only half-eaten.

"No, they are definitely delicious. My mind wandered off some-where, " he replied as he picked up the spoon again.

There was a ring on the doorbell. Upon seeing that Karan had finally resumed eating, Ashu rushed to open the door. A short man dressed in a formal black suit, entered the dining hall. His oblong face was covered with sparse bronze-red hair from the middle of his cheeks till the chin except for a moustache and a dense puff beneath his bottom lip. He raised his eyebrows as his brown eyes glinted with a spark of happiness through the frameless glasses.

"It seems like I disturbed you on the way to your office, Professor Neil," said Karan.

"No worries. Discussions with you are also a part of my work. Tell me what you have got."

Karan hastily wrapped up his meal, washed his hands and joined Neil on the fluffy velvet sofas in the living room.

Karan said, "Ashu, don't bother to make tea. We are about to leave in a few minutes and will get late if we wait."

Ashu nodded his head and left the house after picking up his mobile, which was getting charged on the kitchen counter.

Neil asked, "Where are we headed to?"

Karan bent and whispered in Neil's ear, "Nowhere, Professor. You know that the National Technology for History Organization meetings about this project have to be confidential. I needed an excuse to send him away."

"I get it. You seem worried. What's the matter?"

"Do you remember the locket necklace that the police found at the site of the accident? I think it belongs to the missing son or husband of my friend, Samantha Hughes. I have a faint memory of her gifting it to her son on his birthday a few years ago. She is not admitting it at the moment but her expressions on retrieving the necklace have emboldened my belief. If it is true, her insights could lead us closer to solving the mystery. Also, it feels unfair to deny her the hope that her family might be safe and well."

"How long have they been missing for? What were the circumstances of their disappearance?"

"They disappeared in a plane crash on an aircraft bound for South Africa around a month ago."

"That is around the time we witnessed the first case. She might be able to shed more light on this project if it actually belongs to her missing husband or son. We will anyway have no choice but to reveal the truth once she reports it to the police. Can you please ask her to come here right now?"

Karan gently smiled and nodded on getting the approval to clear him of the guilt, which had been building up inside him since the past week. He dialled the number and called her.

"Hello, Samantha. Would it be possible for you to meet me right now? I know that you have to go to your school but this is critical."

"Karan, you sound tense. Is everything all right?"

"Yes, everything is fine. I just needed your help on some matter urgently."

A small series of knocks was heard before Samantha entered the living room. She was resplendent in a cotton saree with her hair neatly tied into a bun. The slight frown on her forehead was enough to give away her actual mood even with her fake smile.

"I had to take a half-day leave from school to be here. I hope you have a good reason for calling me."

"I do. Samantha, please meet Professor Neil. He heads the zoology department at the University of Mumbai and is currently leading a few interdisciplinary projects in collaboration with the NTFHO as Chief Ornithologist."

Samantha held out her right hand for a handshake, prompting Dr. Neil to stand up and shake hands.

"It is a pleasure to meet you. I am assuming that Karan has already introduced me."

"He has indeed. You are the illustrious teacher of the prodigious student, Aman. We have chosen him for our summer internship program. Please have a seat."

Samantha settled down on the sofa as Karan brought cookies from the kitchen and placed them on the table after offering them to Samantha. With sweat drops on his forehead, Karan asked,

"At the risk of being abrupt, please tell me honestly if the locket necklace actually belongs to you. Are you sure that it doesn't belong to John or Rick?"

Samantha rolled her eyebrows and gave the men a disapproving glance. After a brief pause of reckoning, she asked,

"Why do you ask that?"

"We might get a serious clue about their current whereabouts if it belongs to them."

There was an awkward and long silence in the room as everyone stared blankly at each other. Even though the silence had given away Samantha's secret, Karan wanted to hear the truth from her as a close confidante and friend. He pulled an album from the drawer, opened it and handed it to Samantha.

"Check out these photos. You will understand why we are asking that question."

As Samantha opened the photo album, she observed that all the pictures showed birds of all shapes and sizes with ornaments tied to them. On the first page, there was a photo of a sparrow with a miniature golden bangle strapped around its neck. On the second one, there was a fearsome eagle with a pearl-strung anklet on its claw. The next pages depicted more variety with cranes, crows and even entire flocks of flying birds like geese. As the pages were flipped, the size of the birds grew with that of the ornaments adorning them. On the last page, there was a huge vulture with a small silver necklace tied around its chest.

"Are you implying that the locket necklace came with the gigantic bird in Sanjay Gandhi National Park?"

"Yes, we are. Dr. Neil measured the circumference of the bird's claws. This necklace could fit if tied to one of the claws."

Samantha gazed around the living room. She hadn't realized its grandeur when her primary focus was on finding her family. The main wall in front of her had ornate showcases carved into it. One of the showcases, which was in the shape of a tilted square, housed several distinctly coloured hardcover books. Another rectangular one was covered with a glass pane, allowing one to see the cashew spirit bottles kept inside. The gold-framed painting of a man, wearing a hat and a black long coat, hung in the center of the wall beside her.

As she overcame her moment of awe, she asked, "Why are all these birds covered in ornaments? Where were they spotted? How did the gigantic bird -?"

Karan said, "I know that you have a lot of questions. Let me give you the context of their appearance from the very start. Professor Neil, please fill in any details that I might miss."

Professor Neil nodded his head while Samantha clasped her hands in anticipation.

"The first instance was captured around four months ago at the Dudhsagar Waterfalls in the beach destination of Goa by an eminent wildlife photographer. When the photograph was sent for a publishing contest, it was immediately chosen by the Mumbai Diary magazine's Chief Editor to feature on the upcoming edition's front cover. Thousands of magazine copies had already been printed by the time the police swooped in to halt its production.

A senior crime investigator working with the Indian government, had accidentally noticed a pre-published edition and realized that the unusual bird might be a spying tool by another country. The magazine and the wildlife photographer were duly compensated for the halt and further investigation was launched. Ornithologists and police officers scanned the entire region around the waterfall for three days but couldn't spot any other jewel-bedecked birds. Some people claimed that the bird might be simply collecting shiny objects due to their biological attraction towards them as exhibited by some species like the magpie. Others blamed the photographer for sending a hoax edited photograph. The entire matter was laughed off until …"

Karan took a deep breath and added,

"Can I pass you the baton from here, Dr. Neil?"

"Sure. I was spending a beautiful evening at the Powai Lake with my nephew on a lazy weekend. The fluorescent orange sun was setting behind the clouds as it glazed the clear blue water below."

"You ought to be a poet, Dr Neil," chuckled Karan.

"I know that I am digressing. I had been so enamoured of the surroundings at that time that I get carried away while describing it. Anyway, my nephew insisted on taking a tour of the lake

on one of the tourist boats. I obliged and paid a boat rider to take us on a private tour. He rowed the small canoe to the centre of the lake and then halted it to a still so that we could enjoy the sights and sounds of the lake.

At that moment, a parrot with a thin golden necklace flew into the boat and sat on my nephew's hand. On seeing the sparkling and probably valuable necklace, the boat rider ran after the parrot but tripped and fell into the lake as the parrot flew away. After a frantic rescue operation and return to the shore, I realized that these jewel carrying birds were not isolated cases."

Samantha asked, "Why can't I see a parrot like that one in this album?"

"That is so because we have not captured a live parrot specimen yet. Barring the first photograph, all these photographs are of bejewelled birds, which were tracked and captured for our studies."

"Where did you capture the first live specimen?", said Samantha with her wide eyes betraying her curiosity.

"Considering that the first two sightings were near water bodies, I had a hunch that these birds frequented places with access to water. One of my graduate students captured a spotted eagle with an anklet near the prehistoric Lonar lake, which was formed in a crater created on the Earth's surface by an asteroid collision. However, most of the captured birds were found in freshwater bodies closer to the sea coast in the states of Maharashtra and Goa. In the coming weeks, we captured vultures, cranes, larks and many other species of birds wearing all sorts of ornaments from bangles and trinkets to necklaces.

The collection of around fifty birds gave us a good sample set to study at the University of Mumbai."

After listening to Neil intently, Samantha said, "Did you find an explanation for their attraction towards water bodies or the jewels through your studies?"

"To be honest, we haven't been able to unveil much in this regard. We analyzed the genetic sequence in these birds to see if there was a pattern but we couldn't detect any unusual trend in the sequence. However, we noticed a pattern in the density and type of such birds as time progressed. The birds that we spotted in the initial months were not only fewer in number but also much smaller than the ones we found later. Initially, we chanced upon an occasional sparrow or lark. In the coming weeks, we could observe flocks of five to ten such birds. After that, we began to encounter much bigger birds like eagles or vultures. It seemed as if someone was trying to make these birds more noticeable as time passed. Of course, the last one was too gigantic to be inconspicuous."

"The locket necklace from Rick and John suggests that they might be trying to send a signal. Doesn't all the collected jewellery reveal something about their origin?"

"We carbon-dated all the jewellery after one of my graduate students pointed out that the designs didn't have a very contemporary look. The National Technology for History Organization helped us with the same since my ornithology laboratories weren't equipped for conducting carbon dating. It turned out that every piece was between three to four hundred years old. Since this shocking and intriguing twist to the mystery, I have been collaborating with the NTFHO on this project."

"You already have some clues to narrow down the list of possible places of origin. The answer might lie in any of the historical sites in Goa and Maharashtra, which belong to that period and are located close to a water body."

"Yes, you are absolutely right. In fact, we have initiated an extensive search campaign across all the shortlisted regions meeting those criteria since the past three weeks. We are optimistic about tracing the origin of these birds, which might even lead us to your missing family."

"That is great. Although, there are a few details that you and Karan still haven't told me about. It is impossible that you wouldn't search the closest nature reserve with a water body from the Powai Lake.

Karan wasn't jogging in the Sanjay Gandhi National Park that day to stay fit. Am I right?" she said as she slightly winked at Karan.

Karan nodded and replied amusedly, "Yes, you got me. I was searching for these birds but I hadn't expected an encounter with one of such an enormous size."

Samantha said, "How are you a part of this project? You are a professor of behavioural economics and an aspiring Bollywood actor. Neither behavioural economics nor acting have any connection to the domain of this project."

Karan stammered and struggled to give a response but Samantha stopped him midway and continued, "Cashew spirit is the signature drink of Goa. The cashew spirit bottles in that showcase tell me that you travelled to Goa within the past few months. You tell me about your Bollywood aspirations but your living room is decorated with a large painting of Sherlock Holmes, not a Bollywood actor. Your bookshelf is filled with mystery novels. I think there was no wildlife photographer in the actual narrative. There was just a government investigative officer, who realized the potential implications of his vacation photograph at the last minute. Am I right, Karan?"

"I might be an investigative officer but you outshine me in your skills as a detective. I suppose I can't put up my pretence of a struggling Bollywood actor in front of you any longer. However, I am actually a professor of behavioural economics at the University of Mumbai. I didn't want to draw too much suspicion about my profession so I thought that a part-time guest lecturer position wouldn't hurt, especially considering how my undergraduate major was getting unutilized."

Samantha smirked and said, "Now that I think of it, who would conduct auditions so early in the morning? These auditions were just a pretext for you to get away on your hunt for bejewelled birds in Sanjay Gandhi National Park."

Karan nodded with a wide-eyed expression. Samantha quizzed him further, "If this is a secret mission, why did you tell me about the giant bird at the hospital?"

Karan pointed to the bottles of cashew spirits. He said, "Nobody was believing me. Even my friends at NTFHO. When I am too drunk on alcohol, I spill anything that bothers me even if it is a secret. I had stopped drinking in the presence of people beyond my work colleagues but it was a lapse that day."

Neil chuckled and added, "Despite this lapse, which could have turned into a grave mistake, we have been fairly impressed by his performance at NTFHO. If the bird didn't belong to the supposedly extinct Pelagornis Sandersi species, we would have named the bird species after him. Considering his fake association with Bollywood, the name "Bollywood Bird" is also a tribute of sorts though."

CHAPTER 7

THE AVIARY TOUR

"So, you are basically asking me to forgo a research opportunity of a lifetime for the sake of a distant relative's elephant," said Aman on the mobile call.

Maya replied, "Aunt Maria was not a distant relative. She was my cousin. She had no spouse or children and her only sibling died last year. That leaves us as her closest living relatives to take care of her inheritance, which includes her elephant."

"My condolences are with her grieving pet elephant but I cannot abandon my project at such a critical juncture. Can't the scores of house helpers provide the needed support?"

"Elephants are complex social creatures with a powerful memory. We cannot rely on a worker to fill the void of compassion and love in that poor elephant's life. If the worker decides to discontinue working for us in the future, the second parting would leave it eternally heartbroken."

"Even I wouldn't be with the elephant in Vidika forever. How does my presence in Vidika solve the problem?"

"You don't need to stay in Vidika and take care of the elephant. However, since Maria has named both of us as the joint custodians in her inheritance, your physical presence in Vidika would be needed for me to take custody of the elephant in the first place."

"I understand your noble intentions but it is a tough call to leave Mumbai on a weekday. I will need to think about it. Give me time till the end of today to figure out something."

The shaking bus on the bumpy road screeched to a halt, propelling the passengers towards the seat in front of them. As Karan massaged his bumped head, Samantha handed him his fallen book.

Karan said, "I told you that we should have boarded the next fully vacant bus. It is impossible to read calmly in the constantly shaking back seats."

Samantha cheekily replied, "You won't be a professor of behavioural economics forever. You can quit reading for a bit."

The bus finally stopped at its destination in front of the blue multi-storey building. The shiny LED-lit letters on the top, which were overshadowed by the bright morning sun, read -

"National Technology for History Organization Headquarters."

The passengers de-boarded the bus one by one. Some of them went directly inside the building while the others stopped at the tea stall outside to sip their routine morning masala tea. Aman, Karan, Samantha and Neil belonged to the former cohort.

Inside the ground floor of the building, the lift door opened and the scores of people waiting outside rushed in. The disgruntled crowd, struggling for space and breath in the packed lift, made the insufficiency of four lifts serving a thirty-floor building evident. Sensing this, Aman rushed forward to stop the lift and avoid a long wait for the next one. However, Dr. Neil stopped him by gesturing him to come back.

"We aren't going inside the building, Aman," he said.

He opened his backpack and handed out encrypted identity cards to Samantha and Neil. As they took turns to receive their respective cards, Neil smiled at them and said,

"Welcome to your first day at NTFHO."

As the next queues began to line up in front of the lifts, Neil beckoned everyone to move towards the back door of the building. Two uniformed guards with guns stood beside a conveyor belt in front of the door. Once the guards had checked them with a metal detector and screened their backpacks, they held their identity cards against the door and opened it.

The door opened to reveal a vast courtyard on the other side. The short roof above the narrow corridor gave way to clear blue skies as they stepped out.

The courtyard consisted of several stone-paved paths amidst verdant gardens, which led to and curled around uniformly spread glass domes. The gardens were replete with roses, lilies and marigold flowers, which attracted a myriad of hovering yellow butterflies. The tallest glass dome stood prominently in the center of the park with the other smaller versions in an orbit around it.

"Should we sit down for breakfast or head straight to the tour?" said Neil when he noticed Aman looking at the people who were eating on benches inside the garden.

"No, I had my breakfast in the morning. I was just wondering why everyone is wearing helmets."

"Let us start the tour and you will understand the reason on your own."

As they moved towards the first dome on the circular path, they observed that a cubical room projected from the exterior of the dome. The dome's reflective glass glinted with the blue colour of the sky, creating a sense of mystery as it obscured its internal contents. The team followed Neil through the door of the attached cubical room. On entering the room, they could see various framed photographs of a hornbill on the front well. The photographs depicted the bird in various positions as it fed on apricots, perched on a tree or flew in the skies.

Samantha recognized one of the photographs, which showed the hornbill with a golden bangle wrapped around the yellow crest on its head, as the one that she had seen in the album of bejewelled birds. Beneath the photographs, a vivacious woman with a round face and curly brown hair sat on the reception desk.

"Good afternoon, Professor Neil. How many people will be accompanying you inside?"

"Apart from me, there are three people."

"That works. There's just one more person inside at the moment. Kishan, please don't allow any more visitors inside. The maximum limit of five has been reached," she said as she looked towards a uniformed guard, wearing a dark blue uniform and carrying a rifle. The guard, who stood at the entrance door to the glass dome, nodded.

Aman gasped as he said, "I am seeing an aviary for the first time in my life."

Karan grinned and said, "I hope that you stay as excited when spending time at an aviary becomes a routine part of your life."

The guard handed each one of them a helmet and a whistle. He explained, "The helmet and gloves will protect your head in the off chance that the bird gets violent. If you sense or face even the slightest of troubles, do not hesitate to whistle. I will tranquilize the bird."

"Dr. Neil, are you sure that we will be safe?" asked Samantha as she rolled her eyes with doubt and anticipation.

He replied, "Don't worry. The Indian hornbill is a fairly harmless bird with no documented attacks on humans. We are just going the extra mile to ensure complete safety of all our visitors. We don't want an unprecedented untoward incident to derail our progress."

Once Samantha's fears had been allayed, everyone proceeded to position their identity cards in front of the security detector one by one. The gate opened for around fifteen seconds when the card was detected, allowing each visitor a small time window to pass through and the gate to close behind them. The dome walls were covered with countless climber plants, which wrapped around wooden supporting sticks.

The blowers attached to the humidifiers on the walls continuously spewed out and circulated misty air throughout the dome. The low-lying fog obscured the view within the dome and one could only observe a few tall evergreen trees jutting out from the white clouds as the horizon slipped into oblivion. Sunlight streamed in through irregular dew-free patches on the upper portions of the dome.

Realizing that they couldn't see each other from a distance, they walked closer to each other to prevent someone from losing track of the others.

As they moved ahead, they saw slender trees with pointed thin leaves, which curled up to form shallow boat-like structures and bent under the weight of accumulated water. Water droplets slipped down the slopes of the leaves and dripped from their narrow tips.

Neil remarked, "Notice the curved shape of these leaves. It has been specifically adapted for the humid climate. Their shape ensures that the leaves can release water for the purposes of respiration and perspiration."

Samantha further drew everyone's attention to the glossy barks with white deposits. As she felt the smoothness of the bark on touching it, she said, "This is wax. Does the slippery wax also aid the release of water?"

"You are right. The wax also serves a similar purpose as the pointed leaves. Wax is not just slippery but also hydrophobic or water-repelling," said Neil.

"Are we trying to simulate the real-life environment of the Indian hornbill's natural habitat inside the dome?"

"Yes, Samantha. We are attempting to recreate similar environmental conditions as observed in the tropical cloud forests on the Western Ghats hills."

Among the dense canopy of green vegetation, one of the trees stood out distinctly with its pale red leaves transfused with shades of green and yellow. A pleasant aroma wafted through the air as they approached the tree.

Aman sniffed it and said, "This aroma seems recognizable but I can't recall where exactly I have smelled it."

Karan said, "Do you remember the last time you went to a temple, Aman?"

Aman recalled the black incense sticks that the priest lit to generate fragrant smoke from their partially burnt orange tops.

A calm smile crossed his face and he asked, "Is this tree the source of camphor?"

"Yes. Camphor is a white substance produced from the wood of the tree. It is not just used to manufacture incense sticks for temples but also insect repellents."

Samantha bent forward towards the reddish green leaves on a lowered tree branch. After a deep breath, she remarked,

"The smell isn't coming from the leaves. I wonder what the source of this fragrance is."

Karan said, "The smell is coming from the trampled leaves below. Try plucking and crushing these leaves. Then, take a whiff."

Samantha plucked a small leaf and smelled it before holding out the crushed leaves on her palm towards her three companions. The tranquil smile on everyone's face reflected their approval. Karan said, "It is not difficult to understand why it is used to induce spiritual contentment and build concentration while praying in temples."

Beyond the crushed leaves, two trees slanted towards each other and almost formed an arc over a stone-paved path. As they looked back, they realized that they had already been walking on the path, which had been obscured by fallen leaves and brown soil till that point.

Neil sighed, "I had been searching for this path all this while. Following the path will take us on a circular tour throughout the dome and prevent us from getting lost in the dense fog. Let us keep our eyes and ears open for the hornbill as we walk."

Aman's enthusiasm couldn't allow him to take well-defined paths though. He gallivanted across the dome, marvelling at the sights and sounds from the tiger butterflies on a bright red mistletoe to the squirrels sipping water from an earthen bowl. While absorbing the charisma of his surroundings, he occasionally got so lost in his thoughts that one of his companions had to call him to rejoin the trail.

However, nobody gave him a reminder when he wandered off amongst the trees while chasing an army of hopping tree frogs. The prominently coloured orange and green frogs stood out in the pale green grass for a while but disappeared into the mist after a few minutes of passionate chasing. As he frantically searched for the path, he saw a grey apparition emerge from the dense white fog. Aman momentarily shook with trepidation before regaining his senses to move towards the human figure.

"Aman, what are you doing here?" said a familiar voice.

As she emerged from the shadows, Aman recognized Tisha, who was donning a long white lab coat, protective glasses and a yellow helmet. He said before being abruptly cut off,

"I have been hired as an intern…"

"Never mind. Stay quiet and look there."

Aman looked in the direction of Tisha's finger. He saw a yellow beak, curved like a scimitar, protruding from a tall woody tree's cavity.

The beak intermittently opened to register a reverberating shrill cry. Tisha motioned Aman to follow her and both of them crept quietly to the base of the tree. Aman noticed that the tree was unusually large with its highest branch almost touching the central tip of the dome. It also had a relatively complex structure with umpteen leafy branches and sub-branches spreading out in all directions from the trunk.

Tisha patted Aman on his back and swayed her head in a slanting upward fashion as if she wanted him to look in that direction. Aman partially closed his eyes and concentratedly peered at the spherical purple fruits, which hung from the tree branch. Another magnificent hornbill was perched on the branch. The curved casque on its head resembled a flat sailor cap though its bright yellow colour was closer to that of a golden crown's.

Tisha whispered, "The male bird, perched on the tree, is behaving weirdly. It should respond to the female hornbill's calls and feed her as she broods the eggs in the tree cavity.

However, this male hornbill is being indifferent to her calls and not bringing her food. If she doesn't receive her usual diet of figs and small rodents, she will starve and die."

"Is it the same hornbill that was spotted with the jewels?"

"Yes. It is the same one. We introduced a female hornbill into its habitat to examine its reaction. While female hornbills are known to be extremely selective while picking mates, making it difficult for conservation programs to breed them in captivity, this one easily mated with the male hornbill. However, since the time she found a nesting site and laid eggs, the male hornbill's behaviour has completely not been on expected lines."

"Shouldn't we intervene and help the female hornbill in this case? She could be mechanically fed food by a spoon or any other feeding instrument."

"You are right. We can try that. But first, let us get out of here and move towards the path."

"How will we find it? I have been struggling to find it for quite a while amidst these low-lying clouds."

"We are underneath the centre of the dome. If we move in the forward direction away from it, we will land on the diametrically opposite side of the path where you probably came from. Aren't you an engineering student?"

Aman blushed with a look of self-disapproval as he took a last look at the hornbills and trudged through the deep layers of fallen leaves and squashed figs. The sound of the blowers grew louder as they approached the path besides the boundary walls.

On the way, Tisha said, "It is so wonderful that you bagged the internship. I am so happy for you."

"Thanks. I won the competition that NTFHO conducted, providing me the opportunity to intern with them for the summer. Today is my first day. I believe that the hands-on experience will broaden my perspectives and allow me to make a more informed decision on whether I should drop out of my engineering program or not."

Aman noticed that the boundary walls were loaded with much fewer humidifiers and blowers than before, causing the glass walls to be relatively clearer. He peeked through the glass to see people strolling in the lush grassy gardens outside. However, the dark green mountains, far away in the background, caught his attention.

"The Western Ghats. The natural habitat of the hornbills," gasped Aman as his mind conjured up images of hornbill flocks perched on hilly trees.

Upon noticing his dazed expression, Tisha laughed and said, "You are always so lost in your own world. We need to get out."

They met Samantha and Karan, waiting for Aman at the entrance with visibly tensed expressions. Karan said,

"Glad to know you are alive, Aman. We thought the hornbills ate you up when we couldn't find you."

"I wandered off and got lost but thankfully ran into Tisha."

The face had looked familiar to Samantha and the mention of the name refreshed her memories of her former student. She said,

"I am pleasantly surprised to see you, Tisha. What have you been up to since school? It has been such a long time since I met you at the high school alumni reunion."

"It is a pleasure indeed. I see that you are continuing to shape generations of history enthusiasts. Your lectures were the prime motivator for me to take up history electives and then, a history minor apart from my biology major at Delhi University. Aman wants to work at the intersection of technology and history. Now, destiny has brought us all together to work on this interdisciplinary project."

Karan said, "I am surprised that both of you already knew each other. Samantha, do you remember Neil talking about his first graduate student, who captured the first live specimen of a bejewelled bird near Lonar lake? She was none other than Tisha."

With a beaming face, Samantha said, "Amazing. I am proud of my students. Tisha, are you pursuing a masters degree from the University of Mumbai?"

"Yes, I am pursuing a specialized graduate program, focused on evolutionary biology. I am looking forward to joining a PhD program after graduating. I am working with Professor Neil on this project as a graduate researcher. That reminds me. Where is Professor Neil? I need to inform him about the dire situation of the female hornbill."

Karan said, "Dr. Sourab, the mission director of NTFHO, called him for some work-related matter. He went a few minutes ago to meet him while we decided to wait here for you. Let us get out of here and have lunch."

* * *

"Are you sure that you didn't hire Ms. Samantha Hughes for this project out of empathy for her?" said Dr. Sourab.

Professor Neil replied, "My decision has nothing to do with her lost family even though the connection to it was the reason we met in the first place."

"But do you feel confident about your decision, considering that she hasn't completed and is not even enrolled in a graduate masters program? She only holds a bachelors in history degree from the University of Rajasthan and a bachelors in education degree from the University of Mumbai."

"Nobody is born with qualifications, Dr. Sourab. Remarkable students earn their qualifications through hard work, a keen desire for learning and a first principles problem-solving approach. Ms. Samantha Hughes demonstrates all these traits and will surely be a valuable addition to the project as a part-time associate researcher."

"If you say so, then I believe you."

* * *

The group convened to have a hearty meal at the canteen tables in the open ground. There were all sorts of dishes and desserts on the table from steaming biryani, haphazardly-shaped jalebis to sweet milk in earthen cups.

Samantha said, "A scrumptious meal in an open ground with a cool breezy climate makes the earth a paradise."

Neil held out his glass of lime soda as the others clanged their glasses against his and shouted together, "Cheers!"

Aman remarked, "If these smaller domes are so well-built and spacious, the largest one in the centre of the park must be almost like a full-fledged forest."

Tisha said, "Not exactly. We are trying our best to replicate their natural environments in the middle of a city but we know that their actual habitats are much more complex and gigantic."

Aman asked, "Which bird resides in the biggest dome? Is it the one that attacked Marine Drive?"

Neil said, "No. That one is too large to be caged in any of these domes. The biggest dome belongs to a flock of three tawny eagles. They are territorial by nature and each of them requires a separate space."

Samantha looked bewildered. She asked, "If the gigantic bird is not present in one of these aviaries, then where is it?"

Neil said, "You mean Pelagornis Sandersi, right?"

She winked and said, "Yes, that one. Don't judge me. It isn't an easy name to remember."

"It is literally roaming right beneath us," chuckled Karan.

Looking at Aman and Samantha's confounded faces,

Neil said, "Let me explain. The bird's physical strength makes it difficult to entrap it within an ordinary structure on the ground. It wouldn't take more than a few wing flutters and beak pecks of the bird to burst open these glass domes. That's why it has been caged in a high-security underground facility with earthquake-proof walls."

Aman didn't seem happy upon hearing this. He said, "Isn't it cruel to keep a free flying bird in a harsh and congested space?"

Neil nodded and said, "It is definitely not optimum even though we have tried to keep the facility as liveable as possible. However, we need to monitor the bird closely and conduct a series of safety assessments before we can shift it to its permanent abode - a mega-aviary being constructed on the outskirts of Mumbai. Currently, none of the zoological parks across the country are equipped to house such a bird. Once this new facility passes all the structural tests and we can establish that the bird poses no security threat, the mega-aviary can be opened for public viewing. This will also enable ornithologists to study the bird's behaviour in a more natural environment."

The melody of a song started playing in the air as the conversation was going on. Everyone on the table turned around to look at Neil as he pulled out his ringing mobile from his pocket. He excused himself and went a few feet away from the table for a brief conversation before coming back to announce, "The bird has woken up. Karan, hurry up. You are going down in the underground facility with me. The seating capacity there is limited and exclusive but the rest of you could visit the screen room with CCTV footage. Tisha, can you please lead Aman and Samantha to the room and give them the context?"

Tisha nodded and led Samantha and Aman towards the door connecting the courtyard to the building. Karan hastily gobbled the last jalebis on his plate and ran in the opposite direction towards the other extreme of the park, where Neil stood and waved at him.

Aman and Samantha followed Tisha without any questions but their faces revealed their impatience for an explanation. However, Tisha's attention was elsewhere. She continued to stare at the lift button with disappointment. She sighed,

"The lift is stuck on the 30th floor. Do both of you mind taking the stairs to the 8th floor?"

Samantha said, "I am not exactly a fitness freak but the sudden enthusiasm in the environment tells me that the sweat will be worth it. Let us go for it."

Aman nodded in unison and the three of them commenced the exhausting climb. As they rushed up the stairs, Tisha explained, "We know that our mouth waters when we see or smell delicacies. The smell or sight stimulates the release of saliva to aid the foreseen digestion process during anticipated food consumption. Interestingly, all the bejewelled birds that we have captured till date exhibit mouth watering when they see gold jewellery. However, only around thirty percent of these birds picked up the gold jewellery and none of them tried to wear or consume it. While we haven't been able to decipher the reason for their behaviour, we feel that this behavioural pattern might be a significant clue. The gigantic bird was tranquilized yesterday and a gold wreath was placed in front of it during its slumber. It has woken up now after a long sleep of twelve hours. Everyone is curious and excited to observe the reaction of the bird to jewellery for the first time."

Meanwhile, Karan and Neil waited as the series of steel benches, hinged onto electric pulleys, gradually emerged from the deep well. Karan looked up at the clear blue sky reminiscently as if he was seeing it for the last time. A husky man pushed a stair-shaped wooden pedestal towards the rim of the well. The scientists, historians and government military officials queued up as the man checked their identity cards before letting them onboard the bench seats through the stair installment.

A lady in the queue pleaded, "I am a senior historian from the Department of Archaeology. Please allow me to board my seat. The ride will go down by the time I go to fetch my identity."

The man verifying the cards was unmoved. He said,

"I am sorry, ma'am but the rules are very strict. You can still catch the live recording in the CCTV screen room."

As the woman sat on the park bench with a visibly repentant face, she watched the occupied benches being lowered into the well. A half-split lid bent over the well to completely shut its mouth as the benches vanished into obscurity.

"I know that the chambers are artificially oxygenated but my heart always skips a beat when the lid shuts," whispered Neil as he saw the last strand of the blue sky above him vanish.

There was a moment of pitch-black darkness until the orange bulbs on the circular walls around them began to light up sequentially. First, the regularly spaced bulbs on the upper section of the circular walls lit up. Then, the speed of lighting picked up and overcame the gradual pace at which the bench was being lowered, causing the bulbs immediately around the seated audience to light up. Karan peered down to see the layers of bulbs sequentially light up the depths below them.

"Is there no end to its depth?" said one of the seated men, who looked with horror at the new depths, which were being revealed by the bulbs below him with every passing second.

Finally, the last layer of bulbs at the deepest part of the well lit up and the benches hit the solid bottom a few minutes later. Karan and Neil rubbed their eyes while struggling to open them in the brightly lit room at the bottom. The belts that tied them to their seats automatically sprung open and both of them hopped off the ride.

There were four tunneled corridors leading outwards from the room. Three of them had been barricaded and closed off while one of them was open for entering with a signboard in front of it.

The group began to enter the open tunnel one by one.

The tunnel's ending led to a dimly lit room with cushioned seats arranged in concentric circles, facing outwards in all directions towards the surrounding walls. The seats in the inner circles were raised to a greater height than the ones in the immediately outer circle, making the structure look like a conical pyramid.

Once everyone had assembled in their allocated seats, the accompanying guide entered a password into a kiosk near the wall and pressed a red button on it. The hung films of black cloth on the four walls began to roll up to reveal transparent walls behind them. The room soon resembled a glass aquarium where a role reversal of humans from spectators to exhibits and the animal from an exhibit to a spectator seemed to have taken place.

Some of the audience members in the upper seats shook and repulsed back in fear while others just shrieked out loudly as they came face to face with the peering giant bird.

The guide rushed forward to calm the panicked group and announced, "Relax. The bird cannot see or hear you. The material of the walls has been specifically engineered by our material scientists to withstand high forces without compromising on its internal transparency and external opacity."

The bird's face almost touched the ceiling as it wobbled its head and fluttered its feathers in an attempt to brush off its dizziness. It stood in a grassy field where climbers with red bougainvillea flowers and white jasmine flower shrubs were spread everywhere. The bird's black eyes shone prominently in the pale yellow light as it struggled in vain to look at its neck, which had been restrained by a collar.

Meanwhile, the CCTV screening closely replicated the underground bird observatory in its design. The real-life views beyond the glass walls were replaced by four projector screens.

Aman remarked, "I wish I had such a setup in my college hostel. It takes so much time for my friends to build a consensus on which movie to watch together. A four-screen cinema hall would make it easy. Everyone can just sit together but watch their respective preferred movies."

Samantha said, "That sounds like a perfect recipe for chaos as streaming sounds from all the screens would clash with each other. And if everyone is watching a different movie, then the fun in friendly commentary and post-movie discussions is gone."

Tisha drew their attention towards the bird and said, "Can you see the strap on the bird's neck? It is a metal detector, which will start sending sound signals into the observatory when the bird's face approaches the jewellery lying in the tall grass. There is also a tiny strip at the base of its tongue, which can detect the level of saliva in its mouth."

Inside the underground observatory, the audience's fearful anticipation gave way to passionate curiosity when they noticed the giant bird frolicking in the gardens, oblivious to their presence. The bird's movements abruptly came to a halt after the bird's head bumped into one of the viewing walls, briefly recreating a pandemonium among the audience. However, it didn't try to fly in the direction of the wall again. Instead, it froze in its tracks and moved its eyes towards the grass. A golden anklet gleamed amidst the verdant green shade. Within a few seconds, a cylindrical unlit lamp on a corner of the room began to glow with a faint green light. As time passed, the faint light grew stronger and the upper parts of the cylinder also started glowing.

With excitement betraying his voice, Karan muttered,

"The bird has seen the jewellery!"

Neil looked at the numbers etched on the side of the lamp and after a few moments of whispered calculations, gasped, "This is the highest level of saliva that we have seen in any of the birds when adjusted for bird mass."

The brightness level of the lamp light started falling as soon as it had risen and the lamp soon completely faded into oblivion again. However, the shining golden anklet that the bird now held with its peak drew more attention from the wide-eyed audience. The room was soon reverberating with beeping sounds of the metal detector. However, the bird's fascination with the piece of jewel was short-lived as it flung the anklet away with its beak, sending a few of the attached beads into the air. The beeping sound of the metal detector stopped.

Aman looked dreamily at the turn of events, which was unfolding on the screens in front of his eyes. Tisha looked at her watch, which had struck 5 PM. She said,

"Considering that the reaction of mouth watering saliva in the bird's beak to its jewellery observation has been established,

I don't think there is anything left to watch. The bird has discarded the piece of jewellery and doesn't seem interested in picking it up again. Do both of you want to stay or leave?"

"If you say that there is nothing left to see, then we can leave for the day," said Aman. "Most of the other people also seem to be leaving. Let us hurry or else we will miss the bus, which leaves at 5:15 PM."

Samantha nodded and the three of them proceeded to step out of the room. They had barely reached the exit when a beeping sound filled the room again. Tisha turned back and saw the bird lowering its neck again. It seemed to be preening its feathers with its beak.

Samantha said, "Didn't the bird fling away the anklet to the other side of the wall? Why is the metal detector making that sound when the bird isn't even close to the anklet?"

Tisha remembered that Samantha was right and asked the assistant, who was handling the projector screens, "Can you please focus the right screen downwards so that we can peer closely at the grass around the bird's claws?"

As instructed by Tisha, the assistant diverted the CCTV screen closer to the grass. The sharp talons on the bird's claw covered the entire screen but the jewellery was not in sight. Tisha requested the assistant to tilt the camera by a few degrees upward. The screen showed a mound of bird droppings. As he zoomed in on those droppings, a shiny gold coin stood out in the massive heap.

While the few people in the remaining audience struggled to read the script inscribed on the coin, the sideways posing elephant and dog caught Samantha's attention immediately. She said,

"It is an old coin issued by the kingdom of Vidika. Is Vidika covered under the list of archaeological sites that are being currently investigated for the origin of the bejewelled birds?"

Tisha gasped for a moment, regained her breath and then said, "No, it isn't. We were prioritising cities, which were not only seats of power in medieval India but also housed a freshwater body since all the previous birds had been captured near a lake, pond or waterfall."

Aman smiled as he knew where they were headed next. He heaved a sigh at the resolution of his dilemma.

"Grandma, I am coming home!" he cheerfully announced on the phone.

CHAPTER 8

CHAMBERS CONDITIONED FOR CHATS

"Dad, I want to go on the roller coaster moving around the Bollywood bird's enclosure. The stadium seats are too far to offer a proper view of the bird," said the five-year old girl.

Her father looked at the wide signboard in front of him, which illustrated the outline of the amusement park. The photograph showed an ellipsoidal glass dome sparkling in a glossy blue shade under the sun. The winding roller coaster track, composed of wooden planks, passed over the centre of the dome, allowing the roller coaster riders to get a close peek at the giant bird's new residence. The enclosure was surrounded by a circular wall, elevating the stadium seats behind it. There was a narrow strip of golden seats in the front, which was followed by successively broader strips of gray and bronze seats in the back.

At the ticket counter where the father stood, only the dome and the coaster track were visible. However, they weren't seeing it for the first time. The dome had started getting visible from as far as 30 kilometres on the highway during their weekend drive to the park. Standing tall at more than 200 metres, the dome towered over the apartments and farmhouses in the coastal town of Alibag.

"Dad, the counter is getting crowded. We won't be able to get in on time," the young girl reminded her father.

His father nodded and glanced worryingly at the ticket prices. The 15-minute roller coaster ride was exorbitantly priced at Rs. 7000 per head. The price of a golden seat for the same duration was only Rs. 3500 per head. The silver and bronze seats were even cheaper at Rs. 2000 and Rs. 1000 per head.

He wasn't as enthusiastic about the bird as his daughter. As an architect, whose interest had been sparked by witnessing architectural marvels like the Meenakshi temple and the Taj Mahal in his childhood, he understood the importance of inspiration though. Reluctant to disappoint his young daughter's dreams, he emptied the cash notes in his wallet and proceeded towards the queue for roller coaster rides.

While the roller coaster riders screamed upon climbing the dome's peak, Neil sat in his observatory with a dull face. The bird flapped its wide wings, making the screams even louder.

Neil heaved a sigh as the structure maintained its integrity. Despite several stress tests in the week before, he was still concerned about an unforeseen compromise in the structural strength of the dome. He didn't want to witness a conscience-shaking human injury or fatality because of his oversight. The smooth operations for the past five days since the park's opening had refuted his concerns though. He smiled and said to Karan, "The park is running fine. Our presence is needed in Vidika now. Even though we sent the team of researchers a week back, we need to oversee and expedite the investigations."

Karan nodded in agreement as he folded and put down the newspaper on the table. The front-page headline read, "Alibag hotels record a high of 99.9% occupancy in March as Bollywood bird attracts tourists from across the world."

* * *

Smoke belched out from the front of the train as it sped forward. Clouds of dust sprung up in the air around the railway tracks, briefly obscuring the bright afternoon shade. A man, dressed in a red uniform, ran towards the escaping train.

Giving up, he flung the small cloth bag in his hand towards the carriage entrance in a last desperate attempt. A girl standing close to the entrance inside the train caught it and almost fell backwards before regaining her balance and waving her hands to the man in gratitude.

The man was one of the several indispensable coolies, traditional luggage porters on Indian railway platforms, who reliably carried heavy bags for overpacked travellers daily.

Aman jumped from the stairs onto the platform and fell flat on the ground after tripping on a potted plant. He looked up and watched aghast as the last carriage left the station. As he stood up on his feet disappointingly, he heard a sound, "Did we just miss the train?" It was Karan.

Neil, who was beside him, fretted as he clicked his mobile phone repeatedly to navigate the Indian Railways app.

"No, we haven't," he proclaimed, much to everyone's relief.

"It was the Shatabdi train. The Rajdhani train, which we are supposed to board, is set to arrive in a minute."

Karan said, "I wonder where Samantha is. Let me call her and ask her to be quick lest she misses the train."

Aman pointed his fingers and said, "There is no need for that. She is sitting on that bench beside the tea stall."

The trio dragged their luggage to the bench and greeted Samantha. They had barely begun to start conversing when the whistling of the train's arrival interrupted them. As the four of them waited in a queue while the arriving passengers de-boarded, Aman remembered, "Tisha hasn't arrived yet. Should we wait for her?".

"We can't," said Samantha. "The train will leave the platform in two minutes and we will miss it if we wait."

"Let us get inside and call her," suggested Karan.

The table in the centre of the coach had three cushioned seats on opposite seats. Samantha, Aman and Neil pushed their luggage into the steel meshed chambers over them while Karan frantically called Tisha. After several failed attempts, he finally joined the others on the comfy velvet seats.

"She isn't picking up," sighed Karan. "I guess she will have to find another way of travelling to Vidika now."

There was a whistle and the train gradually started moving. The shouts of the tea sellers and the chatters of the coolies faded as the train sped away from the platform. The green signboard flashed "See you again in Mumbai" in neon red lights amidst the fading sunlight. The city of dreams had bid its goodbyes. Aman smiled at the irony as he remembered how he had left Vidika for Mumbai to pursue his dreams of being a software engineer. Now, Mumbai was sending him back again.

By the time the stars revealed themselves, the train was speeding through a village as apparent from the huts dotting the lush green landscape on both sides. A group of elderly women was travelling on a wooden bridge across an irrigation canal passing through the fields. Each of them had a school bag strapped to their backs.

"Why are these elderly women carrying school bags?" said Neil as he peeped outside the window.

Karan remarked, "This must be one of those educational initiatives focused on improving the female literacy rate. They generally enrol women, who couldn't complete schooling as children, in night schools. I believe that they are attending one of those night schools."

Aman said, "It is great to be in a time when women can finally avail equal educational opportunities as men."

Samantha said, "There has been massive progress for sure but I doubt that we have attained perfect equality even in this day and age. For instance, my husband was strongly opposed to the idea of me pursuing graduate studies. He wanted me to stick to a teacher's job so that I could reach home on time to care for our son, Rick."

Neil said, "This is unfair. He needs to share the responsibility of raising the child too. The onus doesn't lie solely on you."

"I agree. This was a major bone of contention between us. He simply brushed off his responsibilities as he gallivanted across the country for his business startup, expecting me to sacrifice my career goals and passions."

"I can understand why graduate studies would hold so much significance for you," said Aman. "Teaching history to a bunch of uninterested students is hardly fulfilling. Your calibre is better utilised in furthering the realms of history research."

Karan listened to the conversation quietly, reasoning his friend's disapproval of her husband, John. He could now understand why she had planned to divorce him. However, he didn't mutter a single word as he remembered her fury in the national park. He couldn't make the mistake of being intrusive and presumptuous again.

A smell of food wafted throughout the chamber. A train hostess, clad in a blue uniform with a polka-dotted apron, was pushing a trolley towards them. When she arrived, she handed out plates to the four of them which they placed on the table.

The meal seemed wholesome with curd, rice, vegetables and chapatis with a side of pickles. The famished companions picked up their spoons to dig in while enjoying the view of the full moon over the fields outside.

* * *

Unobscured by the belching smoke from cars and factories, the stars sparkled brightly in the dark sky over the verdant fields. Aman glanced mesmerizingly at the view of the peaceful countryside outside the window as he snuggled in his blanket. What once formed seats had been conveniently folded into cushioned beds for the night, allowing him to lie down and soak in the views.

The whistle of the train upon halting at a station had woken him up. He deliberated whether to sleep or step out of the train to buy a snack before dozing off. The vegetables served at dinner hadn't satiated his taste buds. They had been too bitter for his liking and he craved something spicy and tangy.

There was a tap on his back. He turned back to see Tisha. She wore a woollen sweater with an embroidered scarf wrapped around her head.

Tisha noticed Aman gazing at her scarf. She said, "It is quite chilly outside. The widespread vegetation in rural areas apparently leaves lower greenhouse gases to trap the heat."

"That was quite random but okay. Where have you been? We have been trying to contact you since the afternoon."

"It is a long story. Aren't you sleepy now? Let me tell you in the morning."

"I was planning to head out to buy some snacks. The train stops here for another ten minutes, right?"

"Don't worry about that. I have got you covered. Have these chilly-flavoured popcorns," said Tisha, beaming with pleasure as she dangled shiny packets.

They proceeded to fold the blanket and pull apart the two halves of the bed from the middle. Within no time, the bed had been converted to two seats facing each other beside the window.

Tisha said, "After running, huffing and panting on the bridge across the railway tracks, I saw the Shatabdi train moving on the platform. My watch told me that it was just one minute before the scheduled time. I reached out for the mobile phone in my pocket to confirm the train number but it wasn't there. Guessing that it was in my purse, I realized that the train would leave the platform by the time I searched for the mobile in the purse's numerous pockets. I trusted my instincts and sped after the escaping train to board it."

"Gosh!" exclaimed Aman.

"Exactly. I needed the ticket SMS for the seat number and looked for the phone in every pocket of my purse. After a few minutes of scrummaging, it became apparent that I had left it in the taxi. What was worse was the fact that I had boarded the wrong train. I managed to get off at the next station and connect my laptop to the station Wi-Fi. I got the contact number of the cab company and called their support centre using the cheapest mobile that I could get my hands on at the store outside the station exit. They confirmed that I had left my mobile in the taxi and offered to keep it safely at their Lost and Found centre for me to collect whenever I could."

"That is a great relief."

"It was indeed. My next task was to catch this train at the next station in Thane where we are currently. The twenty-minute stop here provided enough of a time window for me to board a taxi and catch the train."

"You had a great adventure," chuckled Aman.

"I would prefer to call it an interesting ordeal," said Tisha while smirking.

As they looked out, they could see the bright orange sun of dusk shoot out from the horizon behind the neatly planted tall poplar trees. Aman and Tisha yawned as they watched the spectacular interplay of colours on that cold and breezy morning.

* * *

"It is 2 o clock' already. Aman is still asleep. Should I wake him up?" said Karan.

"The lunch boxes have also arrived," said Samantha.

"The meals will get cold and tasteless if not eaten in time. I am not sure when he slept but he could eat and sleep again. Let us wake him up."

As they stood up from their seats, they noticed that the berth below Aman's, which had been reserved for Tisha, had been occupied. The girl faced the window as she slept, preventing them from seeing her face.

"I wonder who came in the middle of the night to sleep in Tisha's berth," said Neil.

The mystery wasn't concealed for long. Tisha took a turn in her sleep to face the corridor, revealing her face to her visibly shocked companions. Before any of them could wake up either Aman or Tisha, a loud verbal spat in the neighbouring compartment woke both of them up. Apparently, a young man had slipped into the train without a ticket and was refusing to pay a fine to the ticket checker. As Aman precariously made his way down using the tiny ladder beside his bed, Tisha's first impulse was to check Benji's cage.

"Benji isn't here!" she exclaimed. "I forgot to close the cage. He must have gallivanted off."

The group ran and searched every nook and cranny in their compartment, including the luggage spaces beneath the feet of passengers, inviting some disgruntled expressions. Benji was nowhere to be found. The sound of the departure whistle was heard as the train picked up speed to leave the station.

"What if Benji got off at the station? Should I pull the chain?" said Tisha with an aghast face.

"The emergency chain can be pulled only for genuine reasons," suggested Samantha. "You will be sent to prison if Benji is found within the train premises. Let us keep looking."

However, there was no success despite further frantic efforts to trace the endeared dog. Tisha unzipped the pockets of her purse and pulled out a whistle. She announced,

"This will be embarrassing but it is our last resort."

She put the whistle to her mouth and let out a series of low-pitched and high-pitched sounds. She persisted in making these sounds for a few minutes despite the stares of onlookers in the whole coach. Soon, they heard a slight bark from the next coach. Benji slammed the swinging entrance door of the coach and made his way inside. He leaped forward and crept close to Tisha's feet. The ticket checker arrived to check the source of the shrill sounds but the whistle had already been tucked away in Tisha's purse by then. He had to contend with a lower fine collection for the day and walked away in disappointment.

"That was impressive," said Aman. "How did you train him to respond to the sound of your whistle?"

She replied, "As a puppy, I wanted him to roam freely without leashing him. Enclosing him in a confined chamber seemed cruel. However, I didn't want him to get lost either. I knew that he always came running to me whenever I offered him food. So, I made a habit of whistling in a certain way whenever I fed him. He gradually remembered the pattern and recognized my signal as an invitation to a meal."

"That is brilliant," said Karan. "You actually deployed the Pavlovian model to train Benji."

Seeing the confused expressions, he went on to explain, "Pavlov was a Russian physiologist, who conducted an experiment in which he fed a dog while ringing a bell. The dog didn't respond to the bell's sound initially but over time, it began to associate the bell's ringing sound with food. As a confirmation, Pavlov recorded salivation in the dog's mouth when he rang the bell even without providing it food."

At that very instant, Neil slid his hands through both sides of his scalp, raising a tuft of hair in between. He momentarily closed his eyes and sat down on the seat with his legs stretched out.

He yelled, "We have solved a part of the mystery finally.

I had been wrecking my brains over it for the past few weeks. This is so relieving."

Karan took a while to reconcile Neil's reaction to the mention of the Pavlovian experiments. But once he had the same thought, he screamed 'Eureka' with the same ecstasy.

He explained, "The birds are subconsciously associating jewellery with the concept of food but not exactly equating them to food. They could have been trained this way. Or there might be a more natural explanation for it."

The train shook to a halt, plunging Karan forward as he held a seat corner to regain his balance. This was followed by a commotion among the people. Some were simply astonished while some panicked with fear. Aman noticed on his mobile phone that the next station of Palakpur was still 30 kilometres away and this stop wasn't a part of the train schedule. The view outside the window was of a mustard field with yellow flowers swaying in the fluorescent orange backdrop characteristic of sunsets. There was a narrow water canal beyond the fields with a bridge over it. A few small, thatched huts dotted the landscape on the other side of the canal.

The ticket collector arrived to calm the passengers and clear the air. He announced, "A buffalo has died on the tracks. It probably belongs to one of the farmers and just happened to wander off. Nobody knows how it died but a few railway workers are coming to clear the corpse from the tracks and find its owner. Since we are still some distance away from Palakpur, they will take some time to arrive and clear the corpse. Please be patient till then."

"How much time will the whole process take approximately?" asked Samantha.

"It will take around 3-4 hours," replied the ticket collector.

With palpable consternation on his face, Karan said, "Vidika is only a 2-hour drive from here. Why don't we just hop off and rent a taxi to Vidika?"

"This seems like a very remote town," said Tisha. "How do we even get a taxi here?"

"There is a car rental shop only 500 metres from here," said Aman as he looked up after checking the online map on his mobile. "We can rent a jeep and drop it at their Vidika centre by tomorrow in return for Rs. 1000."

"What are we waiting for?" said Neil with a gleeful smile.

"The scenery seems panoramic in any case for a brief walk."

The rest nodded and picked up their bags. Tisha signalled to Benji to follow her as they hopped off the train onto the deserted fields. They carefully trod on the bridge one by one lest it collapsed under their combined weight. It had gone dark quickly and one could see kerosene lamps in the front yards of the huts.

"The map says that the car rental centre should be exactly here but I can only see a scarecrow in an empty field at this spot," sighed Aman.

"Let us not get disappointed too early," suggested Karan. "The map might be inaccurate but it might be located somewhere around here. Let us ask one of these villagers."

Karan stepped on the raised front yard of a hut beside the road. He knocked on the door and an elderly man with a long and white moustache stepped out. He was holding a cane and wearing a turban on his head. Karan greeted him and said,

"We are a group of travellers, who are looking for a car rental centre around here. Are you aware of any such centre nearby?"

"Yes. There was actually one centre located right on the opposite side of my house. They have moved to a new location, which is not too far from here. You need to walk further down the road and you will see their shop besides a neem tree. They have a large sign board which is hard to miss."

Karan thanked him and proceeded to leave but realized that something had been stuck to his shoes. He stood on one leg and raised his other leg to inspect. He noticed that a sticky golden coin had been almost glued to his soiled shoes. He jerked his shoe for a while and the coin finally fell off onto the floor below.

"Sir, I think you misplaced your gold coin here," said Karan as he waved to the old man, who was about to close the door.

He stepped out again and laughed for a while. Then, he explained, "This is not exactly a valuable gold coin. This is a coin-shaped chocolate, wrapped in a golden wrapper. Actually, it is a sacred month and we honour our dead ancestors during this time. We are supposed to offer food and valuable jewels to local birds around our house. It is said that the souls of our ancestors descend from heaven in the shape of birds to consume the food and peck at the valuables as a sign of their blessings for our prosperity."

Aman whispered in Tisha's ear, "This is it. Now, we know why those birds associate shiny gold with food."

Tisha muttered to him, "There is one problem with this hypothesis. Chocolate contains theobromine, a substance which is toxic for birds. They are mostly likely to die from consuming it and not want to eat it again even if they manage to survive."

The old man continued, "The food and jewels are supposed to be offered separately but we can't even afford silver jewellery. My granddaughter thought of this innovative idea to combine the two concepts through an edible gold coin. This allows us to continue the tradition without burning a hole in our pocket. The general trend is to offer both jewels and food though, especially in bigger cities like

Vidika."

Aman whispered again, "That explains why those birds might have started associating the presence of jewels with the presence of food. Because they were finding both at the same place."

Neil's phone rang. One of his graduate students had called. He nodded in excitement as he heard the student's exciting revelation, "We have been studying random bird specimens in Vidika for a while.

More than 60% of them exhibit salivation in response to a display of shiny jewels."

CHAPTER 9

A HAVEN FOR TUSKS AND PAWS

Vidika was a quaint seaside town with visible contradictions of modernity and medievalism in every nook and cranny. The curvy blue glassed skyscraper could be seen far away in the distance on the right side of the road while a decommissioned lighthouse towered amongst the thatched huts on the left side. As cars and riding elephants halted at the zebra crossing, the tourists donning straw hats and sunglasses moved in the opposite direction of the formally-dressed professionals. The seven-floor luxury hotel with a rooftop infinity pool stood next to a palace-converted hotel, where people could be seen swimming in the moat surrounding the palace.

All the hotels weren't grandiloquent though. Tourists, looking for a more real and traditional experience, thronged the elephant stables of Vidikan residents offering their homes to guests.

Some of the houses had adjoining mud pools and tube wells in their courtyard, where people could be seen taking a bath with dogs and baby elephants.

Benji peeped out of the window and wagged his tongue as the car sped by posh dog resorts where leashed poodles, Labradors and German shepherds accompanied luggage-carrying tourists on the front yards. Tisha pushed Benji's face inside and patted him on the head.

She said, "Benji, I am guilty of not bringing you to this place earlier. You can blame Aman though. Aman, you never told me that Vidika is such a paradise."

Aman, who sat in the backseat beside her, said, "I guess it is human nature to always undervalue what they have."

Tisha nodded and said, "That's why the grass always seems greener on the other side."

Raindrops started splattering on the windshield and lightning flashed through the air. The roaring thunder woke up Karan, who was dozing off in the front seat. The driver switched on the rotating wipers to show a partially clear view of the winding road ahead with sugarcane fields on both sides. The decommissioned lighthouse that could be earlier seen from a distance, stood immediately on their left. The group wiped the droplets on the left-facing car windows to get a clear view of the lighthouse. Their enthusiasm doubled when they saw sea waves rising and falling in tandem on the vacant white sand beach beyond the sugarcane fields.

"This is the famous Shakti lighthouse," said Samantha.

"'Shakti' in Hindi means power or strength. This tower was built by Queen Loma to commemorate the military victory of Vidika over Magadush. Considering that it was built on the sea coast, there are speculations of it being a lighthouse too. In the absence of proper evidence, nobody really knows the complete truth though."

In front of them, an isolated mansion with intricately carved marble balconies stood in the middle of the fields. A grey-haired woman stepped out from the main gate with an umbrella in her hand.

Aman proudly proclaimed, "That's my grandmother. She is as thoughtful as ever."

Maya rushed forward with the umbrella as the car halted in front of the mansion. She accompanied them inside while holding an umbrella over their heads.

The rain stopped and gave way to a charismatic rainbow over the wheat fields. Aman, Karan, Samantha, Neil and Maya sipped warm tea in the terrace garden on the roof while a cool breeze calmly brushed past them. They sat beneath an ornate colourful umbrella, which provided shade in the centre of the terrace.

Karan said, "I like the way that you have added a mild amount of spices to the tea, Ms. Gill. When we were young, my grandmother used to sneak out such tea for me and my cousins since our parents disapproved of kids drinking tea."

"That sounds relatable. All grandmothers spoil their grandkids," chuckled Samantha.

Aman said, "Since my parents passed away, my grandmother has juggled multiple alter egos. She disciplined me like a 'bad cop' parent. Simultaneously, she played the 'good cop' grandma too by teaching me to break the rules when needed."

Sensing the serious atmosphere, Neil changed the topic,

"Ms. Gill, the location of your mansion is really amazing. You can wake up to see a famous lighthouse, which tourists come to see from all parts of the world, right outside your window. The lighthouse blends beautifully with the panoramic views of the fields and the beach. Whenever you want to relax, you can simply set out for the beach and lie down in the white sand. If you are hungry, you can just grab a sweet bite of a fresh sugarcane from the fields below."

"I agree," said Tisha. "Aman, why don't you spend more time in Vidika? You seem to be in Mumbai most of the time even during your vacations."

Aman replied, "Vidika is a mesmerising and peaceful town, which makes it perfect as a tourist destination. However, I cannot pursue my ambitions of a technological career here."

Once the rainbow faded completely, glaring heat returned to haunt them on the roof. When Maya saw everyone panting and sweating, she

asked everyone to move downstairs to the living room on the first floor. She pointed to the sofa and said,

"Have a seat in the living room. If any of you want to relax, I can show you to your respective guest bedrooms."

The welcoming comfort of the living room seemed difficult to let go for the guests though. They reclined on the traditional Indian bamboo sofas in the living room, whose backs had been contemporarily redesigned to be flexible. The seat cushions and mattresses were bright orange and adorned with blue and green peacock illustrations.

The walls were adorned with a series of miniature paintings depicting dancing men and women in gardens under the night sky. There was a compartmentalised showcase with a framed photograph of a young Maya wearing a khaki uniform and holding a gun. Aman's numerous school trophies and hung medals were displayed beside each other in the other compartments.

Once everyone settled, Aman parted the curtains aside to reveal a scenic view outside. The receding rains had drawn tourists with umbrellas towards the cascading circular balconies around the lighthouse. Playful children and partying hipsters could be seen heading towards the beach. Everyone silently stared in admiration until Karan broke the silence,

"Ms. Gill, do you know of any jewellery shops in Vidika, which might be selling counterfeit historical gold coins?"

Maya replied, "Interestingly, Aman asked me the same question earlier. There are a few jewellery shops near the Great Palace and the Shakti lighthouse, which sell such gold coins. They serve as gimmicky souvenirs for rich tourists, who already know that they are fake though. Why are you investigating fake gold coins?"

Neil showed her a photograph on his mobile and said,

"Ms. Gill, we actually found a gold coin in the Bollywood bird's droppings. It is engraved with the royal Vidikan signage - a dog and elephant symbol. The inscription letters on the coin also resemble archaeologically excavated coins from Vidika belonging to the reigning period of Queen Loma. Our scientific dating techniques indicate that this coin was manufactured only fifty years ago. This is confusing because according to historical records, Queen Loma's kingdom perished in the early 18ᵗʰ century due to a devastating tsunami. The anachronism is extremely puzzling."

"I see," said Maya. "I don't think that there's a huge demand for actual gold replicas of historical Vidikan coins. Gold coins are too expensive for most tourists who are only interested in cheap trinkets. You will probably find such gold coins only in a few jewellery shops, which cater to such niche affluent customer bases."

Tisha suggested, "Why don't we split up and visit the jewellery shops near the two tourist attractions - the Great Palace and the Shakti lighthouse? If we carefully inspect and match the coin designs in all these jewellery shops, we might be able to trace the origin of the coin."

Maya said, "Aman has to go with me for an in-person registration process to take custody of his deceased aunt's elephant. However, the four of you should definitely visit these shops. You might also want to visit the monuments. Be quick because they will be closed for public viewing after four hours."

Samantha drove Maya's blue hatchback on the rain-washed road as Tisha fastened the seat belt beside her. Meanwhile, Karan and Neil picked up their umbrellas and started the walk on the cobbled path towards the lighthouse.

* * *

Samraagi Bazaar, also called the 'Market of the Empress' in English, was full of makeshift stalls and hand-driven carts, which displayed all kinds of items on sale from cashew milk ice creams, artificial jewellery, stuffed toys of elephants and dogs to memorabilia shirts. The sandstone fortress walls of the Great Palace, adorned with intricate ruby red patterns, could be seen perched on the hillock at the end of the market. Samantha and Tisha found it difficult to concentrate on their mission without getting swayed by the charms of the bazaar. A large jewellery shop with a dazzling signboard and fancy bright lights caught Samantha's attention.

"How can I help you ladies today?" said the shopkeeper behind the counter as Samantha and Tisha walked in.

"We are looking to buy gold coins with replicated designs from medieval Vidika. My daughter is a huge history buff," said Samantha.

The shopkeeper smiled and pulled out velvet cases from the shelf one after the other. Each subsequent case displayed coins portraying different scenes from the palace court, battlefields and royal stables. Tisha checked the photograph in her mobile phone to match the coin with the shown pieces. None of them matched even closely.

In the third case, one of the coins highlighted a tuskless elephant standing sideways raising its trumpet in the air.

A puppy stood near the hind legs of the elephant with its head facing the other direction. Tisha compared it to the photograph in her mobile and observed that despite the similarity, they didn't exactly match. The elephant in the photographed coin had tusks and its trumpet faced downwards.

"Didn't you like any of these coins, Ma'am?" said the shopkeeper.

Both refused and disappointingly walked out through the door. They ran from one store to the other and checked every set of coins that the shop offered to sell. However, their attempts to find an exact replica of the coin in question bore no fruit. Sometimes, the corresponding directions of the animals didn't match. On other occasions, the appearance of the animals was starkly different.

"This has been a disappointing day. The Great Palace is also closed now," said Tisha as she wiped the sweat on her forehead while swinging her head to find a bench to sit on.

"It is only as disappointing as you make it to be," winked Samantha as she held out the second cashew milk ice cream in her hand towards her.

They drudged away towards the car while licking their ice creams as the sun set behind the dome on the hilly palace.

* * *

Tisha, Samantha, Karan and Neil reassembled in the living room. The disappointment on their faces was palpable from the complete silence. Samantha tried to cheer everyone up,

"I know that none of us were able to find an exactly matching coin in the market. However, we know that the clue lies somewhere in Vidika because the coin exactly matches one of the excavated historical coins. So, let us not give up hope so quickly."

"You are right," said Neil. "It would be a great idea to visit both the monuments of Vidika tomorrow - the Great Palace and the Shakti lighthouse. Revisiting the rich history of Vidika will refresh our minds and hopefully also lead us to the next clue."

Karan said, "Samantha, did you click the photographs of the coins that you saw in the market? My detective brains are curious to investigate them."

Samantha said, "Tisha meticulously clicked photographs of every coin that we encountered in the market. We got them printed at a shop on the way here."

Tisha took out the bundle of photographs from her bag and laid them beside each other on the table. Karan did the same and the table was soon covered with shiny images of coins, which glistened in the moonlight streaming in through the window.

Karan said, "It is interesting to note how each of these coins has a unique inscription below it. Modern coins generally have uniform titles etched into them, which highlight details like the name of the country, type of currency or even country mottos. I obviously don't know the language. But I am guessing that these inscriptions describe the depicted imagery in the coin. If you look closely, you will notice that coins with similar depictions have similar inscription letters below them."

"Haven't we had any success in understanding the Vidikan language, Samantha?" said Neil.

"Unfortunately not," said Samantha. "Efforts by historians over the years to decipher the script have been largely unsuccessful. The language has gone extinct completely, both in written and oral form. If the script was similar to any existing language, it would have been much easier to pronounce those words.

Most current languages have words derived from each other, so you can find similarly pronounced words in other languages. Once those words have been mapped to their source words in contemporary languages, you can uncover their meanings and make strides towards a complete interpretation."

Karan said, "Isn't Shakti a Hindi word for power or strength? Considering that Queen Loma named the victory lighthouse after it, it must be a common word in Vidikan and Hindi."

"It is a common word," said Samantha. "However, that hasn't helped historians much beyond understanding a handful of alphabets in the Vidikan script. If there were more such words, which we knew how to pronounce, we could map all the alphabets in Vidikan to their counterparts in Hindi and understand the language. However, historians have struggled to unravel such a coherent mapping for several years."

The brainstorming session was interrupted by the arrival of Aman and Maya. Aman was carrying a plastic blue sack in his hand, which was adorned with images of fishes.

"That looks like an inflatable swimming pool. Are you going to bathe in the moonlight on the roof?" asked Tisha with a smirk.

Aman replied, "I wish but this is meant to serve as a drinking pool for the baby elephant. It requires huge amounts of water to drink and we need to ensure that it does not feel thirsty while we are sleeping."

Everyone's eyes brightened with interest. They followed Maya and Tisha through the winding circular stairs leading to the porch downstairs. The courtyard between the porch and the sliding entrance gate was lit by hanging kerosene lanterns on the surrounding walls. A tall neem tree with widely spread branches stood in the centre of the courtyard. They heard a trumpet.

A small elephant was tethered to the woody trunk of the tree. It raised its trunk above its tiny protruding tusks as the group approached it.

As Maya affectionately patted the elephants' head, she said, "Meet Jolly, the elephant known for spreading cheerfulness. Unfortunately, the demise of his previous owner has led him away from his happy self. It is our responsibility to nurse him back to health and shower him with love so that his life can be brought back on track."

Aman said, "That is Tisha's area of expertise. She has rescued countless abandoned animals and given them new lives."

Benji barked as if it approved of Aman's claims. Tisha moved forward and slightly bent on her knees. She gradually held out her palm with caution and kept it on the elephant's head when the elephant didn't object.

Tisha said, "Elephants are intelligent animals. They will not forget the loss of a loved one but their brains can be diverted towards engaging tasks to keep them from thinking about it. Let me think of such an activity for him."

Aman said, "You don't need to look further. It seems that Aunt Maria used to give him kindergarten puzzles to play with. We found this in her belongings."

He held out a wooden board with carved voids in various shapes on the surface. Some of the voids were filled with stamps, which consisted of protruding handles attached to surfaces having the same shape as the void.

Tisha said in an admiring tone, "Elephants are renowned for their intelligence but I didn't know that they are intelligent enough to solve elementary puzzles for human kindergarteners. Why don't you lay it out in front of Jolly to see if he can solve it?"

Aman said, "The noble elephants of Vidika have been getting trained in traditional techniques passed over generations for several centuries. These techniques are highly effective in honing their mental and physical prowess. Obviously, these elephants are no longer required to fight in military battles. Yet the practice has been passed on for the sake of preserving tradition. Wait for Jolly to astound you with his extraordinary talent."

Jolly peered down and then bent on his knees to sit on the ground. He felt his trunk on the surface of the board and curled it around the handle of one of the stamps. He picked up the stamp and tried to fit it in each of the voids. Once he found a fit for the stamp, he released the stamp from his trunk to place it firmly within the void. He repeated this routine until all the stamps had been fitted within their respective voids.

Samantha, Karan and Neil gasped with astonishment at the marvel. The other three, who were accustomed to such displays of wit by pets, simply smiled with appreciation.

"I have an idea to decipher the Vidikan language!" exclaimed Samantha. "As humans, we have grown to appreciate complex and sophisticated approaches to solving problems. However, the elephant did not overthink and deployed a simple trial and error approach to solve this kindergarten puzzle. A large-scale trial and error might help us to arrive at the answer faster than any of our conventional methods."

"And this is where artificial intelligence comes in," said Aman.

The others looked on with glee at the resonating epiphanies between the teacher-student duo. The day's exhaustion extinguished their enthusiasm soon though.

They decided to retire to their beds. The brain battles were left to be fought for another day.

* * *

The dark room faintly lit up when the night lamp beside the bed was switched on. Karan rubbed his eyes and struggled to find his slippers on the ground. He looked up at the clock. It was 3 AM. Karan hated waking up in the middle of his sleep but the dehydration had broken his slumber. When he realized that he had forgotten his water bottle in the kitchen, he grumpily headed out of the room.

The shrill howls drew his attention towards the windy weather. When he parted the curtains in the living room, he could see the swaying branches of the neem tree. However, the lighthouse stood as calm and resilient as ever as it bathed in the moonlight.

As he looked out, he was struck by a beam of white light streaming from one of the lighthouse's open windows. He knew that the lighthouse had not been known to be functional at any point in recent times. He also knew that regulations required the lighthouse to be closed to visitors after 5 PM in the evening. He couldn't think of an explanation. The beam of white light rotated towards the mansion and lit up his peeping face at the window.

CHAPTER 10

THE PALACE DUNGEONS

The magnified photo of a coin, depicting two big cats standing on their hind legs with their claws interlocked in each other, appeared on the big screen in the center of the hall. The same image flashed on hundreds of computer screens spread in rows throughout the hall. Some of the graduate researchers, who sat in front of the computer desks, continued to closely observe the image on their screens while others raised their heads to check the big screen for a better look.

The image on each computer screen had a caption beside it - 'Describe the image in two words.' The coin on the screen also had two indecipherable Vidikan words etched under the image.

The elicited responses were diverse - 'fighting cats', 'warring tigers', 'two leopards', 'standing lionesses' and several others.

The responses were even more diverse during a similar exercise underway in primary and middle schools across India. Karan felt that young students were less prone to biases formed by real-life experiences and hence, were more likely to come up with creative and possibly accurate answers. The opportunity to collaborate with a prestigious national organization was a golden one for schools, who immediately accepted the offer in return for a fully sponsored five-day workshop for their history and science teachers at NTFHO's Mumbai headquarters.

The image was changed after a minute. The screens now depicted a short and plump animal with a small snout. The solicited one-word answer mostly received the same response - 'pig', owing to the strong resemblance. This was one of those few questions where the variance across responses was low.

However, the diversity of cohorts among the responders was too high for a completely uniform answer. A middle school student, who was raised in Malaysia but had returned to India after a decade, could relate more closely to the Malayan tapir that he had spotted in Malaysian rainforest safaris. While the tapir wasn't endemic to India, he entered the name of that animal species in a seemingly naive attempt.

As these responses were entered, they were translated from English into 23 major Indian languages. Even though the lighthouse name suggested that Vidikan was a derivative of Hindi, Samantha guessed that Vidikan could be an amalgamation of several Indian languages due to cross-border cultural exchanges through trade and commerce. The alphabets of these translated responses were being mapped to the alphabets in the Vidikan inscriptions. The aim was to find a mapping, which would most coherently explain the meanings of all the images simultaneously. The enormous task was being accomplished by an artificial intelligence model, which had been developed by Aman after a week of strenuous work.

* * *

Samantha hung up the call and said, "Karan called. He and Neil are at the NTFHO office in Vidika. They have to complete and submit some documentation around the language deciphering project. They will join us in the evening."

She beckoned her former students and the local tourist guide, Sanjay, to move forward. Samantha, Aman and Tisha stepped precariously on the wooden drawbridge over the deep and empty moat.

Sanjay reminded them, "If you walked on this bridge two centuries ago, you would have seen the trenches on both sides brimming with stinking foul water. The Japanese traveller, Akari Nomura, described the sharks swimming in these waters as *fierce and elephant-sized beasts who turned the seemingly calm blue waters into a red bloodbath when fed with their daily dose of silver-coloured fishes and occasional criminals, both of whom were thrown from the turret with the Vidikan flag as a spectacle for the people.'"*

Aman looked at the turrets beside the entrance and froze in horror upon imagining a half-alive human being thrown from that height to be gulped by blood-thirsty sharks below. The Vidikan flag was notably missing from the pole on the turret.

Tisha wasn't convinced. She said, "Aren't most sharks around the same size as a human? Comparing them to the size of an elephant doesn't seem right."

Sanjay smiled and replied, "Writers in those times were known to make sensational and exaggerated claims to arouse the interests of their patrons back home. It might be one of those cases."

A pair of green pigeons flew in circles above them as they approached the creaking gates of the Great Palace. The entrance tunnel was composed of red sandstone painted with ornate patterns of indigo flowers. The group passed the dark roofed passageway to enter a semicircular open-air hall with a choice of four slopes to reach the elevated terrace above them. The floor was laden with laterite bricks and had tiny leafy plants sprouting in the gaps between the bricks. A mahogany tree could be seen on the edge of the terrace above, which cast a shadow on the floor below.

"There seems to be a hanging garden there," said Samantha as she pointed towards it. "Let us start the tour from there."

Everyone nodded and proceeded to climb the steep slope on the left. They held onto the steel railings attached to the wall for support during the hike. After a few minutes of huffing and panting, they reached the elevated terrace at the end of the slope. They noticed that the terrace was home to many more mahogany trees like the one they had seen from below. An earthen plate, which stood on top of a rod-shaped stand, was kept beneath the wide canopy of each tree.

Sanjay remarked, "Do you see the earthen plates on stands beneath each tree? Most of them are currently empty but in earlier times, they were used to provide drinking water to local birds under a shady refuge. As you must have witnessed in other ways as well, serving local animals was an important tenet of Vidikan culture."

Four stone-tiled paths started at the middle of each side of a square courtyard to converge at a pillared monument in the centre. The four squared enclosures, separated by the paths leading to the monument, were filled with clear blue water.

Pink lotuses floated on the water and a frog could occasionally be seen hopping from one lotus leaf to another.

Sanjay explained, "The monument that you see at the centre is the Temple of Mahi. Mahi was the Vidikan Goddess of Wealth. The lotuses have been planted in these small water ponds only in recent

times for beautification. However, Vidikans referred to these ponds as the 'ponds of fortune'. It was said that dropping a gold coin in these ponds around the temple was a way of seeking blessings for good luck from Goddess Mahi. Hundreds of Vidikan devotees would arrive here everyday to drop coins and pray inside the temple abode. The ruling dynasty believed in equal access to places of worship and therefore, the temple was open to all commoners in the Vidikan empire."

They crossed the path across the ponds towards the pillars surrounding the abode. As they approached the dull grey stone pillars, they realized that the temple was larger than they had envisioned from its outer look. Light barely entered the inner premises beyond a few steps and it was pitch dark inside. Sanjay reassured them of their safety and guided them through the darkness with the flicker of his torch. The torchlight didn't reveal much more than the stone-paved flooring initially but when it was directed towards the wall in front of them after a few steps, it revealed a dazzling sight.

As everyone came face to face with the formidable tall statue of Goddess Mahi, the sparkling gold used to carve it blinded Tisha, Aman and Samantha. The smug expression on Sanjay's face showed that he was accustomed to the routine of taking visitors by surprise. It wasn't just the gold that brightly stood out in the dark chambers. The ruby-studded crown and the emerald-studded spears in both her hands further added to the shine.

"I am surprised that such valuable items have been left unguarded for anyone to…," said Samantha.

She had barely completed the sentence when she bumped into someone. She let out a mild shriek as an apparition emerged from the dark.

"Don't worry," reassured Sanjay. "She is Constable Priya. She is on guard duty for these valuable relics today."

He swerved the torch to reveal a woman dressed in a khaki uniform with a gun strapped to her waist.

Samantha remembered the time when she had fled from Jaipur to Mumbai on a 24-hour train journey as a twenty-year old girl. She remembered persevering despite struggling to make ends meet. She recalled how her bravery and determination had eventually melted the hearts of her parents, who had finally agreed to let her pursue an undergraduate program from the University of Jaipur. The nostalgia of a time when she could control her destiny brought a smile to her face. She resonated with the timeless and inspiring energy radiating from her surroundings - a fearless woman constable defending the valuable statue of a fierce medieval Goddess in a city once ruled by a valorous empress.

"I want to see a depiction of Queen Loma," said Samantha. "Where can we find it in the palace?"

Sanjay nodded and led them out towards the temple entrance on the left, which was opposite to the one through which they had entered. As the darkness gave way to sunlight again, they noticed that a portion of the palace wall was pierced by a sandstone staircase. Statues of resting lions were carved on adjoining slabs on both sides of the stairs. The trio followed Sanjay up on the stairs.

The final step afforded them an elevated view of the temple enclosure behind them. They could see a handful of tourists strolling around in the formerly vacant premises. It was no longer the morning time reserved for exploration by overenthusiastic early risers.

They could also see what lay in front of them. There was a winding rectangular spiral of walls below. Most of the red sandstone walls were decorated with intricate attached sculptures and bas-reliefs. The wall surrounding the smallest rectangular chamber at the centre was different though. It was slightly taller than the rest of the walls and possessed a stark white colour because of its marble composition. It consisted of a unique sieve-like surface with hexagonal holes.

There was another staircase leading downwards into the outermost section of the spiralling walls. When Aman landed on his feet after jumping from the final step onto the floor below, he couldn't see any of the inner walls except the white one at the centre. The tunneled gallery with enclosing walls, twice as high as him, made him realize the importance of the sky view.

Sanjay narrated, "Akari Nomura called it the 'Queen's Maze of Stories'. You can think of this as a medieval cinema hall with stationary depictions showing subsequent scenes of the movie. The outermost walls feature childhood visuals of Queen Loma. As we progress into subsequent inner chambers, we will see visuals from the next stages of her life."

The first painting in the gallery showed two short girls in pigtails. Both of them swayed clashing bamboo sticks, which were around twice as tall as themselves, towards each other. A middle-aged moustached man, recognizable as the King, from his golden yellow crown, clapped his hands in the background.

Sanjay explained, "This is King Surma with his two young daughters,

Loma and Soma. As we can see here, both of them were fond of combat since their childhood. While most rulers of King Surma's generation didn't want their daughters to play with swords, King Surma began encouraging his daughter's talents from a young age."

They moved a few steps forward and turned around the arc. The walls in this part of the spiral were irregularly dappled with ochre-red and dull grey colours. Sculpted illustrations, which appeared flat from a sideways glance, could be seen slightly projecting out from the walls when viewed from the front.

The first section of the sculpted illustrations highlighted a pack of hounds chasing a panic-stricken antlered deer far ahead of them. An arrow was struck on the deer's hind leg, which had been apparently shot from the raised bow of a charioteer behind the dogs. The limping deer's bent legs suggested that it stood no chance of escaping. The subsequent section showed two young girls with long hair playing with another hound beside a campfire. The trees around them suggested that the princesses were on a hunting expedition to the forest.

"I can see where this story will lead to," said Tisha. "I remember your grandmother narrating this story on my birthday. It would have been great if she had been able to accompany us."

"Yes, it is the same one," said Aman. "You know Grandma. She is very disciplined. She wouldn't reschedule her self-defence classes that she teaches weekly without a serious reason."

The next illustrations depicted the hound lunging at the throat of a tall man with a drooping moustache. One of the girls was holding a dagger in her hand while the other one was standing behind her.

"You must have already guessed," said Sanjay. "This is the hound saving the princess from her vicious uncle who was planning to assassinate her. The elder princess, Princess Soma, is trying to shield her younger sister. However, the hound has stolen the show in this case. Unfortunately, this is the last gallery image in which the two sisters are depicted together."

"What happened to Princess Soma?" said Tisha.

"Considering that she didn't inherit the throne despite being the eldest offspring of King Surma, the most logical guess is that she died. However, nobody is sure of what actually transpired. Most of the historical information on Vidika comes from the travelogues of Akari Nomura. As a foreigner, he has been able to offer us only limited details that Queen Loma must have felt comfortable divulging to an outsider."

There was a morose silence among the visitors as they trudged ahead towards the inner sections of the spiral. The next series in the gallery consisted of colourful paintings again.

The first painting depicted a dusky woman with kohl-tinted long eyes, who was resplendent in a yellow sari and wore a multilayered golden-beaded necklace. She was sitting on an elevated velvet throne in the royal court where courtiers sat on seats below the throne on both sides. The armrests of the throne were designed in the shape of elephant faces. An elderly grey-haired man could be seen placing a ruby-studded golden crown on the woman's head.

"This is the coronation ceremony of Queen Loma," said Sanjay. "Her father, King Surma, is passing on the crown to his daughter."

Samantha found herself lost in the mystical eyes of Queen Loma, a brave woman who claimed a rare high position for herself in a patriarchal society. As an ardent reader of history books since her childhood, she had grown to appreciate the occasional female rulers that she could look up to as role models. Witnessing the story of Queen Loma unfold before her eyes grew her admiration for the formidable empress.

The next scenes, alternating between colourful paintings and dull bas-reliefs, depicted the Queen riding an elephant in a white suit with a turban. She was accompanied by a military contingent of sword-carrying men and women and the royal stable's elephants and dogs. The elephants came in various shapes and sizes. There were baby elephants and full-grown elephants; tuskless elephants and elephants with long ivory tusks; elephants with tiny ears and elephants with large fanning ears.

In contrast, the dogs were mostly homogenous. All of them had long snouts and slender bodies.

"Very few breeds of domesticated dogs were actually found to be fit enough to fight in a battle," said Sanjay. "Hence, mostly hounds were bred in the royal stables for military induction."

"These dogs seem to be receiving the utmost care in these stables," said Tisha, pointing to another illustration. "The idea that the Queen would have maliciously deployed them as carriers of an infectious disease seems weird."

Aman, who stood a few feet ahead of her, pointed to the raised illustration in front of him. He said, "The dogs in these images are being specifically trained to bite. Look at the man holding a piece of meat hooked to a string. He is inducing them to plunge in the air and bite at the meat. Once they have mastered this art, they can replicate the same attack on a soldier during battle."

"We haven't seen any attempt to infect the dogs with any virus in these images," said Tisha. "Biological warfare anyway seems very advanced for her times. Doesn't your idea seem like too much of a logical leap?"

"If this gallery was open to foreign visitors like Akari, then the Queen would be careful not to represent any information about her state secrets like confidential deadly weapons. So, maybe she just hid the virus transplantation part," said Aman.

They finally reached the second innermost section of the spiral. As they stood outside the entrance to the white marble chamber at the centre of the spiral, Samantha immediately recognized the final painting in the whole gallery.

She said, "This is the famous painting depicting the battle of Vidika in which Queen Loma recorded her biggest triumph against the Magadushian troops."

Aman cheerfully nodded as a smile of nostalgia crossed his face. He said, "Yes, it is the same one that I showed during my presentation at the NTFHO case study competition. I remember being drawn to this painting while visiting the Great Palace during my childhood in Vidika."

"The gallery has given us a close peek into the life of Queen Loma," said Tisha. "The whole experience almost seemed like travelling through time."

Sanjay shared a sobering realisation as he said, "The insightful revelations from this gallery make historians even more repentant when they realize that the last painting stops at the battle of Vidika. The last years of Queen Loma's rule remain shrouded in mystery. The earliest brick in the Shakti lighthouse has been dated to around a year after the battle of Vidika.

This shows that construction of the massive lighthouse was undertaken only after the battle. Akari undertook a sea voyage to leave for Japan after the battle of Vidika. The last passage in his travelogue describes how he witnessed a foundation ceremony for a victory monument called Shakti near the seashore as he took a final glimpse of India from the ship. The wide belief that it was a reference to the lighthouse explains its current name."

Samantha said, "That's why we haven't been able to understand the reason for the abrupt collapse of the Vidikan empire. I read that none of the excavated Vidikan coins have been dated beyond ten years from the battle of Vidika. All signs of a thriving kingdom somehow just disappeared from the face of the earth."

"You are right," said Sanjay. "There is absolutely no evidence or record to tell us what transpired. If a massive tsunami or earthquake had been responsible, the palace and the lighthouse would have also crumbled to the ground or at least shown signs of severe physical damage. However, both of these monuments remain almost intact till this date. There were almost no human skeletons excavated for a period of fifty years in Vidika. This suggests that there was a mass exodus of residents from the kingdom followed by rediscovery and resettlement."

"If it was an exodus, the refugees must have assimilated so well into their new settlements that they even forgot their local language," said Samantha. "The fact that the language is not even barely understood by people in contemporary times proves that the language's extinction was brutally complete."

As they finally reached the centre of the spiral, the white marble of the meshed wall glistened in the sunlight. The holes in the wall were wide enough for anyone to peek inside the royal court.

"Welcome to the Queen's court of justice," said Sanjay. "Everyone, irrespective of their social stature or wealth, could seek a fair hearing here. These meshed walls enabled ordinary citizens to witness the court proceedings from outside without posing any safety risk to the Queen."

The craftily spun cobwebs on some of the holes gave an eerie and deserted appearance to the royal court. A dense layer of dust had settled on the floor. The golden throne, embedded with rubies and emeralds, anomalously sparkled in the gloomy atmosphere. The throne was elevated on a short pedestal with stairs leading to it. The staircase was fenced with velvet ropes and a signboard hooked on one of the ropes declared - "No entry beyond this point".

"Would anyone really notice if I stealthily hopped over the ropes and sat on the throne briefly?" said Tisha.

Sanjay laughed and said, "Do you really think the administration will leave such a gap in their security of such a valuable historical treasure? The staircases are fitted with sensors which will set off a blaring alarm when you step on them. On top of that, there are guards stationed right underneath the throne."

"Underneath the throne?" said Samantha with a puzzled expression.

Sanjay pointed to a dark opening on the floor. It was immediately right to the base of the throne. As the group circled around the throne to get a closer peek, they noticed that it was barely wide enough to allow an average-sized human to wriggle through it. Aman sat on his knees and bent over the opening to peek inside. It was pitch dark and he couldn't see anything. However, he could hear faint mumbles of conversations.

"I can't see anyone down there but I can hear voices," said Aman. "How do the guards even enter through this narrow crevice without any staircase?"

"This isn't the entrance," said Sanjay. "Although, it is believed that there is a makeshift staircase inside, which allows guards to climb up to the throne room and respond to security breaches. The entrance to the network of underground cellars is through the Queen's own royal bedroom."

"Will we be able to visit these underground passages once we reach there?" asked Tisha.

"Unfortunately not," said Sanjay. "These passages historically served as a backup provision for the royal family to escape to safety in case of a fortress invasion. Currently, they are closed off to the public. Only a select few researchers and security staff are allowed there."

Disappointed with the news, the group strode off towards the exit as they proceeded to undertake the long walk through the circular spiral to the opposite end. As they saw the series of paintings and sculptures once again, it felt like a movie playing in reverse mode from the end to the beginning. The shape of the maze was coincidentally not too different from a curled up movie reel. The scene of an adolescent Queen Vidika playing in the mud with elephants was being played out in front of them when they were stopped in their tracks by Sanjay. He said,

"If you go further around the circle, you will see the childhood scenes and reach the entrance where we came from. However, we will take the opposite exit gate from here and move to the courtyard for the next phase of our tour."

Tisha looked at the clearing outside. She sighed in relief at the clear blue sky above them. Hauling herself through the shady mazes had caused her to run out of breath. She ran her eyes across the whole courtyard to find a bench. There were only huge stone vessels, resembling crude bathtubs, carved arbitrarily throughout the place. However, what struck her most was the grand stone statue of an elephant trampling a man, which stood in the middle of the courtyard. On seeing a wooden bench at the foot of the raised elephant, she rushed towards it while beckoning the others to follow her.

As everyone scrambled to take a seat, Tisha asked, "Sanjay, isn't there a shop nearby to buy any cold beverages? Like juices or soft drinks? The heat is debilitating."

Before Sanjay could answer, Samantha interrupted, "There is no need. I have brought a bottle of sugarcane juice in my bag."

She felt her back for the bag and instantly realized, "I left the bag in the court at the maze's centre. Let me go back and fetch it."

Aman offered to help her but she insisted, "I have been skipping my exercise routine since I left Mumbai. Some extra physical workout won't be too bad of an idea."

As Samantha sped off into the darkness of the maze, Tisha's mind wandered off towards the surroundings. Tisha looked at the elephant statue beside her. Only one tusk had been carved on the elephant's face. One of the fanning ears was much smaller than the other one. She was contemplating the incompleteness of the sculptural design when she noticed peculiar patterns engraved irregularly on the elephant's feet. She struggled to recall where she had seen similar patterns earlier. After a brief introspection, she remembered.

"Monkey paws," she gasped.

CHAPTER 11

LITERALLY BURIED SECRETS

Samantha entered the core of the spiralling gallery after a long walk. An eerie calm prevailed in the court with no signs of any human around. The slapping of her heels against the floor reverberated throughout the hall with echoes. She glanced around for the bag while circling around the throne's lower pedestal. Her foot struck something soft and she recoiled in fear at the imagined prospect of crossing a snake's dark lair. She remembered Sanjay warning them to be careful of snakes which occasionally sheltered in these dark chambers.

However, it was the bag she had been looking for. Her foot struck it so hard that it got pushed close to the dark opening that they had seen earlier. She looked around for any security guards and then quietly bent forward to pick it up. A closer peek made her realize that the holding straps had fallen halfway into the hole. She reached out for the straps but her hands disrupted the delicate balance on which the bag was standing, pushing it into the deep recesses of the hole. She stood up on her feet and turned back with the hope of meeting a security staff, who could help her. Unfortunately, instead, she came face to face with her worst fear.

A king cobra snake was slithering towards her with its body

undulating in a wave-like motion. Upon approaching her, it raised its spectacled hood while baring its venomous fangs. Samantha shrieked at the top of her voice and stepped back, momentarily forgetting the existence of the hole behind her. Her feet slipped and her body was halfway stuck in the hole due to its narrowness. The snake was darting towards her.

If she wriggled out of the hole, the snake could reach her and bite her lethally. She was scared to wriggle into the hole since her freely hanging feet couldn't gauge the depth of the hole. The shiny black eyes of the snake, which were looking more prominent and scarier as time passed by, forced her to take the risky latter choice. She struggled and pushed with both of her hands to finally succeed in letting her body free and allowing it to fall through the air. She landed with a thud after a few feet with the bag cushioning her descent. It was pitch dark and she could only see light streaming through the small hole several feet above her. She felt her hands around the bag and pulled out her mobile phone from it. There was no network signal and her attempts at calling Aman or Tisha failed. She switched on the torch in her mobile, lighting up a small section around her. Her eyes fell on the rusted iron bars, which partially shone from her torchlight. The bars partitioned a chamber behind them. As Samantha swerved the torch around, she realized that there were several such chambers arranged sequentially throughout the passage.

"The royal dungeons," she muttered.

* * *

Sanjay said, "In case you haven't already noticed, you can see how the areas become more exclusive as we enter deeper into the palace premises. The temple was open to the general public. The royal court was open to justice-seeking petitioners who had an appointment with the Queen. This courtyard was accessible to only the royal family, ministers and palace staff."

"I don't understand the purpose of this courtyard," said Tisha. "There are crude bathtub-like vessels spread across the floor in the open. The elephant statue seems incomplete and has monkey paws imprinted on its back."

"This is the royal kitchen," said Sanjay. "These vessels are believed to have been used for cooking. The elephant statue has been shown to be a relatively recent addition to the royal kitchen through scientific dating. Believed to have been constructed in the final years of Queen Vidika's reign, it stands as a symbol of justice. The man that the elephant is trampling with its raised foot represents the criminal. Elephant trampling and shark feeding were the two most extreme punishments meted out in Vidika. They were reserved for only the most heinous criminals."

"Why are there monkey paw imprints on the statue though?"

"I don't think that these are monkey paw imprints. They just seem to be holes left due to incomplete construction of the statue in later years. Nobody knows why this statue wasn't completed in the same way as nobody has a clue about the sudden desertion of this thriving city-state."

Tisha was convinced that the imprints were of monkey paws indeed. She had spent the last summers studying the nocturnal behaviour of gray langurs, a species of monkeys native to the Himalayas, besides the turbulent river Kosi at the foot of the mountains. Her eyes had become trained to recognize the footprints left by them on the marshy riverbanks even in the dark.

"I wonder why Ms. Samantha is taking so much time," said Tisha. "The winding path to the centre is a bit long but still…"

"Why don't I show you around while she comes back?" said Sanjay. "The monument will close in half an hour and we will have to leave the palace premises then."

"I didn't really want her to miss out on the guided tour but it seems that we are short on time," sighed Aman.

"Did you try calling her?" asked Tisha.

"Yes, I couldn't reach her," said Aman. "There is a general network issue in the whole area."

Tisha nodded her head in approval and beckoned Sanjay to continue the tour. After a few steps, they arrived at an almost pyramidal structure with a flattened surface on the top. There were four stairs on each side leading to the room atop the flat area. It was built of grey granite and was embellished with silver and golden kite-shaped patterns. There were four bronze resting lion statues at the base corners of the pyramid.

"This is the most exclusive part of the palace," said Sanjay. "Queen Loma's personal chamber. Its height allowed her to keep an eye on all parts of the palace. You would have witnessed a heavily armed regiment of soldiers roaming at the base of this pyramid in those times. The archaeological body recently built a mini museum inside this room."

Aman checked his mobile. He had walked almost double the number of steps that he usually walked everyday. He didn't need to say anything to convey his exhaustion to Sanjay. His reddened sweaty face gave it away. Sensing Aman's dread, Sanjay said,

"Don't worry. It is a short climb. You won't even notice when you reach the top."

After a short ascent on the stairs, they entered the royal chamber.

A faint scent of aged wood and incense filled the room. The velvet sofa, intricately designed lamps and the huge plush bed were elements that they had already expected to see. What they hadn't expected were the turquoise blue walls with green and brown spots. Upon seeing them, Aman remarked,

"These walls look like a giant world map with tiny islands spread all over the sea."

As they looked around, one of the walls caught Tisha's attention. It had a glass case mounted on it, behind which one could see a pattern composed of mirror beads.

"What is this strange illustration representing?" asked Tisha.

"Nobody really knows but the locals think it symbolizes a flower," replied Sanjay.

On a closer peek, Aman realized that the mirror beads were indeed arranged like a flower with several layers of petals.

"If this is a flower, it looks bizarre," commented Tisha.

"This seems like the flower's stem," added Aman, pointing to the thin rectangular mirror attached to the flower.

"Then, the circle on which the stem is hosted must be a flower pot," said Tisha, hovering her finger close to the circle attached to the slender rectangular mirror.

"Some tourists tried to peel off the mirror beads engraved on the wall," said Sanjay. "That's why the illustration has been protected with this alarm-fitted glass case."

Noticing Aman and Tisha's puzzled expressions while observing the flower illustration, he commented,

"This illustration on the wall belongs to the later years of Queen Loma's reign. It is shrouded in mystery too like the rest of the elements during that period."

He led them around the room while pointing his fingers at and talking at length about the various swords, armoured suits, headgears, attires and coins housed in showcases throughout the room. They finally stopped to rest at the window as Sanjay slipped his legs through the window to dangle in the free air outside the room. He stretched out and waved his fingers across the vast expanse of the palace sections below. He said,

"As you can see, we have the moat on the far extreme in all directions. You can notice the canopy of a bunch of trees and a red flag in the front. That is the temple and the garden. The gallery is also visible from here. Its spiral pattern looks even more vivid when you witness it from this height."

"Why can't I see Samantha Ma'am anywhere inside this spiral?" said

Aman with his squinted eyes carefully scanning the whole area.

"Yes, it has been almost half an hour," said Tisha. "Something seems fishy. I am getting worried now. Let us check what is taking her so long."

The rest of them nodded and hastily followed her as they descended the grandiloquent stairs.

* * *

Samantha's nose couldn't recognize the terrible smell as a familiar one and her eyes failed to see the source amidst the darkness. She moved precariously as she assessed the floor for any holes or hidden traps with each step. Her mobile phone battery had run out, forcing her to proceed with only optimism as her guiding light on that invisible and unfamiliar path. She heard a cracking sound on her next step, causing her to repulse in fear and almost trip. Her hand hit a greasy wall section and she was struck by the smooth feeling of fungus on both her palms. She realized that she was in a tunnel. The cracking sounds grew louder and the stench started becoming worse but Samantha paid no heed. Her journey was getting more difficult but she could also see the darkness ebbing away with each step. The tunnel gave way to a dimly lit clearing with a solitary candle at one corner of the room.

As she walked towards the candle, tapping sounds of footsteps suddenly started echoing behind her. She didn't know whether to run towards them or away from them. She had a spectrum of expectations, spanning from the possibility of being rescued to the potential of encountering a violent crime.

Before she could decide, she turned back to a strong beam of light flashing on her face. The source of the light, a torch, was held in the hands of none other than her friend, Karan. Their mutual wide stares made the unexpectedness of the encounter apparent.

Samantha almost screamed, "What are you doing here?"

Before he could have a chance to answer, the room lit up with a white light as the bulbs and tube lights in the hall buzzed and gradually lit up. The room was much bigger than anticipated by Samantha. On the extreme diagonal end of the hall, Dr. Neil stood with a scraping brush beside a gigantic skeleton of a four legged animal. The tunnel also brightened to reveal numerous bones underneath it. Some of those bones had been trampled by Samantha's feet, much to her disgust.

"Something weird is going on here. Can anyone explain?" said Samantha, shocked to discover the source of the cracking sounds and the stench.

"It is a long story," said Karan.

"I am all ears."

"It all began the night of the day when we arrived at Aman's house in Vidika. I woke up in the middle of the night to drink water. I was walking towards the kitchen to fetch water when a flicker of light suddenly beamed on my face. It came through the window and quickly vanished. When I peeped out, I noticed that every floor of the lighthouse was lit up with a faint white colour. Considering that it was supposed to be closed by the archaeological department after dusk,

I was curious about the source of this white light. The lights also flickered in different directions with time, creating a spectacular yet spooky show of lights. Scared out of my wits, I woke up Neil immediately and asked him to accompany me to the window."

"I remember how annoyed I was at being woken up and dragged out in a half-dazed state at midnight," chuckled Neil. "The sight was worth the trouble though."

Samantha's dull expression conveyed that she wasn't amused though. Sensing her annoyance about their secretive activities, Karan continued,

"We wrapped our shawls and stepped out to face the chilly night wind waiting to lash us. We walked across the winding gravel path to arrive at the base of the lighthouse. There was nobody to be seen around but we managed to catch a close glimpse of the first floor from the ground. A series of mirrors were swerving in random directions, apparently without any external human force. White light streaming in through the moon on one side and the streetlights on the other were being reflected off the mirror surfaces."

"Weren't there any security guards around the lighthouse? Historical sites like these are usually closed off to the general public after dusk."

Neil replied, "You are right. It closes at 5 PM. There was a wooden guard house outside the lighthouse and we knocked at its door. On getting no response, we peeped through the glass window on the side and observed a burly uniformed man sleeping with his face resting on the table. We banged the window and shouted out to him. He woke up with a startle and stepped out.

When he realized that Karan is a senior investigative officer, he started apologising for sleeping on duty. He informed us that there was an alarm stationed at the entrance of the lighthouse, which creates a blaring noise if a trespasser tries to break in. So, he became lax since he felt that the alarm would already be vigilant enough to protect the lighthouse."

"What did he have to say about the swerving mirrors when he saw them?" said Samantha. "If he stays on regular duty there, he should probably have a logical explanation for it."

"That is the funny part," said Karan. "By the time we woke him up, the mirrors somehow vanished. There was no sign of the flickering lights and all the floors were back to being pitch dark as expected. The guard was shocked to hear about the mirrors and the lights. He had never seen such lights in the night before."

Neil added, "We wanted to get to the bottom of this immediately. However, we needed special approvals from the Archaeological Department of India to get inside at that hour. After a series of calls to vexed sleepy officials in the middle of the night, who were fairly unconvinced about our claim because we hadn't captured any photographic evidence, we finally received conditional approval.

The condition was that we couldn't let anyone know in case this unverified information got leaked to the news channels. Such news coverage could scare off potential tourists to Vidika and adversely impact the local economy. There was also a fear that some external adversary organization might be deploying spying capabilities and the leakage of information might give away our plans to catch them red-handed."

"So, which is why none of us were told about it?" remarked Samantha.

"You are right," said Neil. "We kept up our investigation and research for a few weeks after that day. We uncovered some clues and sent some of our findings to the Archaeological Department. After a lot of convincing, they finally agreed to let us share our findings with the broader team. We highlighted how important it was for us to be aided by the knowledge and expertise of the other team members to proceed further in this study."

"Then, why didn't you tell us?" asked Samantha.

"We were about to discuss this in tomorrow's convention at the NTFHO regional headquarters in Vidika," said Karan.

"As you know already, the work on deciphering the Vidikan language has been underway for a while. The first set of results are expected to be delivered tomorrow. Since you witnessed our secretive activities beforehand, I suppose we will let you know now itself."

Neil said, "But before that, how did you manage to reach here? The entrance has been guarded by a robust security system."

Samantha replied, "The central throne room in the middle of the spiral has an opening which leads here. While escaping from a snake, I fell into it and landed into these dungeons. So, what did you two uncover?"

"That this is not just a dungeon," said Neil. "This seems to have served as a part of a highly complex interconnected infrastructural system. A system meant to advance the scientific and military interests of Queen Loma."

"Sorry, I don't understand," said Samantha.

"Let me start from the beginning," said Neil. "A cordon of local police personnel accompanied us to the lighthouse chambers that night. We searched every nook and cranny but there was no sign of any mirror. They just vanished in thin air."

"That's crazy," gasped Samantha.

Karan added, "We had almost given up hope and descended to the first floor for a quick rest. The sunrise was about to happen and Neil insisted that we watch the sun ascending behind the sea's horizon. My lousy self wasn't too keen but I agreed nevertheless. On the wall, we noticed a large window, which was sculpted with exquisite human statues on its borders. I was feeling lazy and didn't want to take a few extra steps to the balcony entrance door on the opposite side. I placed my hands firmly on the window and lifted my body with the hope of hopping onto the balcony floor below. I didn't anticipate that a spoked wheel sculpture would be jutting out from the wall immediately below the window on the other side. I tripped over the wheel and fell with a thud on the balcony floor. My feet got entangled in the narrow space between the wheel and the balcony wall. I shrieked for help and Neil came dashing towards me. He struggled to lift and free my heavy body. As he pulled my dangling hands towards him, my shoes rubbed against the narrow rod connecting the wheel to the wall. To our surprise, we noticed that the wheel slightly rotated and a rumbling sound was heard from the centre of the floor…"

Samantha had listened with deep concentration while imaginatively picturing the adventures that had played out. But an epiphany forced her to interrupt the thrilling narrative,

"I forgot that we should inform Aman and Tisha that I am here. The poor souls must be worried and searching for me all over the place."

"Since we are several feet below the ground, the network signal is extremely weak," said Neil. "Let us get out of here and call them. We are done with our work for the day anyway."

Samantha and Karan nodded. Neil led the way by lighting up the path with his mobile torch while the two of them closely followed. The floor was muddy, forcing the trio to pull up their jeans in response. Bulbs had been installed throughout the passage but around half of them didn't glow while the other half glowed with only dim yellow sparks.

Observing the eerie silence, Karan continued, "When we noticed the simultaneous thudding sound and the wheel's rotation, we rushed inside to check the source of that sound.

A square-shaped part of the central pillar inside the lighthouse was slightly tilted with the upper half projecting outwards and the lower half projecting inwards. The square piece hinged around its centre in a clockwise or anticlockwise fashion depending on the direction we rotated the balcony wheel in. The wheel was apparently a part of a complex system of pulleys and wasn't merely an ornamental sculpture. It took us a lot of huffing and panting to rotate the wheel further. Rotating it moved the square piece inside. When the square piece completely flipped, it revealed a shiny mirror that had been plastered on its backside."

"That's a lot to process in one day," said Samantha with wide eyes and raised eyebrows.

"It gets even more interesting," said Neil. "It wasn't just that single wheel. Four such wheels, equally spaced from each other, could be found on every floor balcony. There were four square wall blocks on each floor's central pillar facing those wheels. Each square wall block had a hidden mirror on the backside. All these wheels were somehow connected to the square blocks."

Karan added, "Not to forget, every wheel had spokes. Every arc within any two spokes faced a unique symbol. And noticeably, one of the arcs was always darker than the others.

The symbols most probably denoted the angle of rotation of the square wall piece it was somehow connected to. For example, when the wheel was rotated to allow the darkest arc to face the star symbol, the corresponding square piece inside shifted to an almost horizontal position. When the darkest arc faced the circular symbol, the square piece completely flipped to reveal the mirror."

Misty water dripped from the leaves of wild shrubbery growing on the walls. Even a single drop touching the skin felt like a jolt in the freezing weather. Samantha was fairly gripped with the narrative to not care about the drops though. She asked, "Were you able to recreate the scene of that night finally?"

"We were able to but not on our own," said Neil.

"Quite exhausted, we received the support of work staff who tirelessly pushed the wheels on each floor while the monument was closed for the day."

"If it took so much physical effort to move those mirrors, how did they swerve so smoothly that night?" said Samantha.

"We still don't have a clue," said Karan. "The fact that the alarm didn't capture anybody entering through the front gate made it even more puzzling. Peeping inside the hollowed out ground floor pillar with horizontally tilted mirrors gave us an idea though. A flight of stairs could be seen leading to a cellar inside. Armed with oxygen masks and helmets, we delved into the deep depths of the secret basement. Shoving spades and setting aside irregular dumps of accumulated soil, we observed that there was a whole mile-long concrete tunnel leading directly to these dungeons. The purpose of this passage, connecting the lighthouse to the palace dungeons, is still unclear. However, we noticed a few interesting specimens here. You will witness the most prominent and complete one among those on your way ahead."

The buzzing sounds of electric sparks and the whirring sound of electric drills almost tuned melodiously with the monotonous thuds of hammer swings. The trio realized the inadequacy of their two hands, which failed to shield them from the bright sparks in the wide hall as they had already been invested into covering their ears from the noise.

"We are building a makeshift living space and lab to host resident scientists studying these specimens," yelled Neil at the top of his voice as Samantha managed to catch only a few words over the loud sounds.

Her eyes turned towards the magnificently tall skeleton of a four legged creature, carefully perched atop a wooden pedestal in the centre of the room. Two thick metal rods supported its broad rib cages which precariously hung from the spinal cord. The skull had an oblong shape, making it look like a helmet. Two slightly curved fangs, resembling scimitars, dangled from the jaws.

Samantha said, "I would have guessed that it was a tiger, judging from the skeleton's ferocious demeanour. Especially reflected in these flesh-tearing teeth. However, tigers usually aren't this big so I don't know what to say."

The trio had moved closer to each other so that they could hear each other clearly. Neil smirked and replied, "You could have never guessed it though you were close. It is a liger, the hybrid of a male lion and a female tiger."

"I didn't know that tigers could breed with lions," said Samantha. "This is so strange and unheard of."

"It is an unusual case in the wild indeed," remarked Neil. "Tiger and lion habitats rarely intersect. Tigers can be found in many parts of India but the habitat of the Asiatic lion has been restricted to the Gir National Park for several decades. However, such cases of crossbreeding have been noticed in captivity and ligers actually exist in certain zoos around the world. Interestingly, ligers typically grow up to be larger than both adult tigers and lions."

"Where did you find this liger skeleton?"

"We found the fossil bones in one of these underground chambers. It took us several weeks to piece all of them together in the right positions to recreate this skeleton. Genetic sequencing of the bones revealed that it is a liger. As you might notice, the tail bone at the rear is missing. It was shipped to NTFHO's headquarters in Mumbai two days ago for carbon dating. It revealed that the liger died around a few years after the battle of Vidika."

"The existence of this liger further adds fuel to my curiosity. Maybe it could tell us something about the last little-understood years of the Vidikan empire."

"You are right, Samantha. We also found the skeleton of a Malayan tapir, which is endemic to Malaysia and has never even existed in India. These findings corroborate Aman's hypothesis. Queen Loma was a visionary for her time and understood the potential of biological warfare. These old peculiar specimens seem to be a result of her ambitious experiments. If we are right, the level of sophistication of her biological warfare is even higher than we previously thought.

Maybe even higher than current standards."

"Are you saying that this grand palace hosted advanced laboratories below its seemingly normal gardens, galleries, courts and kitchens?"

"Kitchen. That is what the guides have learnt to call them over the years. The finely-ground bone powder that we found in those bathtub-shaped vessels suggests otherwise. Documents tell us that the royal family strictly followed vegetarianism. Even if we could give a benefit of doubt for the occasional meat, there has been no historical evidence for human consumption of grey langur monkeys. The bone powder belonged to monkeys!"

"So, the 'kitchen vessels' are actually test tubes for some God knows what type of quirky biological experiments."

The combined noises of the electric sparks, hammers and drills suddenly came to a halt. A man dressed in a khaki uniform had just entered the room and beckoned the workers to stop their activity. The formerly curbed shouts could then be heard from the entrance staircase, which led to the roof. Listening intently could help one discern the distinct voices of a boy and a girl.

"Let us inside please. A lady by the name of Samantha Hughes has fallen inside and is possibly injured."

CHAPTER 12

THE LAST LETTERS

Karan immediately recognized the arguing voices as Aman and Tisha's.

"Seems like your young fellows came to rescue you," said Karan as he winked at Samantha.

Neil rushed up the stairs. This was followed by a few mutters that could be heard from the hall below. After a few minutes, Neil escorted Aman and Tisha inside. They sat down on wooden chairs that the staff dragged for them into the dimly lit room. Aman and Tisha nodded excitedly and gasped intermittently as Neil made big reveals while recounting their ordeals.

Aman said, "As crazy as my elephant-rabid dog war theory might have sounded, these incidents and the resulting theories seem even wilder. It is interesting how they sound unrealistic individually but they lend credibility to each other. They seem to be adding up to a common narrative."

"Exactly," said Tisha. "I actually noticed monkey paw prints on the partly finished elephant statue in the so-called 'kitchen', which I now know is a laboratory. The tourist guide refused to attribute those marks to monkeys but I was confident about my belief. Everything makes more sense now."

"We have unravelled only a part of the mystery," said Samantha.

142

"Many crucial questions are yet to be answered. I believe that an accurate interpretation of the Vidikan language will provide deeper insights into the events that unfolded during this glorious kingdom's last years."

Neil informed everyone, "We should have the results by tomorrow morning hopefully. We will visit NTFHO's office in Vidika tomorrow right after breakfast."

"I have a feeling that we should further investigate the purpose of the mirrors in the lighthouse," suggested Karan. "I can make sense of a hidden passage for the royal family and senior loyalists to another part of the kingdom. In case of an invasion, it would have helped them flee to a harbour and escape through the sea. It probably also allowed them to keep their advanced research secretive so that they could enjoy an edge over their rivals. The purpose of installing a mirror behind the door to this secret passage is still lost on me though."

Aman said, "We actually saw a bizarre illustration of mirrors on a wall in the Queen's personal chambers. It might have a clue about the lighthouse mirrors. I clicked a photograph. Let me show you."

"It is getting late," said Neil. "Let us get in the jeep first and drive back to Aman's place. We can review the photograph during the drive."

The rest of them agreed. Seeing Tisha proceed towards the stairs to the palace floor, Karan signalled her to step away and said, "We aren't going through the conventional route on the road. Come back."

Raising her eyebrows in a puzzled look, she asked, "How are we going then?"

"Through the underground tunnel to the lighthouse besides Aman's house. Wait a minute."

Neil ran off into the darkness. A few moments later, the loud blare of a horn was heard, shattering the calmness inside the chamber. Two distinct yellow light beams moved towards them.

When the beams crept closer, they revealed themselves to be the front lights of a jeep. When the indoor lights were switched on, Neil could be seen at the helm in the driver's seat. The door opened and he beckoned the others to step in. Hemispherical orange bulbs, interspersed throughout the walls of the winding tunnel, flickered for a while and then lit up. Once everyone was settled inside, the jeep kicked up clouds of dust and whirred with a roaring sound as it sped forward.

"Can you show me the illustration you saw in the palace, Tisha?" asked Karan as he relaxed in the backseat.

Tisha nodded and took out her phone to show it to him.

While Karan was observing it closely, Tisha explained, "It is believed to be a flower hosted on a flowerpot."

Karan nodded his head sideways and said, "It is anything but that. Which flower has different kinds of petals in each layer? It looks like a cryptic pattern with symbols. We should find a way to decipher it."

* * *

The ultra-modern NTFHO regional headquarters building was in stark contrast to the historical aesthetic of Vidika. The cars moving on the road looked like tiny ants from the glass-paned walls of the conference room. The building was the second tallest architectural structure in Vidika, eclipsed only by the historical Shakti lighthouse. The rival lighthouse could also be seen far away in the distance with the calm blue sea forming the backdrop. Tisha diverted her attention from the scenic view to the presentation screen when a man in a professional black suit entered the room and projected his laptop screen. He announced,

"Hello everyone! I am Raj Kapadia. I am the Chief Data Scientist at NTFHO. Aman and I have been collaborating on developing a model to interpret the Vidikan language. We have made some progress and so, I will be sharing some updates."

Everyone in the room took their seats. He continued,

"As you can see on the screen, there are three varieties of coins with distinct illustrations in the first column. In the next column, you will see the inscription at the bottom of the coin, which has been magnified and isolated for a clearer view. Since we know that the Vidikan language was a derivative of Hindi, Marathi and some other regional languages, we aimed to map the Vidikan letters to their corresponding letters in these understood contemporary languages. The mapping was arrived at by trying to map every Vidikan word to possible words in known languages that could be used to describe these illustrations.

For example, the guesses for the image of a pig-like animal were pig and tapir. The Vidikan word used to describe the image was tried and mapped to the translations of the word 'pig' and 'tapir' in 20 major languages. The idea was to try similar combinations simultaneously for the image of a lion and a tree and arrive at the most coherent mapping of letters which could simultaneously describe all the images.

In this mini simulation on a sample set of three images, you realize that the combination of letters that can simultaneously explain all three illustrations comes from using the Malayan word *badak*, meaning tapir for the pig image, the Sanskrit word *vriksha* for the tree and the Hindi word *sher* for the lion."

"This is excellent research," said Neil while clapping slowly. "However, it sounds too good to be true. Were we able to find a matching word in a known language for every illustration based on the derived mapping of letters?"

"We weren't able to find a corresponding word for roughly 11% of the illustrations," said Raj. "89% accuracy was the best that we could achieve after trying every permutation and combination. This is a good level considering the benchmark for studies of these kind."

"I agree," said Neil. "The performance of this model is commendable indeed. Kudos to your and Aman's perseverance and intellect in developing it!"

His broad smile and glowing eyes betrayed an even higher level of appreciation than his words could convey.

"We are very grateful," added Karan. "This will be a decisive achievement in our quest to understand these bizarre incidents which are somehow linked to past events in the history of Vidika."

Aman and Raj thanked everyone as they received a round of applause from the team of historians, engineers and scientists in the room. Raj proceeded towards the third empty seat on his right side as Samantha took his place beside the presentation screen.

"I am Samantha. As we know, the traveller, whose memoirs form the basis for most of our knowledge about the Vidikan kingdom, had left for his home country before the kingdom's demise. This has left a void in our understanding of the events that transpired in the final years of Queen Loma's reign. Due to this breakthrough translation technique, we have been able to translate three excavated Vidikan letters that belonged to the period. I will be presenting and discussing them."

She pressed a few keys on her laptop and the pale white screen lit up with the picture of a wheatish-brown and slightly crumpled paper with black inscriptions on it. The edges were bordered by purple ribbons and a red blob, presumably a royal stamp, was present at the bottom. The English translation was shown in the space to its right. She read out the translation loudly for everyone to hear,

"Commander Ratla,

I am sending a new batch of prisoners with Commander Bara to the Island of Mos for the next advanced stage of biological trials today. The ship will leave from the harbour near the lighthouse this evening. The prince of Tikri will be arriving at Vidika with a royal procession to marry my cousin, Princess Priya, within the next seven days. Many guests from the royal families of neighbouring kingdoms will also be present for the week-long festivities. We cannot risk anyone knowing about the island. Therefore, you have to make the return trip to Vidika only after fifteen days from now since we can safely assume that the guests will have left by then.

Use this time judiciously to find an isolated and safe spot for the new animal shelter and direct the crewmen accompanying the hostages to start building it.

Regards,

Queen Loma"

She continued, "This letter throws light on the stealthy operation carried out by the Queen. Since she didn't want other rulers to know about the operation, it was most probably geared towards the development of a new war technology. We do not know where the Island of Mos is but the letter hints that the tunnel was developed to transport prisoners from the dungeon to the seashore near the lighthouse secretly. The mentions of the biological trials and the animal facility tell us that the island was a site of intensive research on developing biological weapons. We have already had an inkling of such efforts from our knowledge of the battle of Vidika and the excavated fossils. This letter confirms this suspicion and hints at an even greater intensity and scale of these efforts than we had imagined."

"This seems surprising," said a man in the audience. "There are no islands close to the coast of Vidika. The only islands on the Arabian sea, which are close to India's eastern shores, are the Lakshadweep islands. However, they are offshore from the city of Mangalore, which is more than one thousand kilometres south of Vidika. Even by conventional naval standards, traversing such a long distance over sea would take more than 20 hours. Regular communication and coordination would be really difficult between Vidika and the Lakshadweep islands. Moreover, we haven't found evidence of any historical research centre there in all these years."

She said, "Yes, it seems improbable based on the distance. There is no current evidence of the presence of such a facility on any other island too. I believe that we will have to dig deeper here. The next letter might have such clues."

She pressed a key on her laptop and the visual on the screen switched to that of a new letter. Its outer design was remarkably similar to that of the previous one. She continued,

"Commander Ratla,

I understand your concern about travelling through the night. However, the lighthouse has come under scrutiny by the general public. A resident of Shakti town came to complain about shimmering sunlight emanating from the lighthouse on the suspicion of enemy spying. Knowing how gossip spreads, we have switched off the source during the daytime when everyone is awake. Since it is highly unlikely that anyone would be awake at the late hours of the night, it is important for you to plan your arrival around those hours. I will have soldiers cordon off the area around the lighthouse. I have deliberately chosen a full moon night so that the glimmers across the sea are at their brightest and guide your ship safely to our shores.

Regards,

Queen Loma"

Seeing the amused expressions on the audience's faces, she smiled and remarked, "I was as piqued by this discovery as you. The mirrors were probably used to reflect light beams to guide ships over the sea. They wouldn't emanate very far though so their effectiveness must have been limited. I believe that we need to make a research trip to the lighthouse and investigate the link between those mirrors and the illustration in Queen Vidika's chamber."

Tisha said, "I agree. I have been examining that illustration for a few days. I have a hunch that the spatial patterns are related to the architectural design of the lighthouse. If my hypothesis is right, examining the architectural intricacies closely would reveal that link to us."

Karan said, "I will secure the necessary documents and approval to close the lighthouse for general public viewing tomorrow. We can make a private visit there for investigation."

The others nodded as Samantha displayed the next and final letter on the screen. Noticeably, this one was on a seemingly ordinary white piece of paper with tattered edges. She read it out,

"To

Her Highness

Queen Loma of Vidika,

Our village, Panipur, has been ambushed by a group of ferocious abnormally huge langur monkeys. They band together to launch surprise attacks on unsuspecting villagers who are alone. We have been able to save lives in most cases as the shrieks alert other villagers who come to the rescue of the victim. We even formed a vigilante group to find, track and kill these monkeys. After a few successful hunts, the attacks began to cease. However, we realized that the success was short-lived when a woman, who went to collect water from a well during the night, never returned and was found dead near the well the next morning. Sensing our lack of alert during the night, these monkeys have started coordinating attacks on our people during the night. We have no clue about their origins and are finding it difficult to carry on with our daily activities due to the menace. We request your support in helping us to ward off these monkeys and restore normalcy and peace in our village.

Regards,
Sanjeev Singh
Village Head
Panipur"

Samantha noticed Tisha's nodding face upon completing the narrative. Tisha's fists were clenched and seemed ready to thump on the table with excitement at any moment. Samantha looked Tisha in the eye and beckoned Tisha to reveal her epiphany by waving her hand.

Jumping at the opportunity, Tisha said, "These vicious monkeys, bred to fight in battles, may have gone out of the royal administration's own control in the later years. The incomplete elephant statue with monkey paw prints might be a result of these monkeys scaring away the statue builders before they could complete its construction. The fact that the prints got embedded in the statue makes it clear that the paste hadn't solidified when the monkeys arrived and the statue was still being built. This letter further corroborates my belief about the kingdom's inability to control these hyper-intelligent and powerful monkeys that they had bred themselves."

Aman added, "The unexplained desertion of the Vidikan empire without much physical damage to the infrastructure might be a result of an invasion by these animals. Even though the disappearance of those animals from human society later props up more questions."

The constant mutters and whispers in the room made the burst of energy palpable. They hushed up as Neil began to speak.

"The appearance of the gigantic Bollywood bird might be a testimony to the fact that the scientists behind this biological warfare passed on their knowledge to someone. Someone who is engineering these genetically modified animals. This knowledge could have been passed on over the generations to a descendant of these scientists. It is also possible that someone excavated historical documents, detailing their scientific techniques, and managed to interpret them. There doesn't seem to be a malicious intent at play till now but we can't be sure. At any rate, it has become imperative to understand the motive behind sending these bejewelled birds."

Aman had been watching the inscriptions closely all this while. As the conversation was going on, he walked up to the screen while intermittently gazing at the photograph on his mobile. He ran his hands over the inscriptions shown on the screen and peered at his mobile screen. He was oblivious to the stare of the audience in the room, whose attention had shifted towards him.

Looking at the curious and bemused faces in the room, he held up his mobile screen for everyone to see. It showed the image of a bright golden necklace with some engraved inscriptions.

He announced, "There is one more type of artifact that deserves our attention - these jewelleries brought to us by magnificent birds. Doves preceded postal letters and telephones as the primary means of communication for several centuries. These birds aren't doing anything different. They also carry messages for us albeit in a less conspicuous and unconventional style."

Tisha gasped and almost yelled, "Let us find a translation for these jewellery inscriptions!"

CHAPTER 13

AN ANCIENT CALL FOR HELP

"This is a very manual and exhausting process," complained Tisha. "There has to be a smarter and less time-consuming way to do this."

"I would have helped but I have already done my share in the morning with those letters," chuckled Samantha as she sat back on the curved armchair while sipping lemonade using a funky spiralling straw.

Tisha sighed and resumed matching every letter of the hazy inscription on the anklet to one out of thirty letters in the deciphered Vidikan alphabet displayed on the laptop screen.

"It is a temporary makeshift mechanism," said Aman. "We are developing an image recognition software to recognize the letters from a photograph of any inscription and directly give the translated output. Meanwhile, we will have to work with this."

After a few minutes, Tisha announced, "The sentence on this anklet is done. I am translating it. See this."

The white bar on the TV screen began to grow progressively orange like orange juice flowing through a pipe. The results were being loaded. The white bar turned completely orange quickly.

The screen read out, "PLEASE HELP US."

Samantha cupped her lips with her hands. Aman raised his hands in the air. Karan and Neil crept closer to the screen to confirm. Everyone had their unique way of processing the surprise.

"Who needs our help? And what kind of help?" said Neil, breaking the silence.

"It might be Rick and John," said Samantha as her eyes lit up with a renewed optimism. "They might be trapped somewhere. Their plane disappeared close to the Lakshadweep islands."

"We might get more details in the next pieces of jewellery. This was the first piece of discovered jewellery with the shortest inscription," said Tisha.

"It makes sense now," said Aman. "The size of the bejewelled birds grew progressively with each subsequent discovery along with the size of the worn jewel. Someone was trying to send more detailed and conspicuous messages."

The broad grins on the faces in the room showed their smug satisfaction at the revelation of a significant clue. They sank in their chairs for a moment, revelling in their success with the knowledge that their efforts were finally paying off.

The laboratory had long tables with sequentially placed laptops. In the centre of the room, there was a metallic storage chamber sealed off by a securely locked door. Tisha overcame her lethargy almost instantaneously and paced towards the chamber.

She entered the password as asked on a tiny digital screen besides the door and flung the door open. As she took out the contents of the chamber, the room was flooded with a myriad of shiny colours. There were gleaming rubies, emeralds and diamonds embedded in intricate designs on numerous gold anklets, necklaces and bangles. Each piece of jewellery was placed in a separately locked glass case. As Tisha looked starstruck at the cases, the others rushed in behind her. Their visibly raised spirits indicated their collective resolve to aid Tisha in her erstwhile tiring endeavour. They took a key each from the bunch in Tisha's hands and began to take out the jewellery and heap it onto the table.

Within a few minutes, each of them was sitting in front of a separate laptop with equally distributed jewellery ornaments lying beside their respective keyboards. Their routine of inspecting the pieces and matching the Vidikan letters on the jewels began to yield results.

"Rescue us from the Island of Mos," yelled Neil as he read out the translation in front of him.

"Come to the Island of Mos for many more such treasures," said Karan.

"The responsible citizens of Vidika stuck on Mos want to return," said Aman.

With a puzzled frown, Neil said, "Why would you call yourself a citizen of Vidika? The kingdom existed hundreds of years ago. Why not call yourself Indian citizens?"

Samantha said, "The jewellery pieces also belong to the Vidikan era and the language used is also Vidikan, which is a dead language today. We are missing something."

Everyone sat in silence for half an hour until Aman came up with a potential explanation. He suggested,

"Some captive shipped off to the island several years ago might still be there and could be asking for help."

"Any captive would be dead by now. They weren't taken to the island yesterday," chuckled Tisha.

"It could be a descendant," suggested Karan.

Samantha nodded for a moment and said, "But the last piece of jewellery belonged to Rick. Might be Rick or John. Although, why didn't they build a ship and sail off? Seems easier than training birds to send mostly indecipherable messages with the hope of getting aid."

"It isn't clear but let us inspect the remaining ones and discuss them," said Neil.

Unfortunately, most of the new messages turned out to be repetitive, much to the disappointment of the group. However, the longest inscription on the last discovered piece of jewellery before the arrival of the Bollywood bird, a multilayered necklace, caught everybody's attention.

"We are innocent citizens of Vidika," translated Samantha with her eyes widening at the utterance of every phrase. "We have been stuck on the Island of Mos for ages. Let the Shakti mirrors lead you here and we will shower you with treasures for rescuing us."

Karan almost yelled, "Pack your bags. We are travelling to the Shakti lighthouse right now."

* * *

A pair of eagles was circling the roof of the towering Shakti lighthouse when Dr. Neil looked up from the base. He noticed a tuft of hay straw slightly projecting outside one of the square windows on the top floor wall. The brief desertion by humans had apparently given way to the occupation of animals, who had found their residence in forgotten nooks and crannies. Neil startled and jumped as a striped squirrel carrying a walnut scurried across his shoes. The sea waves created intermittent roaring sounds as they rose and splashed against the golden sandy beach. The bright orange sun gradually plunged behind the sea horizon while the sky dimmed and the darkness of the night grew more imminent.

A moustached man with a rifle strapped to his belt checked the cards that Karan showed him. After a few close peeks, he nodded and beckoned the group to cross the barricades to enter.

The peripheral circular walls of the ground floor were embellished with alternating sculptures of men and women with palms pressed together in the *namaste* greeting style. Random specks of yellow and red paint could occasionally be seen on the loincloth of a carved man or the saree of a carved woman. However, the colours had mostly faded away, causing the human reliefs to blend with the terracotta brown colour of the walls. Aman's attention was caught by the cuboidal pillar in the centre of the room. In stark contrast, the mosaic art on that pillar, consisting of vividly coloured roses, seemed to have withstood the ravages of time.

Recognizing the pillar as the one described by Dr. Neil, Aman asked, "Is this the pillar from which mirrors popped out?"

"You are right," said Neil. "Notice the slightly uplifted squares at the four centres of the pillar walls. Tilting the corresponding wheel for any of the squares causes it to flip around its centre, revealing a mirror on its internally facing side."

"Why don't we show you a demonstration?" said Karan as he began to move towards the doorway leading to the balcony. Samantha's concern caused him to rein in his steps though.

"Where is Tisha?" she reminded the others about her absence in the room.

Aman's phone rang with a melodious tune, which echoed between the walls of the vacant chamber. Aman picked it up, had a brief chat and slid the mobile into his pocket. He declared,

"She was excited to see the panoramic view of the sea and the city of Vidika from the balcony on the top floor. So, she went upstairs."

Neil said, "Let us go upstairs too. The wheels are identical on each floor. So, we can show you the demonstration there."

Their eyes fell on a winding staircase which curled around the central pillar to reach a small opening to the roof. While climbing the stairs, Samantha realized that the sun had set completely once she popped her head through the opening leading to the second floor. Darkness filled the surroundings for a moment, freezing Samantha in her tracks. Before she could contemplate how to take the next step, dim yellow lights began to light up the hall on the second floor. She moved her head around to see wide torches installed throughout the periphery of the room. Noticing her confusion, Karan remarked, "This is a recently installed automatic lighting system. It notices the sunset and lights up the inner chambers to annihilate the darkness."

Neil added, "These lights have been purposely kept dim so that the onlookers on the outside cannot observe them. While Vidika is renowned for its rich history, not many people know that some of its beaches are important nesting sites for Olive Ridley sea turtles. The natural instinct of turtle hatchlings is to move to the brightest area, which is usually the reflection of moonlight in the ocean. However, such artificial lights can confuse them and mislead them towards the city. In the city, these young turtles can't survive as they fall prey to humans and predators. That's why the presence of artificial lights on these beaches has been curtailed to a great extent."

* * *

The huts and bungalows appeared diminutively as bright orange and yellow blobs of light dotting the grassy landscape. The occasional car seemed like a wading firefly in the pitch darkness as it moved on the empty roads. Tisha guessed rightly that Vidika was a sleepy town where most people still went to bed early and woke up at the crack of dawn.

She peered down and took a moment to gauge the height at which the tall lighthouse stood. Realizing that she was uncomfortably too close to the edge of the balcony, she retraced a few steps backward.

"Isn't the view very serene from up here?" a chirpy voice came from behind.

A startled Tisha turned back to see Aman standing outside the door to the highest balcony. Karan, Samantha and Neil followed him as they emerged from the darkness into the moonlit balcony. The calmness of the city at night was in stark contrast to the roaring waves which rose and crashed onto the beach on the other side of the balcony. It was a full moon night. The bright stream of white light emanating from the moon lit up a narrow section of the sea. The lit section looked like a white bridge over the ocean which disappeared into the horizon.

Karan called out, "Friends, pay attention here. We will start the demonstration of the rotating mirrors now. Can someone please flash their mobile torches? The automatic lights on this floor seem to have gone dysfunctional."

He stood next to a window which had its wooden doors flung towards the balcony outside. Beneath the window, a wheel projected outwards from the wall. The austere appearance of the wheel was at odds with the grandiloquence of the paintings inside the chamber.

As Aman flashed his mobile's torchlight onto the wheel, Tisha pushed the wheel clockwise from one end while Karan did so from the other end. After a few seconds of huffing and panting, the slightly uplifted section of the pillar opposite to the window began to tilt with a grating sound. Seeing the weariness of the duo, Neil and Samantha joined the strenuous activity.

Within a few minutes, the wheel had been rotated halfway from its initial position and a flat mirror appeared in place of the pillar's submerged section. The moonlight streaming in through the window got reflected by the mirror as a dim glint on the concrete floor. While everyone was gasping at the spectacular display of the covert mirror, Tisha's attention was diverted somewhere else. She peered closely at the spokes of the wheel and its outer rim. She yelled,

"Aman, can you flash some light on the rim of this wheel?"

Although taken aback a bit, he did so without any question. Different shapes could be seen on the immediate exterior of each arc formed by the spokes.

With her face betraying awkwardness at a second request, she meekly announced, "My mobile phone battery died a few minutes ago. Does anyone else have the flower-like mirror illustration that we saw in Queen Loma's room on their mobile phone?"

Samantha pulled out her mobile phone from her pocket, swiped her fingers on the screen for a few seconds and handed it to Tisha.

The screen displayed the photograph of the intricately designed mirror beads pattern.

Tisha peered at the wheel again and looked at the illustration as if she was comparing them. At Tisha's behest, Aman rotated his mobile torch around the wheel's rim. She looked at the distinct geometric shapes around the five arcs again. She smiled and then shrieked with excitement,

"Oh my goodness! The five symbols on the wheel arcs are identical to the five shapes that form each layer of the petals."

Everyone else moved closer and realized that she was right. Aman muttered a silent 'woah' under his breath. They watched each other's confused yet delighted expressions for a bit.

"Brainstorming time," announced Neil.

They sat in silence for about half an hour, sometimes gazing at the sky and sometimes towards the sea. Tisha was the first to break the silence.

"Shakti lighthouse has exactly five floors. The mirror flower also has exactly five layers of petals. I think each layer of petals corresponds to a floor of this lighthouse. Also, there are four petals in each layer and four wheels on each floor. So, each petal could represent a wheel."

"That is a fascinating coincidence. Do you have a hunch on what it could mean?" asked Samantha.

"I am not sure. The floor area of the lighthouse slightly reduces as we progress to the next floor starting from the bottom. If you would observe this lighthouse from the sky, the balconies on each floor would appear as concentric circles. I think that every layer of petals on this flower of mirrors corresponds to a distinct floor of this lighthouse. Keeping in mind the sky view, the innermost layer of petals should correspond to the four wheels on the top floor and the outermost layer should correspond to the four wheels on the ground floor."

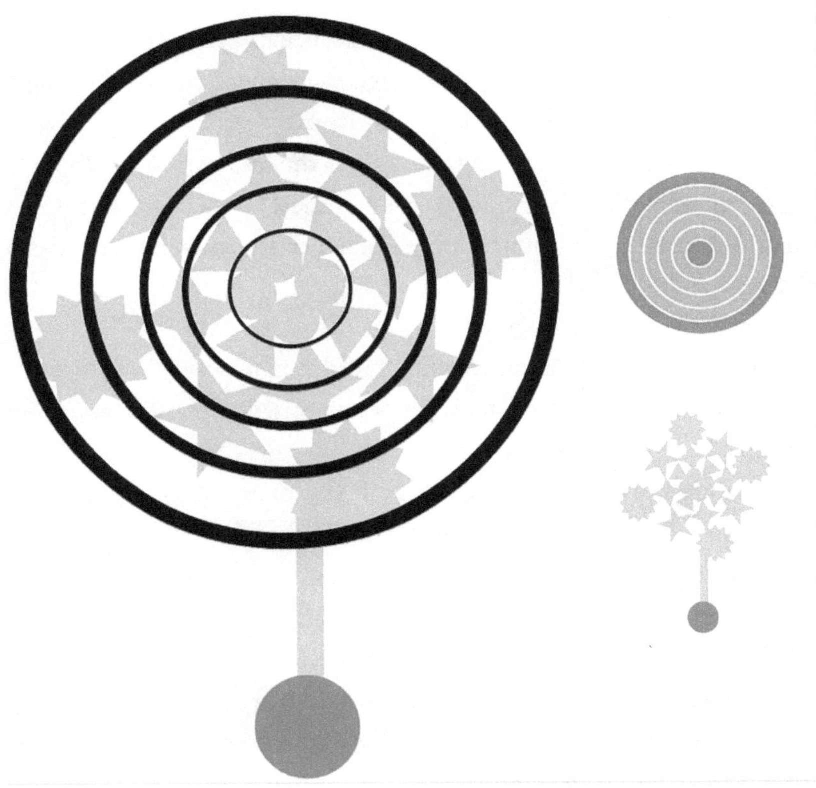

Neil added, "Considering that each layer is composed of distinct shapes, I think this illustration is assigning a shape to each floor. For example, the innermost layer has four circles. So, the four wheels on the top floor should be assigned a circle. The second innermost layer has triangles, which means the wheels on the floor beneath this one should be assigned to triangles."

"How do we assign the wheel to a shape?" said Aman. "Every wheel has the same five shapes on its exterior."

Karan moved towards the wheel and pointed his fingers towards a section of the wheel. He said,

"Notice how one out of the five arcs within each wheel is darker than the rest. We might be able to assign each wheel a particular shape by rotating the prominently dark arc towards that shape."

Aman said, "So, considering that this is the highest floor, which is represented by the innermost layer of circles, all the four wheels on this floor need to be rotated so that each of their dark arcs faces a circle."

"Exactly!" replied Karan.

"What happens when you do that?" said Aman.

"That's what we will find out when we do this, young man," chuckled Karan.

Everyone's face brightened up with the prospect of an exciting discovery. The excitement was all the higher for Samantha. She clasped her hands together with nervous anticipation as the hope of reuniting with her family flooded her mind.

While resting his legs on the floor, Neil said,

"I am highly enthusiastic about the prospect of a significant discovery here but no amount of enthusiasm can fire up my stamina enough to rotate 20 wheels in this lighthouse."

Karan smiled at him and said, "Don't worry. I will call the investigative bureau to get some help. We can take a break."

The others nodded in gleeful agreement.

As Karan went downstairs to make a call in a quieter environment, the rest of them started chatting.

"I still don't understand one aspect," said Aman. "What does the long rectangular mirror attached to the flower-like pattern represent?"

"Look across the sea. You will get your answer," said Tisha and her lips broke into a broad smile.

She led the group to the edge of the balcony and raised her hand to point her fingers towards the roaring waves. The narrow section of the sea brightened up by the moonlight seemed to fit into the puzzle perfectly. She remarked,

"The mirror that we thought was a flower stem possibly represents this moonlit bridge. It joins perfectly with the flower, which symbolizes the lighthouse."

"What about the circle on the other end of the rectangle which we previously thought was a flowerpot?", said Samantha.

"A place in the sea we need to check out next," said Neil.

* * *

Grating sounds filled the air as the wheels on each floor were simultaneously rotated by the collective efforts of numerous staff members. The dust, which had accumulated in the space between the wall and the wheel since the last round of cleaning, filled the air. Neil witnessed the fluorescent orange sun rise from the sea horizon as he paced on the balcony to find a quiet spot. The gentle sound of his mobile's ringtone was obscured by the loud noises and chatter. It grew more audible after his brief search for a quiet spot half-satisfactorily ended on the edges of the balcony.

The next minutes saw his face expression change from that of mild disappointment to one of worry and panic. He hung up his call and stood silently while processing the news he had just received.

He hastily made a few calls. The arrival of Karan, Aman and Tisha was announced by their treading sounds as they descended the stairs.

"Did Samantha see any of you coming?" asked Neil.

"I don't think so. She is busy overseeing the staff on the top floor," said Aman.

Neil took a deep breath and declared, "Okay. I have some bad news. The Bollywood bird is dead."

Feelings of shock and gloom, reflected in their long collective silence, prevailed over the group. Karan was the first to break the silence.

In an almost whispering tone, he asked, "How did the poor bird die?"

Neil said, "The post-mortem reveals that there was a rupture in its intestines, most probably caused due to abrasion with an indigestible coarse object. There must have been a minor wound initially which got exacerbated when left untreated. Some birds have evolved in a way that they don't exhibit symptoms of even life-threatening ailments until their final moments. This is done to avoid being hunted by predators which can recognize their weakness and assume them to be an easy target. That's why this health issue went undetected from our side. The most disturbing part is that undigested pieces of human bones have been found in the bloodstream of the bird. Considering that the bird arrived with Rick's locket necklace, I am fearful that the bones might be his. I don't know how to break this news to Samantha."

With her hands cupped over her face, Tisha said, "I don't think we should do so at the moment. It might be better to wait for a more final confirmation."

Neil said, "It sounds unprofessional and unethical. I have realized the follies of withholding crucial information from specific team members. Doing so weakens their trust. Also, it delays their valuable contributions and impedes the overall investigative research. I do not want to repeat the mistake that we committed earlier by hiding the finding of the secret tunnel."

"But…"

Tisha's objection was cut off by a loud shriek coming from above. Everyone looked up and listened to the words and voices intently. It was Samantha's voice.

"Rick. John. Can you hear me? I am here."

CHAPTER 14

TURNING THE WHEELS OF FORTUNE

The grating sounds of wheel rotation and mirror tilting finally stopped, giving way to an eerie silence. Everyone expected an exciting discovery once the wheels were rotated to positions supposedly prescribed by the mirror illustration. Yet, nothing could have prepared them for the sight they witnessed on that chilly morning. As they rushed into the chamber on the ground floor, they saw Samantha screaming at a mirror. They gathered around her and couldn't believe the vivid scene being played out in the mirror.

The mirror, slightly tilted downwards, offered a view of a lush forest consisting of palm trees and shrubs. Behind the trees, the faint outline of a small stone-built house, having walls overrun with moss, could be seen. A slim child with matted black hair, wearing a half-torn blue rag draped over his noodle-thin arms and a red sarong over his waist, could be seen in the centre of the frame. He was vigorously striking the base of one of the trees with a sickle in his hands. It was unclear if the greater credit was deserved by the sickle's material or the boy's strength as the mighty tree quickly fell with a tremor onto the ground, kicking up a huge cloud of dust as it touched the ground. The mirror slightly shook for a moment and the middle section of the view was covered with patches of soil. One could only see wooden slippers and a tiny tuft of hair on the boy's scalp as he walked away from the scene, presumably with the chopped barks of the tree.

"Where is this reflection even coming from?" said Aman as he squinted his eyes to examine.

"Only one way to find out," said Neil.

He proceeded to cautiously slip into the narrow gap in the pillar created by the tilted mirror.

"Be careful," warned Tisha.

"Don't worry. It just leads to the underground tunnel," he said with one of his feet slid into the gap.

He managed to squeeze himself into the gap and a loud thud was heard next. This was followed by a weak groan. Neil had landed on solid ground.

"Are you okay down there?" said Aman as he rushed forward and peered down the gap.

He saw Neil holding up his fingers in a thumbs up position and felt reassured.

Trying hard not to get any attention, Samantha stealthily stepped out to sob on the balcony. Nevertheless, Karan noticed and joined her. He patted her on the back. She shared her mixed feelings with him.

"He was Rick. My young boy is alive. I am so thankful but he seems starved. We need to rescue him from that wretched place."

Nobody could have guessed if the tears reflected her agony of being separated or her gladness on seeing her son. Karan handed out a handkerchief to her so that she could wipe her tears. He tried to reassure her.

"We will find your son soon. We have come a long way in unravelling this mysterious chain of events. Let us not lose our willpower in the final phase."

Meanwhile, a shout was heard from the underground floor.

"Pass me a shovel please."

Aman and Tisha looked at each other. The exchange of glances conveyed their mutual curiosity to each other. Instead of finding a shovel, they decided to run and slip in through the gap.

They landed with a thud and bruised legs. Neil almost jumped in fear, only to realize that it wasn't a giant shovel. Just his two eager impatient companions.

"Did you find anything?" asked Aman as he struggled to stand up.

Neil didn't say anything. Instead, he shone a torch, revealing a vertical black cylinder piercing the soil.

"What is that?" said Tisha.

"The source of the reflection. The mirror is covered by this cylinder on all sides. The mirror is reflecting something present within this cylinder," said Neil.

"It seems partially buried underneath the ground," said Aman.

"Precisely why a shovel would have been helpful," said Neil.

"Well, how do we get back up?" said Aman with an embarrassed grin and one hand on his scalp.

After a few yells, the trio saw a temporary ladder being lowered towards the underground floor. Aman hastily climbed it and returned with three shovels. They began fervently digging around the cylinder. After an hour of relentless digging, they discovered the buried section of the cylinder. At the bottom end, the cylinder curled into a horizontal pipe. They were able to unearth only a section of the horizontal pipe. It seemed to be extremely long and headed towards the sea.

"I am confused," said Tisha. "The mirror should have just reflected the curved edge of this cylinder. How was it projecting that entire scenery?"

Neil scratched his head for an answer but he couldn't think of anything. The lack of oxygen didn't help. He said,

"I will go upstairs for some fresh air."

Realizing that it was no easy task, he said, "Aman, can you please help me climb the ladder?"

No response. He swerved his head in all directions. He couldn't see him. Tisha looked clueless too. They heard the familiar thud of falling again. They looked around to check but there was no sign of Aman again. This was followed by a muffled echo. Neil walked closer to the cylinder to hear clearly. It dawned on him soon.

"Aman, are you inside the pipe?" said Neil.

"Yes…and there is another mirror around the curve…. reflecting the first one. Wait. Found another mirror parallel to the second one. Oh, my goodness. There's another," said Aman with his echoing intermittent sound.

Tisha yelled, "Aman, get out of there before you suffocate yourself to death."

"I figured it out," said Neil. "This is one giant periscope. Or more appropriately, a series of periscopes joined together. We need to find the original mirror whose reflection is being transmitted all the way here."

"That would lie on the other end of the pipe. We don't even know where it ends," said Tisha.

"I have an idea."

* * *

"I don't remember the last time I slept," said Samantha after a loud yawn.

"Me too. I wonder where the others are," said Karan as he glanced around.

The afternoon sun had become blinding and the soaring heat prompted Samantha to pull out sunscreen lotion from her purse. She handed it to Karan after applying it on her own face.

The winding stairs offered a view of the beach, which was abuzz with undeterred tourists swimming, making sandcastles and collecting seashells.

As Samantha looked down from the balcony, she noticed a huge crowd of irate tourists. They had assembled at the gates of the lighthouse and were haggling with the security guards. The security guards were struggling to explain why the most-visited tourist spot of Vidika had been closed to the public for a second consecutive day.

"We didn't pay for expensive flights and hotels to miss the Shakti lighthouse. Please let us in," came a yell.

"We have come to visit this historic monument all the way from Toronto. Please open this for a while," came another.

"I feel bad for them," said Samantha. "Can't we do something about it?"

Karan's lack of response made it apparent that they couldn't. There seemed to be no solution to this crisis. Or he was just too tired to care. It took only a few minutes for both of them to doze off on their chairs.

* * *

Karan rubbed his eyes as he struggled to wake up from his nap. The loud tourist noises didn't let him sleep well even though his body kept forcing him to close his eyes. Giving up the battle, he stood up and looked across the seashore. The screaming tourists at the lighthouse entrance seemed to have given up their battle too as none of them could be seen anymore.

The quietness didn't prevail for long though. A roaring mechanical sound filled the air. Samantha woke up, startled by the screeching noise. As they looked across the beach to inspect, they noticed a strange phenomenon. Initially, it appeared as a long shadow across the sand and the sea.

With each passing second, it became wider. Something seemed to be emerging from the sand.

"What is happening?!," said Samantha.

A black wide pipe was piercing through the sand and the rocks on the beach. It extended far into the ocean and disappeared across the horizon. The pipe wobbled with the waves when a section of the pipe struck a rock on the beach. After a few minutes of struggle, the pipe managed to break free and hurtled the obstructing rock away. The rock landed with a strong force on a kid's beach sandcastle, completely decimating it.

The girl, sitting beside the sandcastle, shrieked and fled away. The voices of onlookers turned to loud chatters and soon, evolved into a full-blown pandemonium. The courageous ones crowded around the broad black pipe, which was abruptly cutting its way through the beach sand and the ocean. The others fled away with their backpacks and umbrellas, shouting and creating panic wherever they went.

With a frown on his forehead, Karan rushed into the inner chamber. He saw Aman, Tisha and Neil circled around the pillar. A series of pulleys passed through the pillar's interior. The other end of the pulley was tied to a tractor on the beach outside, which was moving away.

"What is going on here?" shouted Karan, trying to make himself heard over the mechanical sounds.

Neil smiled at him and replied, "We discovered a pipe underneath the pillar that is connected to the mirrors. It transmits reflections over long distances through a series of mirrors embedded inside it. We are just trying to pull it up."

Karan didn't seem impressed. Neil had anticipated that he would be jumping with joy on hearing about their discovery.

Instead, Karan retorted,

"You need to follow a safety protocol before carrying out such an activity. There are unaware tourists on the beach whose lives are getting endangered by this. You might also compromise the structural integrity of this historical monument."

Neil couldn't make eye contact. He felt careless and realized that his impatience had gotten the better of him. He apologized and instructed the tractor to stop. The giant pipe had arrived on the surface anyway.

* * *

After a well-deserved sleep that calmed everyone's nerves, they were back at the NTFHO office for further discussion.

Aman said, "How did nobody ever notice a giant periscope buried deep within the beach and the sea?"

Karan explained, "The lighthouse and the beach surrounding it are important tourist attractions. The local government didn't initiate any excavation or construction projects in the area. They didn't want to disturb tourists, who support the economy here."

"Still quite strange," said Tisha. "This pipe seemed to extend quite far into the ocean. I wonder where it ends."

"The place where we saw Rick," said Samantha. "The reflection of that place is getting transmitted all the way here."

Tisha sighed, "We should have captured a photo of the reflection. It might have thrown up some clues about this place."

"I was unfortunately too stunned even to move," repented Samantha.

"Don't worry about it. I clicked a photo," said Aman, grabbing everyone's attention at the conference table.

He took out his mobile phone and looked at the picture again.

There was a modest-looking house with the forest trees in the background. Rick could be seen chopping down a tree in front of the house. Aman inspected the photo for a few minutes until his eyes fell on a hazy inscription on the house.

"I can see something written on the house wall," he said with a beaming smile betraying his sense of accomplishment. "Let me use my language translation model to decipher the text in this photograph. It is finally ready."

Everyone immediately stood up from their seats and huddled around him. There was a circle on the screen that started rotating to indicate that the translation was in progress. There was absolute silence in the room. No sounds could be heard except the heavy anticipating breaths of onlookers, waiting for a big reveal. When the results didn't load immediately, their initial exuberance gave way to a calm yet optimism-filled patience. However, when the circle still kept on rotating for 15 minutes, they began to lose hope in the promising technology.

"Why is this taking so long?" said Tisha.

"Maybe because the text is really hazy," said Aman.

Samantha bent forward for a closer look at the screen. After a few minutes of inspection, she let out a loud laugh, much to the puzzlement of everyone else.

"No, that's not the reason," said Samantha while trying hard to suppress her laugh.

"Then, what is it?" said Aman.

"It is not Vidikan. It is plain old English. It is just written by Rick in his quintessential bad handwriting."

She announced the words,

"Mos Island research centre."

* * *

The security guard at the Vidika lighthouse sat on the chair after a long day of confrontations. He had to face the wrath of hundreds for a decision he had no role to play in. Another instance of the powerful delegating the guilt of their decisions to the powerless. He tried to think about it that way. Yet, the numerous faces of disappointed kids that he turned away kept haunting him. Unfortunately, the heart sometimes forgot logic.

As he sat buried in these thoughts, he heard a grating sound. He turned around to see a bunch of glimmers in all directions. The lighthouse mirrors were flipping on their own. As far as he knew, no investigation was scheduled in the lighthouse for that day. He rushed towards the lighthouse to inspect the source of their movement. To his surprise, not a single soul could be seen on the premises. While wiping the sweat from his brow, he fervently ran up the stairs. No sign of anyone again. The mirrors were somehow rotating without any external intervention. This was too much to take for him. His head spun for a bit and darkness took over his eyes within a minute.

CHAPTER 15

OVER A DESERT OF WATER

Tisha, Aman, Samantha and Neil huddled around the self rotating mirrors. Their conscience had taken a hit from seeing the unconscious security guard being escorted into an ambulance.

"Too bad that he has to bear the brunt of angry visitors alone," sighed Tisha.

They had been called to investigate the source of the mirror's movement. Yet, they stood there, completely clueless, gazing at the rotating mirrors. Aman diverted everyone's attention towards a scene playing out in one of the mirrors. He said,

"Look at the reflection of sand on this mirror."

Tisha said, "This looks like beach sand. But where is the seawater?"

Samantha chuckled, "Even without a sea view, I would appreciate the solitude that this beach seems to offer. It doesn't seem like the tourist-overridden one on which we stand."

As they immersed themselves in the scenery, a green coconut fell and settled on the plain sand, unperturbed by footsteps and sandcastles. On peering closely, Aman noticed tiny white deposits on the sand and realized that it was salt left behind after the evaporation of previously contacted seawater.

He remarked, "Since the first reflection showed us a place on Mos

Island, this reflection could be from another place on the same island."

Tisha said, "I think this network of mirrors is more complex than we had imagined. Changing the orientation of these mirrors seems to connect it to different places on the island."

Karan rushed into the chamber from the balcony and announced a discovery,

"The wheels that we titled to flip these mirrors are also rotating by themselves."

Neil said with a solo finger raised in the air, "That leaves just one option. There is a mechanism on the other end of the pipe that allows these wheels and mirrors to be controlled."

Karan said, "Are you implying that someone is rotating the mirrors from the island of Mos?"

Neil nodded with a sober expression. He recalled the inscription on a jewellery brought by one of the birds - *"Let the Shakti mirrors lead you here and we will shower you with treasures for rescuing us."*

He added, "The island residents know the mirrors can guide us there. They probably noticed the raised pipe and realized that they had caught our attention. So, they are probably trying to send us more views of the island. Visuals that could help us to track them down."

As the team inspected other mirrors, they witnessed a few more scenes. One of the mirrors showed snow-white fog blowing across the screen. Sometimes, the fog wafted gently and sometimes, its pace seemed almost violent. The dense fog occasionally parted in places to form clear patches, allowing one to see the clear blue sky.

In another mirror, Tisha and Neil looked at the irregularly raised grassy mounds in a verdant meadow. The light green grass was interspersed with tiny yellow flowers. There was an inkling of a mild rainbow in the clear blue sky, which Tisha confirmed by bending forward with her face almost touching the mirror.

She squinted her eyes to focus them more sharply on the faint streak of light in the sky. No sooner had she bent forward that she pulled away her face with such alacrity that she would have almost tripped and fell, had Neil not intervened with his arm support. Both looked in the mirror with an aghast expression as Tisha struggled to regain her balance. The erstwhile plain mirror on the other end revealed a deep crack, resembling a spider web.

As the commotion caught the attention of the others, the sharp black talons of a bird appeared on the relatively unscathed bottom section of the mirror. Aman looked at the photograph of the Bollywood bird on his mobile and rechecked the talons. He muttered under his breath, "Pelagornis Sandersi."

* * *

Samantha gazed out of the window from Maya's living room. The half moon lit up a section of the sea with a faint white light. The black pipe floated exactly in the middle of that moonlit section.

"I have a hypothesis. The black pipe led the Queen's regiments to the Island of Mos during the day. However, it would be rendered useless in the night. That's why they relied on the moonlight to travel in the dark."

On hearing no response, she read a sentence aloud from Queen Loma's translated letter,

"I have deliberately chosen a full moon night so that the glimmers across the sea are at their brightest and guide your ship safely to our shores."

She sipped the masala chai from the cup in her hand as she leaned back in the orange bean bag in the living room, waiting to hear everyone's thoughts.

Aman was the first to speak out,

"The mirrors would have also helped. Their constant rotation creates a kind of light show as it throws shimmering sunlight and moonlight in all directions. This would certainly be a good guiding signal for ships."

"Queen Loma alluded to that in her letter. Remember?" said Samantha.

Seeing everyone's lost expression, she held out the printed letter translation and placed it on the table in the centre of the living room. She led her forefinger over the phrases as if she was underlining them to draw everybody's attention towards them.

"A resident of Shakti town came to complain about shimmering sunlight emanating from the lighthouse on the suspicion of enemy spying. Knowing how gossip spreads, we have switched off the source during the daytime when everyone is awake."

She continued, "The black pipe and rotating mirrors were the usual guide for those travelling to and from the Island of Mos across the ocean. However, the elaborate system of rotating the mirrors and raising the black pipe to the surface probably attracted unwanted attention. Therefore, the Queen suggested travelling on a full moon night so that the moonlight could compensate for the low visibility of the black pipe."

Everyone's eyes lit up with surprise and admiration at the explanation. It was time for a break. The pitter patter of raindrops could be heard outside. An aroma of freshly fried *pakoras* wafted through the air as Maya entered the living room from the kitchen with a tray in her hand. She gently placed the irregularly-shaped pakoras with an assorted combination of hot sauces on the table.

She said, "I would usually ask my grandson to cook this rain time delicacy since that is his area of expertise. But he seemed weary and exhausted today, pretty much like everyone else here. I guess you all worked very hard last night. What did you stumble upon?"

Aman turned to Neil and Karan for cues on the secrecy of their findings. Out of respect for Maya's prominent role in the Indian navy, he found it difficult to refuse. Realizing that her profession had taught her the significance of sensitive information, he requested her not to reveal what he was about to tell her.

As the merry group feasted on the sumptuous *pakoras*, Neil narrated the incidents in detail as Maya listened with facial expressions of awe and surprise. When Neil finally paused his narrative, she said,

"This sounds like quite an adventure. Samantha, I hope that we can find your family soon. I am presuming that the next step would be to take an expedition to the Island of Mos by following the pipe. Am I right?"

"To be honest, we haven't thought much about it," said Karan.

"I still can't fathom how such an island, if it exists, has escaped discovery by seafaring explorers or conventional satellites all this while. Let us look at the satellite images of the sea along the guiding pipe."

Tisha pulled out a laptop from her bag and started typing something fervently. After a while, she put the laptop in the centre of the table for everyone to see. Maya and Aman, who sat opposite to her, stood up and dragged chairs to sit beside the sofas facing the screen.

After a brief period of close observation, Samantha remarked,

"There seems to be nothing except the clear turquoise-green and blue water on the straight path shown by the tube. There are occasional white clouds looming over the ocean but not a single green or brown blob, highlighting the presence of an island."

Karan said, "I think it makes sense to fly in an aircraft to visit this spot. We just need to follow the black pipe. The actual view might tell us something that the satellite images are not conveying."

Maya's eyes lit up and her chapped lips curved into a reminiscent smile. Her old age, evident from the numerous wrinkles on her face, had diminished her sharp vision and physical strength but her steely resolve was as steadfast as ever. The mention of aerial flight sent her on a trip of nostalgia. She looked at the framed newspaper headlines, highlighting her achievements as a navy pilot.

The balcony-delivered newspaper, which was unread since the morning to be eventually picked up by Aman, didn't share such pleasantries in its headlines though. The headline on the front page read in bold letters - "Activists to hold rally against NTFHO Research Team to protest negligent care of last living Pelagornis Sandersi aka Bollywood Bird ".

The subtitle, written in smaller letters, beneath the main title read - "The prehistoric bird, rediscovered after millions of years of extinction, passed away on 14 August due to multiple organ failure."

Two hundred miles away, hundreds of environmentalists, animal rights activists and young students had gathered at the Gateway of India as the sun shone its last rays before setting down at dusk.

Some of them held protest board signs with slogans like 'Animal cruelty not okay' and 'Save Biodiversity'. Others held white candles which they lit with matchsticks or the candle flames of their neigh-bours. The protestors were surrounded by one of the largest flocks of pigeons ever seen on the gateway grounds as the protestors threw grains to feed the birds. It wasn't clear if the feeding was a deliberate show of protest to highlight compassionate treatment of birds or the spontaneous response of a group of bird-lovers. But the symbolism of the bird's presence was evident for everyone to see. As if to reinforce the symbolism, a flock of Oriental magpie-robins sat on the arch walls and began to sing in their quintessential chirpy tones. The sea waves on the marine waterfront gurgled in unison as the protestors started their march.

* * *

As she viewed the protest video on her mobile, Tisha said, "It is so unfair to malign our team in the media press, especially after all the progress that we have made in our research. There is mounting evidence that the bone shrapnel was present in the bird's body before its arrival in Mumbai. It went undetected in our medical tests which aren't perfectly equipped to understand the health of gigantic birds. This was an unprecedented situation and we did our best."

Karan reassured her in a calming voice, "You know these facts. The media doesn't. We can't let them know either because of the confidentiality of the matter. NTFHO has released a generic statement to counter the protestor's narrative but they cannot be compelled without complete facts."

Neil added, "We saw Pelagornis Sandersi talons in the mirror view. It is waiting to be rediscovered by us on Mos Island. We just need to reach there. Nullifying the so-called 'second extinction' theory would be more than enough to hopefully quell these raging protestors."

"Why is Aman taking so long?" said Samantha.

She peered out from the glass window in the small passenger airplane. She saw Maya and Aman standing at the foot of the staircase leading to the entrance door of the aeroplane. The relatively vacant airstrip caused the wind to move without obstacles, fluttering their clothes. Maya kissed her grandson on the forehead and then handed him a steel tiffin box with food containers stacked on top of each other.

"Grandma, they will provide me with food on the flight. Why did you go to the trouble of baking so many homemade snacks?"

"I am sure you will get in-flight food but you don't need to starve if you feel hungry in between the regular meals that they serve after long gaps."

"I am not flying on a ten-hour flight to Europe, Grandma. We are flying to the target spot which is probably not far away from here. If we manage to spot the island, we will circle around it for any observations that we might be able to make from a high altitude and return here within two hours. This trip is only to get a cursory idea of what to expect on the island. The observations will help us properly plan a full-fledged expedition to the island with a bigger contingent and adequate preparations."

"I see. Stay safe and see you back soon."

"Anyway, your snacks are always a delight. Thank you."

"Alright. Take care. Call me when your flight lands back here. Goodbye."

Aman waved back to Maya as she bid him farewell when he began to climb the stairs.

"Aren't grandmothers the best?" chuckled Samantha as Aman made his way into the corridor with his bag and shoved it into the compartment above his seat.

Aman sank back in his seat and said, "Yes, I have been lucky.

I never got to see my parents but she never made me feel their absence with her love and affection. Plus, she has always encouraged me to pursue my dreams and been a strong source of support and motivation."

"That is great," said Samantha. "My grandmother was similar. As a young girl, I would visit my grandparents' house in Jaipur during the vacations. She used to take me on visits to old forts and palaces in the city and narrate historical stories hidden in the walls of those magnificent structures."

"Was that your childhood motivation?"

"Indeed. These tours greatly piqued my interest in history.

My grandma didn't get the opportunity to study much due to the patriarchal society in her times but she constantly encouraged me to empower myself through education."

Aman smiled and looked out of the window. He watched Maya board a ferry bus on the airstrip below and the bus subsequently moving towards the airport premises. He took a deep breath and fastened his seat belt.

The airplane shook slightly and a roaring sound followed. The aeroplane lunged forward and picked up speed. After a few minutes of speeding on the runway, it tilted upwards. When a slightly terrified Aman opened his eyes, they were in the air. He looked at the sparkles of orange and white light on the streets and the skyscrapers.

The occasional truck or car that moved in the early pre-sunrise hours of the morning looked like a tiny ant on the road. By the time the sun rose, the sleepy scenes of an otherwise vibrant city had given way to clear blue ocean water lit up by the morning sun. Misty white clouds drifted over the choppy water. The enormous pipe appeared as an erratic black streak over the sea due to its constant wobbling in the waves. His appreciative glances of the scenic views were disturbed by Tisha's loud call.

"Is that a school of dolphins?"

Aman and Samantha, whose seats were on the opposite side of the aisle, moved to the adjoining window seats in Tisha's seat row. Tisha pointed her fingers to direct the others to look but the constantly moving aeroplane rendered her effort useless. The aeroplane had crossed a long distance by the time everyone's attention was drawn.

"I missed the opportunity to see dolphins in the wild for the first time," sighed Karan.

"Don't worry. I am not even sure if they were actually dolphins," said Tisha. "I just saw some hazy grey blobs on the surface of the sea."

The aeroplane descended a bit, leaving the clouds several feet above it. Within a few minutes, Tisha yelled again.

"I can see them again. There seem to be more of them."

The descent made the view clearer. There was a swarm of grey and white dots moving over the seawater. Neil instantly pulled out his DSLR camera and clicked a series of photographs as the rest of the group spectated in awe. Once they had been left behind again, Neil zoomed the photographs in his camera. The powerful resolution of the camera allowed it to capture clear photographs from such a high altitude.

Considering Neil's renown in ornithology, his possession of such a camera didn't surprise anyone much. It was the content of the photographs that was more surprising.

The photographs showed large flocks of seagulls with white bodies and black wings flying at low altitudes over the sea. Some of the seagulls were floating peacefully on the chaotic water. Some had their prominent orange beaks dipped into the sea with their wings and body in the air. One of them had a silvery fish trapped between its beak.

"They look beautiful. I feel stupid to mistake them for dolphins," remarked Tisha with an embarrassed laughter.

"Nobody could have made an accurate call from this height. Not your fault," said Aman.

"Funny though," winked Samantha.

"How do these birds drink seawater? Isn't it supposed to be impotable?" said Karan, pointing his finger to the seagull with its beak in the water.

"These marine birds have special glands to process seawater and rid it of salts," explained Neil. "Humans don't have such glands, making seawater unfit for our drinking."

Neil's explanation led to the declaration of a loud epiphany from Aman, startling everyone.

"Nor do any of the terrestrial bejewelled birds that arrived on our shores after travelling several kilometres from the Island of Mos. This explains why we found these birds near freshwater bodies. They needed to quench their thirsts after flying for a long distance over this desert ironically full of water."

The others nodded in agreement. Tisha's deep contemplative expressions showed that Aman's hypothesis had pushed her to think and reflect. She shared her thoughts.

"I have a hunch. We noticed how the local Vidikan birds salivated on seeing jewellery. We attributed their salivation to the tradition of offering food in the presence of jewellery as ancestral homages. The bejewelled birds flying from the Island of Mos, which found refuge near freshwater bodies, weren't related to these local birds. Their similar salivating behaviour suggests that they witnessed a similar tradition on the island they inhabited. Considering that the inhabitants of the island are descendants of old-era Vidikan scientists and prisoners of war, these traditions might have been passed on there too."

"This makes sense," said Samantha. "It seems obvious in retrospect and yet we didn't come up with this earlier."

Neil zoomed the touchscreen map on his seat and said,

"This visit will shed even more light on the matter. I think we have almost reached the spot indicated on the map."

The moving red dot, symbolizing the airplane's location, was moving closer to the stationary green dot indicating the destination spot's location. Barely had he completed his sentence when the pilot's blaring announcement reverberated throughout the passenger seating area -

"We have reached the indicated location. We will be circling around the area for half an hour before starting the return journey. Kindly remain seated and observe the view outside your window."

The airplane took a sideways turn, jolting the group briefly before they began peering outside their window. There was no sign of any island. There were only vast stretches of blue and pale green seawater extending across miles in all directions.

"There is nothing to be seen here. Did we miss something in the clues?" said Aman with dismay.

The aircraft had slowed considerably to allow them to make keen observations but the views remained as monotonous as before, exacerbating the gloomy atmosphere in the passenger cabin. After a while, everyone except Karan gave up and sat back in their seats. They dispassionately watched the empty seas from their windows, resigning to their bad fortune.

In stark contrast, Karan's enthusiasm was as undiminished as ever. He squinted his eyes, opened them and squinted them again at the slightest suspicion. His efforts paid off when he noticed the obvious anomaly right in front of their eyes.

"Look at this particular patch of clouds here. It is situated at a much lower altitude than the rest of the clouds. These clouds also seem significantly denser and whiter than the others. If you notice closely, you will also see occasional bursts of white fog from a few feet below them, fuelling their creation. The fog streams seem to be appearing out of nowhere since there is nothing except the clear sky and sea waves below their point of emergence."

Hearing this shook off the lethargy that had set in amongst the others. They fixated their eyes on the view outside and validated what had been just described to them.

"The satellite images also showed the presence of clouds at this spot," said Aman. "Something's off about these clouds. We need to take a closer look."

As if on cue, the pilot made another announcement - "We will be descending now and flying at low altitudes above the seawater for closer observation."

The airplane nosedived towards the sea, causing everyone to be caught off balance. They clung to the seat in front of them for balance. Neil closed his eyes, only momentarily opening them.

The quick peek revealed an eerie sight of a gigantic sea wave on the verge of approaching his window. The seemingly imminent crash was averted as the airplane slowed its descent and tilted to jet upward. Neil freaked out every time the waves rose but they always crashed after reaching a peak several feet below the aircraft's base. After a few iterations, he was finally convinced enough to let the fear escape him. He observed a flock of seagulls prancing in the water. Their distinctive black-white plumage and their orange peaks were prominently visible from this altitude. He looked ahead and observed a similar flock of seagulls on the horizon far away. After a while, Tisha made a fresh claim that she had seen dolphins.

"I am not mistaken this time. I clearly saw a school of silvery-grey dolphins leap out of the sea with their unique thin and long snouts."

Neil, who sat on the window seat in front of her, looked back. He noticed several curved fins subtly emerge from the water which subsequently slid and disappeared into the water. He heard Tisha's voice from behind.

"I can see another school of dolphins ahead. Look at the fins in the distance."

By the time Neil diverted his attention, those dolphins had leapt out of the water. He looked on the opposite side to observe the same spectacle of leaping dolphins with their slender grey bodies and open snouts embedded with innumerous tiny teeth. It was at this moment that he noticed the pattern.

"There is a giant mirror shielding this spot. Whatever you are seeing in the distance is a mirage of sorts designed to fool you into believing that there is nothing here except seawater. However, the open sea that you see at the location of the spot is simply a reflection of the sea surrounding the spot. Notice how the leap of a dolphin or the flutter of the seagull's wings beneath us gets immediately replicated on the horizon. That's why the fog streams seem to be emerging from thin air since the mirrors hide their source up to a certain height. Till that height, you only see the reflection of the clear sky and the water."

Samantha said, "There does seem to be a random shine around here. The kind that sparkles from a mirror."

Tisha added, "Also, look at the dust particles suspended in mid air. They are probably stuck to the mirror's surface."

Karan said, "Remember the scene of dense white fog in one of the lighthouse mirrors. It was probably from a part of the island behind these mirrors where the source of this fog is located. The mirrors and the fog clouds are working together to effectively render this island invisible from the sea and the sky. Maybe we could ask the pilot to…"

His statement was interrupted by an abrupt and sharp halt, which sent everyone tumbling back onto their seat cushions. The aircraft began to reverse. A faint trembling sound reverberated through the attached speakers meant for dissemination of the pilot's speeches. Karan unfastened his belt and ran towards the cockpit as his new shoes squeaked against the floor. The abrupt reverse drift faltered his steps but he managed to support himself with the seats on both sides. He flung open the entrance door and rushed inside.

The pilot was a young woman, who sat on the black leather seat with a trembling face. She was unaware of Karan's presence and solely focused on the view outside the glass window in front of her. She was shaking but her hands were contrarily steadfast.

She clicked control buttons one after the other. When Karan entered, he saw what the pilot had seen earlier.

A gigantic bird with black wings as long as the aircraft wings itself and sharp teeth sliding over the lower half of its yellow beak. The eyes seemed similar in size, shape and colour to pale green tennis balls except for additional black dots forming the pupils. The black pupils rolled to and fro from the sides towards the beak as if examining the alien object. It stood surprisingly still with slow flaps of its wings. On the other hand, the airplane was drifting backwards and away from the bird.

"This isn't moving backwards fast enough," the pilot gasped as she finally noticed Karan mutely spectating the turn of events.

After a briefly startled expression, the pilot ignored him and rapidly pushed the jockey stick in front of her and pushed a control button. The airplane jolted and swerved towards the left. Within a matter of seconds, it picked up pace and the speeding was accompanied by a roaring sound. Aman and Samantha looked at the Pelagornis Sandersi bird from their passenger windows as it momentarily descended towards the sea and flew up with a bunch of silvery-grey fishes scooped up in its mouth.

The pilot shouted as she saw another airplane speeding towards them, "How did this airplane arrive out of nowhere?"

"There is no other airplane. It is a reflection of our own airplane. Raise the airplane else we will crash into the mirror," shrieked Karan with a voice so loud and terrifying that the rest of the passengers scampered into the cockpit.

"What is going on here?" said Neil.

"No time for explanations," said Karan.

The pilot's decisive maneuver lifted the airplane several feet into the sky and they could not see anything except clouds.

The aircraft shook violently, leaving them to find handles for support. When Aman opened his eyes, he noticed that the airplane reflection in front of them was gone. The ground view was still obscured with white clouds but he could see clear patches of the ground amidst gaps between them. The soil was barren and grey without any traces of vegetation. Jets of steam and water rushed out from the soil with most of the water collapsing back into the ground but leaving jets of steam to linger and ascend into the sky. He noticed that everyone around him was terribly freaked out as visible from the stressed curls and sweat on their foreheads. The exception was the pilot, whose expression was remarkably calm and resolute as she kept her hands firmly on the control panel.

"Ma'am, you are so brave. What is your name?" said Tisha with the smitten expression of a fangirl.

"Preeti Kaur," she said with a smile.

The aircraft began to descend slowly. The Island of Mos had seen its first visitors in several centuries.

CHAPTER 16

A WELCOME OF WORRY

"This was not the plan. Why don't we turn around and fly back?"

These were Aman's first words when the aeroplane skidded to a halt on a vacant plot of land amidst the tropical forest beyond the geysers. Spectating Preeti's courage had contrarily driven Tisha's unfazed spirits to new highs. Brimming with curiosity and excitement, she unloaded her heavy bag from the cabin above her seat and fastened it around her back. As soon as she unlocked Benji's cage, the sleepy dog woke up and leapt into her arms for an affectionate pat.

Neil said, "Don't worry, Aman. We will fly back to Mumbai in an hour. We have successfully reached an island concealed from the eyes of the world for centuries. I am too curious to let a golden opportunity like this slide."

Preeti added, "In any case, I need to check the control system and engines before taking off again. Flying away from giant birds wasn't exactly what I had prepared the flight systems for."

She chuckled at the last sentence and added, "By the time I complete my safety checks, you all can roam around for a while. Don't stray off too far else I will leave you alone on this wretched island."

She laughed again and this time, the others joined in as well. Samantha led the way as she opened the door and jumped onto the ground below. A flock of parrots fluttered from the tree branches into the dark evening sky. There were dense clusters of colossal ebony trees, which formed a dense canopy, on both sides of the clearing.

A fallen tree lay in the middle of the wide vegetation-free path running through the tropical forest.

"This path has probably been cleared by the islanders to facilitate movement across the forest," said Neil. "Does anyone want to take a short walk?"

As they trod slowly on the path, accompanied by the occasional crunching sound from the trampling of fallen leaves, Samantha closely watched the forest on both sides with the hope of seeing her son. A black porcupine with a set of sharp white-coloured quills adorning its back sluggishly crossed the path in front of them. When Benji saw the porcupine, he started barking and chased it into the bushes. Tisha ran after Benji and reined him by its leash.

"It is a dangerous idea to mess with a porcupine. Those quills can pierce your body and cause serious injury," said Tisha as she sternly looked at Benji while the others heard her.

Benji's intelligence ensured that he could decipher what was inappropriate based on Tisha's expression and not repeat those mistakes. Be it not frightening the neighbour's rabbit or not relieving oneself on the sofa, there was little that Benji couldn't learn.

After a few steps, a rustling sound was heard from the bushes, causing the pedestrians to freeze in their tracks and listen closely. The sound grew louder with every passing second. Soon, they realized that it resembled the tapping of several feet against the ground.

"This might be a pride of lions or a pack of leopards. Let us run before we get devoured for their dinner," said Aman as he muttered and gestured to the others to move.

His fears were put to rest when the brown and white striped face of a zebra emerged from the bushes. After briefly shrugging to shake off the bush thorns prickling its body, it completely stepped out into the open and walked across the road while flaunting its majestic body. The zebra didn't look like any typical zebra they had laid their eyes on. Its body was covered with distinctive brown stripes as opposed to the conventional black ones. Most of the zebra's rear skin was plain brown and devoid of any stripes while the front half retained the usual striped skin.

Neil's mouth was left half open. Recovering from his shock, he said, "I cannot believe it. It is the quagga, a subspecies of zebra, which went extinct in Africa sometime in the 19th century. I am keen to know how many more such believed to be extinct species have managed to thrive away from human overexploitation on this island."

He squatted on the ground and watched with mesmerisation as another quagga leapt onto the road from the bushes and crossed onto the other forested side. Within a matter of a few minutes, a herd of around fifty quaggas could be seen crossing the road. Most of them were full-grown adults, some of whom constantly nudged their foals with fragile legs to move forward as they repeatedly fell and stood up. Neil repeatedly clicked photographs using his mobile until the procession finally ended with the last quagga disappearing into the dark wilderness.

Samantha warned, "Dr. Neil, don't exhaust your mobile battery. We should be using our phones to call or message people on the mainland and let them know of our situation. We aren't getting any telecommunication signals here unfortunately at the moment but we might catch a weak signal somewhere."

"You are probably right. As a biologist, who has worked in the domain of evolutionary science for decades, this scene was very euphoric for me though. Imagine how glad you would be if a medieval Indian emperor, say Ashoka, came back to life."

Samantha nodded and smiled. The group turned back and started strolling towards the airplane. Intermittent owl hoots could be heard from the trees but the owls couldn't be seen in the branches of the dense canopy amidst the darkness. When they reached the airplane, there was no sign of Preeti.

"Maybe she is in the cockpit. Let us check inside," suggested Karan.

When they entered, they saw Preeti running around frantically to close every passenger window. Upon noticing them, she whispered,

"Close the entrance door and help me close the windows. Don't you all hear that sound?"

While nobody except her could hear the sound she referred to, they proceeded to close the door and windows as she asked while looking puzzled. Subsequent shrill trumpets and thudding sounds, which grew louder with every passing second, cleared the confusion.

"There is no time to close all the windows. Hide quickly," whispered Preeti.

Everyone either squatted on the leg space beneath an open window or sat on a seat beside a closed window. Clouds of dust swirled up in the air outside the window as Neil noticed a shiny amber-coloured eye in the diagonally opposite open window of his seat.

"Duck your head down," said Karan who sat beside him.

He bent a little but his eyes were still above the seat to satisfy his curiosity. As the dust settled down to allow him a clearer view, he noticed grey skin patches. Within a few seconds, the outline of an elephant's face appeared. The large fanning ears shaped like the continent of Africa suggested that it belonged to an African species. It turned its head towards the window and felt its trunk over the glass. Neil sat down speculating if the elephant saw him. He heard a roaring trumpet which was followed by a series of more trumpets of various pitches and loudness. A mix of bangs and clanks were heard throughout the length of the aircraft walls. Karan relented when he felt the vibration of the wall against which his back rested as he sat on the floor.

The calm within the aircraft couldn't hold up much longer. Tisha impulsively darted across the corridor towards the opposite seat when the noise felt too close. The sigh of relief as she sat on the seat turned into a blood-curdling yell when two elephants, which were probably lurking nearby, met her in the eye as they peeped through the window. She got her first clear view of the elephant's face. The most distinguishable aspect of its face was the presence of four tusks with the broad tusk on each side diverging and splitting into two thinner ones like two crescent moons held together by only one end. The trumpets outside grew shriller and louder. Preeti screamed,

"These elephants will seriously damage the airplane and make it impossible for us to fly back. We need to divert them away."

"But how?" asked Aman.

"We jump out through the entrance door and run into the dense forest. The trees are close to each other and so the narrow spaces between them will impede the movement of the elephants. We should be able to divert their attention yet outrun them with some effort."

"What if we aren't able to?"

"There is no choice. We have to take the risk else we will be trapped on an island cleverly shrouded from the rest of the world."

Aman shuddered but nodded along with the others. They pulled out their bags and strapped them to their backs. Preeti slowly pushed the door and slightly peeked out. Sensing that there was no elephant immediately outside, she popped her head outside for a complete and clear view. A herd of four-tusked elephants stood around five feet away with their faces turned towards the windows and their trunks lashing against them. Preeti gently put her feet on the ground and gestured to the others to follow her. Karan leapt out first and then helped Samantha to climb out by lending his hand for support. Tisha followed her and subsequently caught Benji in her hands when Neil held Benji out for her from the raised door. After Neil jumped out, Aman was the only one remaining. He was jittery about jumping from a height and sat down on the edge of the entrance to skid off it. He gauged the height while looking down and hastily landed with a thud on the ground. This invited the attention of the raging elephants, which were earlier occupied in mounting a collective attack on the aircraft.

"Run into the woods," shrieked Tisha.

The elephants charged towards them as they ran into the dark woods. Aman remembered his embarrassing annual school tradition of finishing last in the marathon. He realized that there was something greater than his self-respect at stake now - his life.

He concentrated his mind on navigating through the narrow gaps between the trees and sped without looking back. He could hear the raging trumpets but he knew that he would freeze from fear if he moved his eyes back to check how close or far they were. Karan, who was outrunning everyone, could afford a momentary glance to check on his folks. Most of the elephants were struggling to uproot the trees that stood in their way or occasionally stopping to inspect broader gaps between the trees to pass through. In the background, tall orange flames rose, belching clouds of dense gray smoke into the sky. The airplane had breathed its last along with their hopes of an imminent escape.

* * *

"I think I am still alive."

These were Neil's first words after taking a small bite from a maroon-red apple that he had seen on the ground. The others sighed in relief. They might have escaped the fury of violent four-tusked elephants but the marathon had left them hungry.

"The risk is worth it. I am so starved that I will even gobble one of these caterpillars," said Aman as he looked at the green caterpillar crawling over the bark.

"Thanks for the blatant exaggeration, Mr. Dramatic," said Tisha as she rolled her eyes at him from the tree bark upon which she stood.

She plucked an apple from the tree and threw it towards Samantha, who deftly caught it. She huffed and panted as she climbed from one branch to another while carefully maintaining her balance. Preeti offered to help but she refused stating that the job was almost done.

Neil remarked, "I wonder how this solitary apple tree is thriving without any sunshine. The other closely packed trees around it are much taller and must be almost completely eclipsing it from sunshine with their dense canopy."

Everyone else was too hungry to care. They huddled beneath the tree and nibbled at the apples furiously. Thoughts of hunger and fear of food poisoning alternated in their minds. Eventually though, the apples were consumed and a few of them were packed for the onward journey. After half an hour of aimless wandering, they spotted a multi-storey treehouse built of parallel wooden planks held together by bundles of bamboo canes on each side. There were winding stairs connecting each floor to the others and the topmost leg of the stairs arbitrarily disappeared as it pierced through the dense canopy above them.

Preeti said, "I think the topmost floor of this tree house is situated above this canopy. Let us go upstairs and get a clear view of this island from the top. It will help us to navigate through the wilderness and think of a route through which we could get out of this island."

"This makes sense," said Karan. "Let us tread carefully and step one by one in case the structure is fragile and unable to support our combined weight. I will go first."

He placed his legs one after the other on the creaking wooden plank on the first floor. Once he had walked around a bit on it, he beckoned Neil to join him. This exercise continued till everyone had joined them on the first floor and it still stood still. They similarly tested each floor with Karan taking the first hit and then ascending to the next floor after an assurance of the plank's carrying capacity. Midway, Aman looked down below on the forest floor. The fallen leaves looked much smaller. The numerous ants swarming over those leaves were invisible to the naked eye. The clusters of white flowers, which looked like tiny spots from the ground below, were within a hand's reach. Aman reached out to touch them only to be pulled back by Samantha to prevent him from stumbling into what looked like a deep valley. On the seventh floor, they were greeted by a family of black-hooded orioles. The birds had formed an almost spherical hanging nest of intertwined fibers on an overgrown branch passing through the space between the floor and the roof. The stark pink beaks and yellow faces of two yelling oriole chicks popped out from the fibers as an adult bird fed them black berries.

"These birds are so adorable and magnificent," said Aman with gleaming eyes.

"They are black-hooded orioles," said Tisha. "They usually form their nests in canopy branches. This means that we are almost around the canopy. The staircase to the next floor should take us above it."

The anticipation fuelled by this revelation caused everyone to skip the traditional testing procedure as they rushed together through the winding stairs.

After battling a few sturdy branches by either pushing them aside or making their way through uncluttered spaces, they eventually reached the top floor. The balcony walls on this one were much higher than the ones that they had encountered till now, allowing them to collapse on the ground with their back resting against the walls.

"I feel for those who dare to climb Mount Everest," said Samantha.

"I am exhausted after this short ascent."

She still struggled to get on her feet and peep over the balcony walls. At this level, the tree house overlooked the dense canopy.

On three sides, the canopy stretched endlessly into the horizon displaying a colourful potpourri - green tree leaves, dangling pale orange fruits on apricot trees, white flower clusters on gum trees and red flowers of a tree species nobody could recognize. On one side, the dense canopy gave way to a grassy clearing with a lake in between. The outline of a mountain range could be seen in the background of the lake. The lake water reflected the stars which glimmered brightly in the absence of polluting air and bright lights characteristic of urban settings. While Samantha continued to gaze at the thriving ecosystem, the others chose to lie on the ground admiring the clear black and star-studded sky.

Samantha said, "We should make a trip to the lake tomorrow since we will most probably run out of the limited freshwater stock in our bottles."

"Yes, we should," agreed Aman. "We also need to figure out a way to get out of here. Shouldn't a rescue party be sent for us when our aircraft goes off the radar?"

Preeti said, "A rescue party is most probably circling around this island as we speak but the clever deception would make it difficult for anyone to spot the island and reach us. We should also explore ways to reach them."

The events of the day had exhausted everyone and they simply gave a slight nod. Lying on the ground, they soon closed their eyes and dozed off, unfazed by the howling wind and the rustling leaves.

* * *

Even Tisha's loud snores ceased to overcome the rustling noise when the tree branch shook vigorously. Unlike the others, who were deep in sleep, Aman had only begun to sleep after a long bout of overthinking that had kept him awake.

He slightly opened his eyes with the hope that it was a temporary disturbance that would ebb away. When it didn't, he gathered the courage to stand on his feet and peep over the wall. Piercing through the canopy during the shady hours of dawn, a giraffe's head tugged at a leafy branch only a few inches away from him. His drowsiness gave way to enthusiasm as he sat back to watch the magnificent creature traverse its head across the network of leafy branches. He had seen giraffes before at the Delhi Zoo but this was the first time that he was seeing one at such close quarters.

The giraffe broke away a long twig from one of the branches with its mouth but failed to hold it in its mouth. The twig wobbled in its mouth and lost balance to crash through the leaves, momentarily exposing the view beneath the dense canopy. An unexpected view. Because Aman noticed not just the giraffe's body but also the hazy figure of a man sitting on its back. Visibly shaken, Aman relented from the balcony edge and slunk onto the floor. As he contemplated whether to wake up his peers, he heard the sound of footsteps. The sound grew louder and clearer with each passing second. Someone was climbing up the staircase to the treehouse.

CHAPTER 17

SHINY SOUP SPRINKLES NOT TO BE SLURPED

"Wake up quickly. Someone is climbing up the stairs."

Aman's frantic whispers, aimed at waking up his sleeping friends without alerting the intruder, failed to elicit any response. The snores were as loud as ever and the eyes were still shut. What Aman's calls couldn't achieve, the sunlight of dawn did.

As the sun rose to eradicate the darkness around them gradually, Preeti's eyes began to flutter. She saw Aman and heard him. She was instantly on her feet. She sharply shook the others and capped their mouths before they could let out a surprised scream.

The panic turned out to be unwarranted. The sound of footsteps ebbed gradually and couldn't be heard after a few minutes. The giraffe glanced around for a while after having its fill and then began to stroll away. Its long neck and head still propped up over the canopy wherever it went. The group except Samantha was relieved when nobody turned up on their floor. Samantha had been hoping against hope to meet her son or ex-husband but the turn of events proved to be disappointing.

"Riding a giraffe. That's new. What did the rider look like?" said Tisha.

"I couldn't see much in the darkness," said Aman. "I only saw the outline of his hands, matted black hair and a peach-ish cape over his shoulders."

Tisha said, "I assume we still don't know much about this mystery man. He must be one of those Vidikans trapped on this island. Why was he riding a giraffe though?"

Neil suggested, "Being perched at that height probably makes it easier to pluck fruits from tall trees or spot animals for hunting."

As they looked over the balcony, they noticed that the giraffe's head, although still visible, looked no bigger than a tiny yellow blob in the faraway distance.

Tisha said, "I think the giraffe and his rider have gone away. So, if they posed any threat to us, we are safe. Let us pick up our bags and move towards the lake in the opposite direction. I am parched and our water bottles are almost empty."

The lake gleamed in a turquoise blue colour in the morning sunlight with light green vegetation surrounding it on all sides. Hills, covered with dark green vegetation, formed the backdrop of the lake.

"Are they boats?" said Preeti, pointing to a cluster of irregularly shaped brown spots on the lake water.

"Can't see clearly. They could also be freshwater islands," suggested Karan.

"I don't think so. They seem too small to be...," said Neil.

His statement was cut off by a loud call from the floor below them. It was Samantha's.

She repeated herself with her words clearer this time - "He was here!"

The group rushed down the stairs battling rigid overgrown branches as they had done while ascending, although with greater curiosity and concern. They leapt onto the wooden floor, creating a flutter among the residing oriole family. They noticed Samantha holding up a soiled polka-dotted green hanky with the letter R embroidered in the centre with yellow fabric.

She said, "I had woven this for Rick. I remember cutting out a piece of cloth from his favourite nightwear that he had outgrown as a child. He was the one whose footsteps we heard. He was here."

* * *

Having convinced Samantha that they would return to the tree house to wait for Rick's return, they started walking towards the lake. After an hour, the shady forest gave way to an open grassy clearing. Unaccustomed to bright sunlight for a while, the group raised their hands to shield their eyes. When their eyes adjusted to the new normal level of brightness, the panoramic vision in front of their eyes became clear. The lake was vaster than they had imagined. Chirping and whistling of birds could be heard all around them. A flock of bright pink flamingos paraded about in an almost synchronized fashion in the shallow waters close to the shore. A peacock waded through the water while displaying its vibrant blue-green tail feathers in a circular fashion behind it, resembling a floating yacht.

"Look at the fishes here," said Tisha, ecstatically clapping her hands.

A shoal of silvery-grey fish swam close to the shore with the clear blue water allowing a close-up look. She had barely diverted anyone's attention towards them when a blue kingfisher with a yellow belly swooped down, caught a fish in its beak and flew away before their eyes. Naturally, the shoal of fishes dispersed and disappeared into the deep waters.

Tisha suggested, "I don't think we will be able to find a reliable supply of fruits regularly. Why don't we go fishing in these waters and roast the caught fish?"

"How will we catch them without a fishing rod?" said Neil.

"We could sharpen the edge of a slim wooden stick and try to pierce it through a fish's body to trap it," said Tisha. "Getting it right will require high precision and a lot of practice. I won't deny that. But it seems worth a try."

"That sounds brutal," said Aman with disgust. "But we can't really afford luxuries on this hostile island. So, let us go for it."

Samantha said, "The solitary tree over there seems nice for relaxing under the shade. We might also be able to use some of its barks as sticks for the fishing operation."

It was a neem tree, which stood alone amidst the open land as a refuge for tree-nesting birds. As everyone sat down on the soil, they noticed that the barks were occupied by nests of all shapes and sizes. The green parrots hovered over the pebble-sized eggs in their cup-shaped nest. A pair of blue swallows struggled to simultaneously feed their noisy chicks in their mud nest. It was the hornbill nest, carved out of a hole drilled into the wall, that caught their attention. The two hornbills would take turns sitting inside the nest to take care of the chickens so that the other could fly out into the forest beyond the grassland and return with berries to feed the family. The distinct colours of their eyes - white and red indicated that one of them was a male and the other was a female. Noticeably, both seemed much larger than even the biggest hornbills that Neil and Tisha had seen in captivity.

Neil remarked, "This explains why the male hornbill from this island that we had captured wasn't feeding the female hornbill from the mainland that we had introduced it to. The hornbill species of this island has a different arrangement when it comes to raising families."

Samantha said, "This equal partnership seems healthier for them. Notice how they are bigger than the mainland hornbills."

Meanwhile, Karan was filling water bottles by dipping them into the lake and waiting for the rising bubbles to stop. This indicated that the bottle had been filled with water and the air inside had been replaced.

While carrying out this tedious exercise, he noticed a basket floating towards him. When it drifted to the shore, he noticed that it had been woven by straws and held wheat grains with a gold bangle half-buried in it.

A sparrow perched on the basket's edge intermittently bent down to scoop up the grains in its beak. Aman witnessed a similar view from a high tree branch, albeit in a much more vivid fashion. He noticed several straw baskets laden with fruits, grains and glittering jewellery floating in the centre of the lake. Various birds flew over the lake to hop from one basket to the other and feast on the variety of food that each offered.

He gasped and said to himself, "Is it any surprise that the birds arriving from this island salivated on seeing jewellery?"

As he looked down, he saw Karan rushing towards them with his long hair flying in the wind. He looked up to smile at Aman, realizing that he had already witnessed the event.

* * *

The mesmerizing views, brought to everyone's attention by Aman and Karan, were a feast for the eyes but such feasts didn't satisfy the clarion calls of their stomachs for literal feasts. Tisha tried in vain to strike at the fish with the sharpened wooden stick but they always slipped away. Her failed endeavours were in stark contrast to Benji's successful exploits. He repeatedly dipped his mouth in the water only to resurge with a bunch of fish trapped between its sharp jaws. Even when there was no prospect of food, Aman was busy plucking twigs from the neem tree since in his own words, 'brushing is very important before a meal for oral hygiene'. In the absence of conventional brushes, he was using the ancient wisdom of rubbing teeth with neem twigs to clean them, imparted to him by his grandmother.

Samantha said, "Considering that these baskets seem to be a part of a ceremony to honour ancestors as we saw in the village in Vidika, I feel that the people must be living nearby. Why don't we try to contact them instead of running away from them? They wanted someone to rescue them so we would be welcomed. We would also benefit from their local knowledge."

"How will we talk to them? They don't understand our language," said Karan.

"Don't worry about it," said Aman. "The translator application has been developed and installed on my mobile. We can speak in English and the microphone will recognize the sentences and repeat them in Vidikan for the person in front of us to hear."

"Why are you telling us about it now? This is so awesome," said Neil.

"I guess that I was too focused on surviving and finding a way to escape ourselves that it never occurred to me."

"I have some good news," said Tisha as she came running towards the group assembled beneath the tree.

"Did you finally manage to catch some fish for us?" said Aman teasingly.

She replied, "Nope. It is an impossible task. I have managed to pull a few of the baskets ashore for us to relish the various fruits."

The baskets contained apples, mangoes, grapes and berries along with gold necklaces and anklets. In a conventional scenario, it was unimaginable for them to get more excited about fruits than medieval valuable treasures.

However, a day of starvation had left them with no desire except a normal meal. They gorged on the fruits while taking care not to waste even a tiny morsel. Samantha's attention also extended beyond the immediate meal in front of her.

While looking at the photograph on her mobile, she said,

"Look at that tiny house atop the hill peak. It looks the same as the one we saw in the lighthouse mirror. The one in the background when we saw Rick in the reflection. I think I have finally found my son."

Neil added, "If it is the same house, there must also be a mirror around it which was showing us the reflection. We can use it to contact someone in the Shakti lighthouse, who might see us in the reflection."

An eagle keenly watched the group as it hovered in circles over them in the sky. When Preeti noticed it upon raising her head, it flapped its wings and flew away towards the hills.

* * *

The steep ascent made the climb a weary one as they held onto rocks and tree branches along the slope for support. The tense perspiration on Aman's face reflected his clear anxiety for all his fellow climbers to see.

"Don't look down. You will only get more nervous. Keep moving on," said Preeti as she braved the climb fearlessly.

Irony had a laugh when Preeti herself froze in horror a few minutes later. A noodle-thin green snake slithered down the hill a few feet away from her. She kept her calm because she knew that the look of fright in her eyes would weaken the spirits of her fellows. Except Karan and Preeti, none of them were accustomed to harsh lifestyles and daunting campaigns. Within a few hours, they reached the edge of a stone-paved winding road around the hill leading to the peak.

As they felt their feet on solid ground and regained their balance, they heaved a sigh and lied down on the road. Benji, perhaps in a sense of gratitude to Tisha for having carried him up in his bag during the long climb, began to lick Tisha's hands and nudged his head against hers. The sun was beginning to set behind the clouds, spreading a fluorescent orange radiance in the sky. The lake reflected these shades emanating from the sky in its still and clear water. The golden jewellery floating around on its surface in straw baskets glowed dimly, looking like shiny spots.

"Don't they look like shiny toppings sprinkled on tomato soup?" pointed out Samantha.

"Vaguely," replied Karan tersely.

He was too absorbed in the view to speak much. The mountains and flying birds appeared as shadows since the sun was on the cusp of disappearing into the clouds. His concentration was disturbed only by the sensation of a water droplet on his face. He touched his face and inspected the tip of his finger to confirm the presence of water. He looked up and noticed the slight rumble in the clouds. The drops sprinkled on everyone else too within the next few minutes.

Neil warned, "If this drizzle evolves to torrential rain, the slopes will become muddy and the roads will get slippery. It will become arduous and potentially hazardous for us to make our way up to the summit. We need to hasten our climb."

The short couple of rounds around the hill felt like an eternal slow torture as they were faced with the paradox of treading carefully to prevent them from slipping while quickening their pace to prevent the situation from worsening. After what felt like a lifetime, they finally reached the porch of the sandstone-walled house amidst the hilly forest.

The fading signboard stood to the right of the porch as they had envisioned it from the reflection in the mirror. It was a double-storey structure with multiple tiny opaque windows on each floor. The ochre entrance door, which had been carved out of oakwood, had dark irregular patches and a rusty handle.

"Should we knock on the door?" whispered Samantha.

"I don't think there is anybody inside. Let us barge in and save ourselves from getting drenched here," said Tisha.

"What if we are deemed to be hostile invaders by the residents? Let us not take our chances here," said Aman.

Tisha raised her voice to protest but the door creaked loudly until the blowing wind eventually flung it wide open. It was pitch dark inside. They stepped onto the porch watchfully.

"Is anybody here?" said Aman. To his relief and Samantha's disappointment, there was no response. The only sound they heard was the rumble of thunder.

Neil lit up a section of the wall with white light emanating from his mobile's torch. The lit section revealed an extinguished bronze torch in a sconce. There were two haphazardly shaped grey tools on a projecting slab besides the sconce. Neil waved the light across the wall to reveal a whole horizontal series of such sconces carved into it.

"I know how to light up these torches. There is a common technique used in medieval times. Neil, can you please focus the light here?" said Samantha, pointing to the slab on which the tools were kept.

Once Neil had focused his torch onto it, she explained, "One of these is a flint stone and the other is a steel tool. The trick is to use the flint stone to scrape off particles from the surface of the steel tool. Once these detached particles come in contact with the air, they spontaneously ignite by virtue of their chemical property. The sparks burn the hay straw stuffed inside these torches."

Within a few loud strikes, she managed to accomplish a live demonstration of her theory. The torch housed leaping orange flames when she was done. She went on to repeat the exercise for every torch in the series across the wall. The formerly dark room lit up enough to reveal its contents albeit the light was considerably dim. The group cast long shadows across the floor in the backdrop of the light radiating from the fires. The wall in front of them was illustrated with a gigantic colourful painting. There was a tattered sofa with a silver rim facing the illustrated wall. A short closed wooden door led outside through that wall. The ceiling was pierced by a staircase leading to the floor above the one in which they stood.

"Isn't this quite magnificent and vivid? I wonder if it depicts the same lake we saw," said Karan as he gasped at the painting.

The depiction showed a round blue lake surrounded by green mountains, similar to the one they had witnessed in the morning. The difference was in the level of activity around the lake. While the one they had seen in the morning appeared to be deserted, this one was surrounded by men and women wearing plain dresses and sitting atop the edge of terracotta slides along the lake coast. They were using these slides to slip baskets, filled with food and jewellery, towards the lake water. Various kinds of birds - sparrows, parrots and even hawks perched on the hands of these people. Some of them were affectionately stroking these birds. Aman said confusingly,

"Why can't they simply drop the baskets in the lake? What is the idea behind using a slide to push them into the lake?"

Tisha said, "I can't fathom that either but these birds seem really close to these people. Could they be pets?"

"Maybe they are," said Neil. "They could also be simply feeding them in the wild though."

Preeti's attention was more drawn towards the wooden door. She felt her hand over the latch until she managed to get hold of the handle. It was firm but her repeated full-force jerks eventually caused

the door to get unlatched. With a slight push, the door was flung wide open. She stepped out onto the balcony overlooking the wide valley. The lake, surrounded by the green hills, could be seen along with the countless trees dotting the mountain slope. The little light that the balcony received came from the flaming torches inside and the full moon. As she looked around, she noticed a silhouette in the doorway.

She whispered, "Karan. Is that you?"

Once he had stepped out onto the balcony and the faint outline of his face became visible, he replied, "Yes. It is me. What are you doing out here alone?"

"Nothing much. I was just curious and decided to explore. Isn't it weird how we sometimes get exactly what we didn't want? After leading a long-drawn military rescue operation in the Himalayas, I was seeking some peace and stability as a civilian pilot. However, the current situation has flung me into the deepest abyss of instability and unpredictability."

"I can understand. I could not have anticipated what happened today in my wildest dreams too. One would think that the past few months would have prepared me for such bouts of unpredictability. But to be honest, I still feel scared about this situation."

"It is great that you could admit that. Honestly, I feel the same. Theoretically, it makes absolute sense to brave the situation with the utmost fearlessness and determination. But the heart doesn't understand theory. It just flutters nervously when it senses danger at every step."

"No shame in acknowledging our fears. As humans, each of us has their own limitations. We can brave this dire situation collectively by complementing each other's strengths and weaknesses."

Karan held out his hand. Preeti briefly looked at his extended hand and then proceeded to hold it. They clutched each other's hands tightly as they stood mesmerized by the ironically calm vista in front of them.

Meanwhile, Aman and Samantha left Neil and Tisha, who were closely observing the illustrations on the wall, to climb the stairs and explore the second floor. To their amazement, they discovered a library dimly lit up by moonlight percolating through irregular cracks in the ceiling. They sat on the floor beneath one such crack to closely examine the contents of a book they had randomly pulled out from the shelf.

The cover was built of tattered cloth. The pages were creaky and dotted with brown spots around their edges. The book that they held in their hands seemed to be a picture book with large colourful illustrations of animals occupying most of the space on each page. On one such page, they noticed the image of a diminutive elephant with four tusks standing beside a regular elephant with two tusks. Beneath them, a regular-sized elephant with four tusks was depicted in the centre. This elephant looked eerily similar to the ones that had violently attacked them. Some sentences were written at the bottom of the page in Vidikan.

"Is it possible that the elephant in the centre was a result of interbreeding between the two elephants depicted at the top of the page?" said Samantha.

Before Aman could reply, they heard a sulking sound in the room. They turned their eyes across the room but couldn't see anybody. Aman silently signalled Samantha to step back. They had barely taken a few steps when a loud thud was heard from the next corridor. When they rushed to the site, they saw a pile of fallen books from the lowermost shelf. Behind the books, they saw a short and lanky boy, presumably between ten and fifteen years of age, with green eyes and matted brown hair. He wore a khaki yellow poncho with plain blue shorts. He seemed to be shivering from fear and froze in his tracks. Samantha made her way around the pile to reach the kid and crouched on the floor in front of him. She raised her hand to pat him but he started retreating. Samantha gestured him to stop and reassured him,

"Don't worry. We mean no harm."

But he didn't understand a word.

"His lips seem chapped. I feel that he is thirsty," said Aman as he followed Samantha.

He opened and held out his bottle, freshly filled with lake water, towards the kid. When the boy saw the bottle, his eyes widened and he let out a shrill scream. Aman was taken aback by surprise and lost his balance as he tripped on a fallen book. As he fell on the ground, the bottle escaped his hands, splashing water everywhere without its lid. Around a cupful of water fell on the kid's face, causing him to let out a second scream - much louder and shriller than the last one. His face and body began to shake as if shocked by an electric current. His shaking legs couldn't hold his body any longer and he fell on the floor.

"You have paralyzed the poor kid," said Samantha as her eyes nervously twitched. "He might be allergic to water."

Aman said, "This might be the hydrophobia that we had expected among the Vidikan-era captives. The ones afflicted with rabies due to the war. How does one treat it?"

There was no answer as Samantha and Aman hopelessly watched the kid writhing on the ground. The boy's eyes betrayed mistrust and anger as they met theirs.

Meanwhile, Karan and Preeti heard tumultuous noises as they witnessed several outlines of human figures rushing into the balcony through the doorway. Neil and Tisha's worried silences were contrasted by Benji's deafening barks when they noticed the crowd of people circling around them. One of them held up a kerosene lamp close to his face, allowing them to get a clear view. A brown-feathered kite was perched on his left shoulder. He had wrinkles on his cheeks and wore a silver nose ring. His squinted brown eyes moved up and down to examine them closely. When the lamp in his hand got slightly lowered, the pistol in his hands, which was pointed towards them, became visible.

CHAPTER 18

AN UNWELCOME REVISIT

The medley of shrieks, creaking and pounding noises grew louder with each passing second as Samantha and Aman frantically tried to calm the paralyzed kid on the floor but in vain.

Crying out in alarm, Samantha said, "It seems like an entire group of people is ascending the stairs to come here. What do we do now?"

"We could put our feet on the bookshelves," said Aman while looking up. "And climb onto the roof through these ceiling cracks. That's our only escape."

"It would prick my conscience to leave the poor kid here."

A series of screams were heard.

"That was Tisha's voice!" said Samantha.

"We are of no help to anyone if we are dead. This kid's parents will kill us when they know what we did. Let us get out of here and take a more informed decision on our next steps."

"That makes sense."

Samantha struggled to lift her weight onto the edge of the emptied bookshelf while Aman's agility aided him in hastily executing his planned manoeuvres. Aman peered down through the crack and lowered his hand towards Samantha. She caught his hand and managed to reach the top of the bookshelf with her feet dangling from the edge. As she sat, her eyes fell on the man who entered the library below her. The stimulated fear caused her to stand on her feet immediately and pull her head out through the crack. She held both her hands on the roof and lifted the rest of her body above the ceiling. Samantha and Aman looked down through the crack.

They realized that the commotion created by Samantha's movement had alerted a horde of people, who rushed to the spot immediately below them. The duo impulsively pulled away from the crack. The group seemed to have assembled around the kid since they could hear several mumbling voices beneath them. Samantha and Aman were deliberating whether to take a peek again when they heard Preeti's yell.

"We are going to be locked in the room opposite the library entrance. Help us later."

This was followed by a whistling sound of the kind that one hears from the movement of an ungreased doorknob.

Aman said, "Preeti is signalling us to unlock the door when this group gets away from here. Thankfully, these people don't understand English. Atleast, I hope so."

Within half an hour, the chatting voices died down and the sound of footsteps began retreating. Aman noticed that the kid had been taken away along with the rest of the group. Samantha ran her eyes across every nook and cranny in the library sections but couldn't spot a single soul.

Aman suggested, "I can climb and descend much faster and more discreetly. Let me handle this stealthy operation. Can you wait for me here? Give me a cuckoo call if you see anyone entering the library."

Samantha nodded understandably. Aman gently placed his feet on top of the bookshelf and slowly descended onto the floor. He tiptoed his way through the numerous library sections while keeping an eye around for any danger. As expected, he saw a door, composed of shiny steel, at the end of the library. He slowly unlatched it and slightly opened the door.

He projected his head inside and whispered before anyone could get a chance to speak,

"It is me. Aman. Quietly get out."

One after the other, his peers stepped out into the library while gently placing their feet as they walked. Aman put his fingers to his lips and beckoned them to follow him with his other hand. When they reached the floor section beneath a ceiling crack, Aman stepped on the bookshelf and jumped onto the roof for a demonstration. The others followed his lead and reached the roof after overcoming a few hiccups like Tisha's fear of heights and Neil's imperfect balancing skills. As a collective, they managed to make up for each other's weaknesses. Once everyone had assembled on the roof, the pertinent question was where to go next. Karan looked up at the sky and said,

"The night is about to end. We need to get out of here while the darkness hides us."

The pitch black star-studded sky was turning plain and greyish. While the sun couldn't be seen, it was apparent that it wouldn't be concealed for long. Preeti lay down on her back and crawled towards the roof's edge like a caterpillar. She pulled back her hair and passed one of her eyes to face the open ground outside the house. She heard some talking sounds and then a scream. She whispered,

"I think someone is still inside and noticed that we escaped!"

She peered again and didn't spot anyone roaming in the deserted courtyard. She heard a hiss and looked back to see Karan asking her to come towards them.

"There is nobody in the grounds to the front of the house," informed Preeti.

Karan added, "Neither is anyone on the back and left sides. However, the front and back sides of this house have windows, allowing anyone inside to get a clear view of the outside. We need to slip out through the left side."

"How do we climb down? It is a steep fall and I can't see any steps or supports to help us."

"I might have felt quite dumb for over packing before the trip but my over-the-top cautiousness will come to our rescue now.

I have a rope with inbuilt knots for supporting our feet as we step down. I will tie a knot by passing the rope through two neighbouring cracks. The other open end of the rope can fall freely to hang over the edge and reach the ground."

The others, listening to the conversation, nervously nodded. If the situation wasn't that grave and urgent, they would have been paranoid about this adventurous descent. When the other clear prospect was to be shot by a gun, they knew that they had to take their chances.

Karan led the way by demonstrating how to get down as he carefully balanced each of his feet on adjacent knots on the ropes. He moved his head sideways to check for any signs of the captors before proceeding to move his feet to the next knot below. He landed with a soft thud on the ground after a while and beckoned the others to descend through a hand gesture. Tisha stuffed Benji in her bag and gently whispered something. She was the next one to follow Karan's lead with Samantha, Aman and Preeti trailing behind her.

The last one to descend was Neil. Neil looked at the elevation at which he stood. He freaked out and promised himself not to look again to stay focused. However, his curiosity kept getting the better of him as he repeatedly looked down to check the elevation. He was midway when a wooden board on the wall in front of him gave way to two flung apart window shutters.

He was met in the eye by a burly man who stared at him with raised eyebrows before hoarsely shouting at the top of his voice. Neil hastened his descent while signalling the others to start retreating.

The sounds of stampedes and commotion grew louder at every step. The final acceleration to his descent was given by a woman on the roof, who cut the rope at its base with a saw, causing him to freely fall into Karan's trembling arms. Once Neil had regained his balance, Karan held his hand to lead him into the woods. The duo could see the rest of their group darting away in the distance ahead of them. The broadly spaced tall poplar trees and the dusk made them easy to spot. Noticing that, Neil asked, "Is this the right way for us to be going?"

Karan didn't answer but the sound of a gunshot behind them did. This was followed by stampeding sounds and more whistling gunshots.

"Don't look behind. Just watch ahead and run," yelled Karan.

They sprinted across the open field at top speed and noticed that the voices had died down after a while. Considering the terror that he had to witness due to over checking earlier, Neil couldn't afford to impede his run and turn back. However, Karan did and noticed how the scores of people following them had abruptly frozen in their tracks. Without thinking about a reason, he simply marched ahead. The scenes a mile ahead provided him with the answer itself. There was a wide turbulent river flowing in front of them with the choppy water creating a roaring sound.

"They fear the water," smirked Aman, who had been waiting for them at the bank along with the others.

* * *

The azure blue water gushing through the hill was crystal clear, allowing one to get a fine peek at the unique creatures inhabiting its waters. Vibrant pink dolphins could be seen from the shore even when they swam close to the swaying weeds in the deep riverbed. They occasionally leapt above the surface of water to catch unsuspecting fluttering birds between their needle-thin beaks, neatly slicing them in half like a fine saw. It was gruesome to watch for Aman and he began to avoid glancing sideways. Neil and Tisha were on the contrary, observing these phenomena with a childlike fascination but talking with complex adult-style jargon. Keen to follow the conversation due to her general thirst for knowledge, Samantha listened intently but could only understand the following part of the conversation.

Tisha said, "Doesn't the dolphin's vibrant pink colour lead to a competitive disadvantage while preying on these birds? It seems counterintuitive to the whole idea of camouflage."

"Maybe not," said Neil. "Some birds are known to be colour-blind to certain colours. The birds they prey on might not be able to see the pink colour, effectively camouflaging them."

The group trudged along the river banks with the comforting assurances of regular water supply and safety from gun-wielding locals. The hunger and lack of sleep soon caught up with them though. Neil rested his back against the trunk of a towering willow tree with leaves neatly arranged like drooping umbrellas. When Tisha saw the fatigue on everyone's faces, she suggested,

"I can't sleep in the day even if I have skipped an entire night of sleep. However, you all can take a nap in the shade here. Meanwhile, I can look around for a source of food."

Samantha remarked, "Good idea. Civilizations have flourished on fertile river banks for centuries. There must be a fruit tree somewhere around here to replenish our food stocks."

The others nodded and watched Tisha and Benji walk away with half-closed eyes. Tisha and Benji had barely walked a few steps when they realized that they had reached the edge of a cliff. The raging water fell off from the cliff into the valley below in the form of a steep waterfall. Benji kept barking up at the enticing bunches of plums hanging from the tree but Tisha's attention was too focused elsewhere to notice. She was crouched on the soil and looking down at the valley.

The valley consisted of grassy domes spread across a verdant meadow. She also noticed tiny moving white dots spread across the greenery and along the banks of the calmed downstream river. She couldn't confirm if they represented zebras or goats. However, she could confirm that the meadow was the same one that they had seen through the mirror in the lighthouse.

* * *

After a hearty meal of plums, thanks to Benji's dedicated attention-seeking efforts, everyone reached the meadow. It was decided that they would try to send a signal to someone stationed in the lighthouse through the mirror. Samantha managed to find a series of stone-carved staircases with steel railings descending into the meadow. Every staircase connected two subsequent roads cutting across the cliff at regular altitudinal levels. The air was sprinkled with the freshness and chilliness of dew drops, owing to the water rapidly gushing down besides them. The stress lines on everybody's foreheads vanished when what started out as a nervous downward hike became a merry promenade. They looked with mesmerization at the milky churning water, smoothening the rocks as it descended into the valley. When Neil saw a kite fly closely over their head, he remarked, "Could that be a spy bird which will give away our presence to the locals?"

Tisha was feeling optimistic though, thanks to the tasty plums or the natural beauty or perhaps both. She said, "They couldn't have tamed and trained every kite residing on this island. That would be a mammoth feat for anyone to achieve."

"In any case, we have no option," said Samantha. "We are stuck in the middle. We can't make a giant leap to the top or jump off into the valley. Let us continue our journey in the same direction but increase our pace."

Once about three-quarters of the distance to the bottom had been covered, they saw a Pomeranian dog hopping around on the rocks. It had impeccably clean white fur. It wagged its pink tongue and rushed towards Benji when it saw them. As soon as the dog came close, Benji started aggressively barking at it. The dog barked back at Benji in a softer tone. Benji's next bark was a milder one and he playfully shook his head sideways while wagging his tongue. The barks mellowed down to murmurs and it almost seemed as if they were long-lost reunited friends catching up.

"What could they be talking about?" said Tisha as she stared at the exchange with a puzzled expression.

"Are you sure they have a language to actually converse in?" said Preeti.

"Benji is an exceptionally intelligent dog," replied Tisha with a proud smile. "I wouldn't be surprised if he understood our language and started talking to me someday."

The supposed conversation ended when the Pomeranian dog retreated and disappeared into a rock cave. The group resumed their walk oblivious to the appearance of a human shadow at the cave entrance.

* * *

The white dots that Tisha had spotted from above turned out to be a herd of sheep grazing all over the meadows. What Tisha hadn't spotted from above were the numerous tiny jasmine flowers sprinkled between the grass, which lent a sweet fragrance to the air. The raging river water had calmed down into a wide pool at the foot of the waterfall. When Aman bent over to refill his almost empty bottle, he witnessed, to his horror, a wire-thin yellow snake slithering on the surface of the water. Overcame by paranoia, he shrieked and rushed away at top speed.

"It is only a snake. Many snakes are not even venomous," said Neil on observing Aman's sweat-drenched face.

"I have an extreme phobia of snakes," explained a visibly embarrassed Aman.

Meanwhile, Samantha and Karan waded through the herd of puffy sheep with overgrown and thick woollen coats. Weighed down by those heavy coats, the sheep struggled to continuously walk for even short distances without regularly stopping to rest their feet by collapsing on the ground.

"Why don't the locals shear these poor sheep? The wool could be used to weave clothes and carpets. The sheep would also be able to heave a sigh of relief," said Karan as he patiently waited for the sheep in front of him to make way.

"I wonder how these sheep even survive. Their lack of mobility makes them such easy prey for predators," said Samantha.

Tisha and Preeti climbed up one of the grassy domes and swerved their heads in all directions to look for any signs of the mirror. They couldn't see anything except grazing sheep in all directions. Spotting a solitary lamb at the foot of the dome, Benji sprang into action by pacing down along the slope and leaping towards the oblivious lamb.

Taken by surprise, the lamb bleated loudly when it felt the sharp claws on its back. It tried to escape but bogged down by its fragile feet and heavy coat, it fell on the grass with a thud. The loud and repeated bleats attracted the attention of Tisha and Preeti, who watched Benji's hunting escapade with horror as he dug his teeth into the helpless sheep, crying for help. However, the object of their sympathies changed by the time they rushed down from the peak. The formerly terrified lamb had got back on its feet. Meanwhile, Benji lay unconscious on the ground.

"How did this happen?" screamed Tisha.

***

Aman stood a few feet away from the pool to look out for the dreaded swimming snakes. He warned Neil a few times when he saw one but Neil didn't seem to care. He continued to walk along the riverbank in search of the mirror. Realizing that he wasn't being of much help, Aman decided to climb the oak tree with its abnormally broad leaves and aid his companion in his search. He had barely gauged the tree trunk for low-hanging branches when his eyes fell on a glinting surface underneath a rotting yellow leaf on the ground. When he removed the leaf, he observed a half-buried tilted rectangular box. Much to his relief, the box housed a slanting mirror inside it. He tried to peer inside but the surface was dirty from the settled dust, rendering the reflection invisible. He shouted out to Neil.

Ecstatic at the discovery, Aman and Neil vigorously scrubbed the mirror surface with fallen leaves until the last peck of dust had been removed. Their determined efforts still didn't pay off when the spot-clean mirror refused to offer them a reflection of anything beyond dark surroundings.

"Maybe the mirror has been shut behind the lighthouse walls again," sighed Aman.

"The lighthouse could also be closed to the general public. What do we do now?" said Neil.

"The police on the mainland must be worried about our disappearance and will inevitably inspect the lighthouse mirrors for any clues. Let us leave a message for them."

"How can we do that?"

Aman pulled out a paper and a pen from his bag and smiled.

"Aren't you resourceful?" said Neil, beaming with excitement.

After a long discussion on the optimum size and content of the message, both eventually settled for -

"THE ISLAND IS SURROUNDED BY MIRRORS. CROSS THEM AND RESCUE US - KARAN"

If they wrote too many sentences, the text would appear very small and might not be clearly visible to the viewers on the other side. But they also didn't want to miss crucial details which could aid them in the rescue operation. They had initially planned on writing everyone's name but later felt that it would take up too much unnecessary space. As the person most well-known within the investigative circuit, Karan's name seemed the most logical choice to put up. The moist riverine soil acted as a glue between the folded part and the mirror's back. Neil sat back with smug satisfaction when he finally managed to strap the paper message onto the mirror by folding its edges around the mirror. They smiled at each other with a renewed hope.

Unfortunately, the cheerful optimism was short lived. It was only when the task had been accomplished that a dreadful memory associated with the mirror came back to haunt Aman. He remembered what they had seen through this mirror from the lighthouse. The recall almost appeared to be a premonition when Aman witnessed the scene that ensued in the following minutes.

It started with a violent storm of dust that blew in their faces. When the dust began to settle down, a giant Pelagornis Sandersi bird could be seen flapping its long wings and hovering above the meadow. A jarring shrill sound filled the air when it opened its orange beak to reveal the sharp teeth in it. The stampeding sound of panic-stricken sheep running around in all directions further added to the noise. The wind sent a rock hurling towards Aman. Neil brushed Aman just in time to avoid an injurious hit. The rock instead went past where they stood and collided with the mirror, smashing it into pieces. Aman felt his soul leaving his body upon witnessing cold water being poured on their hopes. Alas, there was no time to nurse their wounded minds. Frantically searching for any refuge, Neil and Aman stumbled upon a hollow wooden trunk. They bent and crept inside to hide.

Tisha fled away from the centre of the meadow with Benji in her arms as Preeti led the way for the duo through the scampering closely packed herd. Karan and Samantha tried to leap over the sheep which had blocked the sloping path around them. Growing restless due to the terrifying bird flying in circles around the peak on which they stood, Samantha crouched on the ground and rushed through the gap between the numerous sheep feet. Karan didn't seem to have noticed her manoeuvre because he started looking in all directions to search for her.

Aman and Neil began to frantically wave their hands to beckon him to run towards them. Samantha disappeared amidst the herd and was nowhere to be seen. Karan looked at Aman and Neil's gestures and contemplated his next move. The bird vigorously flapped its wings again, sending up another huge cloud of dust into the air. Its faint outline could be seen swooping down towards the meadow through the dusty wind.

Aman and Neil covered their mouths and noses. After a long bout of hysteric sneezing, Neil looked up at the clear view as the dust mostly settled. The bird could be seen ascending towards the sky as Samantha's wide silken scarf slowly drifted downwards through the breeze. Neil's eyes widened when he saw Samantha's face between one of the bird's curled up yellow claws. Her lack of motion indicated her unconsciousness. Karan's shriek reverberated throughout the meadow when he witnessed the same view. But the bird had disappeared into the clouds and flown far away.

Aman tried to run towards it but a cold hand grabbed his shirt collar to stop him. He turned back to see an old man smirking at him with his flashy white but broken teeth. A young woman held a gun to Neil's head and capped his mouth with her hands as he froze and trembled. Two middle-aged men rushed forward to grab each of Aman's hands. The old man moved towards Neil and looked him in the eye. Neil's red eyes betrayed his fear of facing his former captor again.

CHAPTER 19

THE ORATOR WHO OUTSHONE ALL

The horse cart wobbled as it moved on the rocky path. The two brawny horses pulling it neighed and stopped abruptly, sending a sharp jolt to the cage on the buggy. Neil fell with a thud while the others managed to hold onto the cage railings for support. Neil writhed around on the cage floor as his stiffly tied feet and legs made it difficult for him to regain his balance. His companions looked on helplessly while letting out muffled sounds through the piece of cloth strapped to their mouths. The woman riding the chariot jumped off and stealthily walked forward to investigate the horse's unexpected halt. A wildcat leapt out from the bushes on the edge of the unpaved road, looked around with its pale green eyes and disappeared into the bushes.

A bald man with a stark bushy moustache, who was walking beside the cage, turned his eyes towards the hostages. He said something to another man a few feet away, which was incomprehensible to everyone inside the cage. The other man carried Benji, who was unconscious but occasionally quivering, in his hairy arms. Aman tried to reach out for the mobile in his jeans pocket so that he could communicate using the Vidikan-translation application. However, his tied hands didn't budge much beyond a point, making it impossible for him to carry out the operation. The cage door was flung open and the bald man entered the cage. A brown rifle hung from his shoulders. He bent towards Neil. As he did so, the gun slipped from his shoulder and fell on Neil, who shrieked so loudly that it could be heard even through the cloth.

The shriek caused a ruckus among the Vidikan captors, who huddled around the cage to see what had happened. The bald man hushed them away and picked up his gun. He proceeded to hold out his hand and lend support to Neil. Neil hesitated initially but seeing the man's innocuous expression, he clutched his hand, allowing himself to be pulled up. When the woman saw Neil standing up again, she went back to the front seat of the cart and patted the horse. She beckoned the bald man to get out with a hand gesture. He nodded and obeyed, allowing the journey to resume with the tip-tapping noises created by the horse's hooves.

As he peeped out, Aman noticed the ready-to-be-harvested wheat crops swaying in the wind. Their height was around twice that of the regular wheat he had seen in the villages around Vidika. The grains were closer in size to that of grapes than regular wheat. The vast open fields stretched out in all directions as far as his eyes could see. Occasionally, people working in the fields would leave their work and start staring at the procession. Most of them wore plain and tattered clothes, consisting of a single robe draped over them. Irrigation canals flooded water in maze-like patterns through the fields. It would have been a serene view to get lost in if they hadn't been kidnapped and weren't awaiting the uncertain outcome at the end of the journey.

They were passing through a deserted patch of land when a boy darted across the field towards the procession. He was followed by a scampering white Pomeranian dog. Both approached the man holding Benji. Tisha tried to get a clear view but the sunset made it difficult to discern the boy's face. There was only a faint dark outline in the backdrop of the fields. The boy seemed to be whispering to the man.

Tisha pressed her face to the railing with her face flushed red from worry.

The man placed Benji on the ground and the boy crouched over the unconscious dog. The Pomeranian dog pranced in circles around Benji as the boy pressed Benji's belly and proceeded to open its mouth, baring its sharp white canines. Uncertain and fearful, Tisha began to bang her fists on the cage railings only to invite nothing more than a brief stare from the cart-rider. She watched with horror as the boy pulled out a glass tube and orally administered something to Benji. Benji lay still for a few minutes. Then, he mildly sneezed and followed it with stronger intermittent sneezes. His body shook violently but soon, he was back on his feet. The Pomeranian barked at him and Benji barked in return. The to-and-fro exchange of barks took place for a while until the Pomeranian dog rushed away to bark at a blue-eyed woman, who had just arrived on the scene. She nodded and then whispered something into the boy's ears.

The dark outline of the boy and the woman appeared on the cage door. A rattling of keys was heard when the woman pulled out a bunch from her pocket. She unlatched the door, allowing herself and the boy to step inside. When the woman lit the lamp in her hand, the erstwhile hazy view of the unknown boy's face gave way to a clear and recognizable one.

Rick gleefully smiled at them with remarkably white teeth for someone who had survived in the wilderness for months. He wore a loose green kurta, the sleeves of which drooped over his lanky arms. The lamplight shone up the smooth surface of his bald head. Tisha tried to speak to him but her words were muffled by the tightly strapped cloth. Rick hastened to untie Tisha's hands and legs when he heard her, prompting the woman to untie the others.

While he was engaged in removing the ropes, he said,

"I apologize for this inhumane and unjustified punishment that was meted out to you. I was informed a few days earlier that someone from the mainland had been captured. Since none of the locals can speak English or Hindi, they wanted me to come to the hill observatory and speak to you. They didn't mean any harm but had no effective means to communicate that to you. However, by the time I arrived, you all had already escaped."

Aman replied, "We had no choice. The locals were wielding guns. We didn't want to get shot."

"I understand. They meant no harm though. They just didn't want you to escape. As you might know, they haven't had a visitor in centuries and they need your help."

"How did you find us when we escaped?"

"When you all were descending from the path along the waterfall, our dog, Sheru, met Benji and had a brief conversation with him. Benji assured Sheru that you all meant no harm. I was resting in an abandoned bear cave to escape the sharp eyes of lurking predators when Sheru came darting towards me. He waved his head as if to signal me to follow him. When I followed him, I saw no animal or human and presumed that I had misunderstood until we met Benji here again. The lady's name is Alia. She is an exceptional veterinarian and had immediately diagnosed Benji when she saw his unconscious state. She had sent me a message to bring along the medicine for the sheep poison from the city. Sheru told her what Benji had conveyed to him near the waterfall."

Rick's constant effort to untie the tight knot of the strapped cloth on Tisha's face wasn't yielding any effort but it didn't take more than a minute for experienced Alia to free everyone else.

As soon as Karan got freed, he ran towards Rick and hugged him tightly in a warm embrace.

"Benji told us that you all had come here to find me," said Rick. "It's good to see you, Uncle Karan."

"I don't understand. How do you know Benji's name?" said Tisha with a puzzled frown.

"It is written on his dog collar," said Rick with a bemused smile.

"How did he know that we were searching for you?"

"Did you give him any indication regarding it?"

Tisha stood silent for a few moments as she pondered. Then, she said, "Your mother had shown him your photograph so that he could help us in searching for you. Maybe he got the hint. I am still confused how your dog, Sheru, conveyed to Alia whatever Benji told him."

"Sheru belongs to a novel hyper intelligent species of dogs, which was genetically engineered by Vidikan scientists in the 17th century. They have a way of communicating basic stuff to humans with their paw movements. You mentioned Mom. Where is she?"

Sensing that the news might be disturbing for a young kid, Tisha said, "Can we talk to your father? He is with you, right?"

* * *

Samantha's eyes fluttered to reveal a hazy view of the blue sky. The dusty hay on which she lay caused her to sneeze violently and completely open her eyes. She tilted her head leftwards to see extraordinarily long strands of hay irregularly sprouting up from all over the floor.

Towering muddy walls encircled her to form a deep well-like structure. She recollected the moments before she had fallen unconscious. Her memory served a haunting realization - she could be in a nest full of hungry bird chicks, ready to devour her the moment they lay their eyes on her. She stood up on her feet and looked around with wide eyes. There was no sign of any feathery being darting

towards her for its next delicacy. She sighed and looked up. The sunlight was streaming through but the wall seemed too high for her to climb and get out.

Her contemplation was disturbed by a rustle among the straws to her right. She swerved her head and noticed a blackish spot moving amidst the bushy mound. The upward-projecting straws around it were swaying. Samantha plucked a prickly strand of hay and began to brandish it like a sword. The walls made escape impossible, leaving a fight as her last option. Samantha positioned the strand in front of her, ready to stab the creature as soon as it leapt out from the bushes. A familiar voice stopped her.

"Samantha, how did you end up here?"

The beard, which had grown much denser, covered the entire bottom half of his face. The hands and legs were filthy and dust laden. The white colour of the teeth had been overridden by a dark yellow tinge. The black T-shirt that used to fit perfectly seemed loose for his thin body now. Even through those filters, Samantha could recognize John's idiosyncratic round face and fearful brown eyes.

* * *

Rick said, "Dad was kidnapped a week ago by a giant bird which inhabits this island. Earlier, those birds mostly restricted themselves to their habitat in the 'forbidden forest'.

Even when they occasionally flew to other regions of this island, they hunted for only riverine fishes. They have turned violent against us only in the past few months. That's why we have abandoned the lake and the hilltop research facility. The birds frequently patrol that area, making it dangerous to live there. I had gone with him to fetch the leaves of a specific tree, which only grows around the lake and whose leaves are crushed to develop a vital medicine.

We tried to be vigilant but the bird was too swift for him. I got my hands on the crucially needed leaves but Dad was gone by the time I made it to the tree house in the dense forest. We had planned to meet a giraffe-rider near it, who would have safely taken us both to the city. The giraffe can tower above the canopy to look out for the dangerous bird while keeping us concealed beneath the canopy."

"What a coincidence," said Karan. "We were on the top floor at the time. We heard your steps. Your Mom even recognized your hanky on the second-topmost floor of the tree house."

"A giraffe is quite tall so you have to climb up to that floor to get on its back," said Rick.

He paused and then exclaimed, "Wait. You haven't told me yet. Where is Mom?"

Karan hesitated and looked at Preeti. Seeing her nod, he told Rick, "The bird abducted her today. We don't even know where it took her. Maybe the forbidden forest you mentioned? Can't we go there to rescue your parents?"

Rick sank his face into his hands and began to sob. Preeti and Karan bent towards him to pat his head.

Preeti empathised and said, "I wouldn't give you the impractical advice to not feel sad. The heart cannot wipe away all emotions completely even when that might be the best course of action. Instead, I would advise you to direct your energy towards finding a solution instead of repenting."

Karan added, "Don't give up hope. We have a big team of brilliant people from diverse backgrounds. We have come a long way by collaborating with each other and leveraging each other's strengths. There's no reason we can't succeed again."

Rick listened intently and then responded, "The might of those birds can't be overcome by a handful of people. We need to send an entire army and a well-planned strategy to stand a chance against them. That's why we are heading to Mosika to meet the Ranija."

Tisha overheard their conversation and walked towards them. She said, "I and Aman have been trying to talk to these people but in vain. Aman's translator application has also stopped working for some reason he can't understand. We keep hearing these words in their conversations too - 'Ranija' and 'Mosika'. What do they mean?"

Rick said, "You know the Hindi words 'Raja' meaning King and 'Rani' meaning Queen. The Vidikan words for King and Queen are also the same. The word Ranija has been formed by fusing the two words to develop a gender-neutral title for the ruler. It is similar to how we use chairperson instead of chairman now. Their political system has evolved on similar lines as we have seen in most countries across the globe. The Ranija is elected to power by the people every year."

Preeti said, "These developments sound amazing. Is Mosika the city where the Vidikans on this island live?"

Rick replied, "Mosika is the city where most of the population is concentrated. However, there are small settlements spread across all parts of the island except for the forbidden forest. That's home to the giant birds."

Karan said, "I was thinking. Is there any specific reason for the bird's recent hostility towards humans?"

Rick said, "We understand the reason very well. The locals kidnapped one of their eggs last year and raised one of the hatched chickens. They trained it with the impeccable techniques that they have learnt and mastered over centuries. The earlier bejewelled birds, trained to travel to the mainland, failed to elicit any response from people from the mainland. So, they thought that training one of these gigantic birds to send a message was their only shot. While they were able to raise the bird in secrecy and send it away, the birds found out about it anyway…"

Aman asked, "How did they even find out?"

Rick elaborated, "One day, a man was resting by the lakeside and feeling bothered due to the summer heat. He started fanning himself with a giant feather that had been plucked from the captive bird's wings. Coincidentally, one of the adult birds flying over the lake at that time spotted him. It must have raised suspicion that the egg was stolen by the people. The bird swooped down from the sky and chased the man until he fled towards the lake and drowned in it. The man was rescued in an unconscious state later but the birds began to venture out more frequently, especially around the lake. They have been growing increasingly violent since then."

* * *

Formidable high walls, laden with pale yellow sandstone bricks, fortified the city. After traversing for miles through the vast stretches of fields, the cavalcade halted in front of the wooden gate. The woman riding the horse-cart offered to dismantle the cage walls to give them a more dignified entry. However, Neil's insistence that the cage roof protected them from the sunshine caused her to take back that offer. A golden bell hung from one of the numerous prickly metal spikes on the gate. The man leading the procession got off from his white horse and rang the golden bell. The bell gong's heaviness could be gauged from the time and strenuous efforts it took to be shifted from the centre to the edge. The shrill tinkling sound of the bell was followed by a loud and hoarse voice from beyond the gate. The man who had rung the bell responded with a phrase that they didn't understand.

The door creaked as it was slowly opened from within to reveal a battalion of soldiers in velvet tuxedos with sword cases strapped to their pants. There was a hushed conversation between the man and the soldiers, following which the man gestured to the horse-rider to move the cart towards the gate. The horse rushed forward briefly to stop near one of the soldiers. The soldier got inside the cage and declared, "Vzero vachika Ranija. Mosika pala safra."

Rick held his hand close to his ear and nodded sideways. This was meant as a gesture for the soldier to repeat slowly so that he could understand it. It worked. The soldier repeated,

"Vzero…Vachika…Ranija…"

He paused midway when three words were shouted back at him in a foreign language.

"Ranija seeks you."

Everyone's eyes turned to notice that the voice emanated from Aman's phone. He beamed with satisfaction and said,

"The translator is finally working. It wasn't able to decipher the words earlier due to the fast pace at which they were speaking."

The translator repeated Aman's sentences in Vidikan, "Motera hum wo. Kalas ba rant boke entu hush hush vani."

The soldier didn't understand the context and looked at them with a perplexed expression. Rick stood up and walked towards the soldier.

He looked at Aman and said, "Let me talk to him. I understand Vidikan to a great extent by now. I will convey his message to everyone here. The translator will lead to a lot of back and forth."

Aman nodded, allowing them to have a brief conversation. The exchange seemed to be a playful one as evident from the occasional laughs interspersed between their words. Rick looked back and declared, "The Ranija wants to see you in the palace and discuss your intentions and opportunities for mutual cooperation. She doesn't want to create a flutter among the public until the details are sorted out. That's why she wants you to arrive at the palace in concealed palanquins so that nobody notices you. Your language and clothing style will easily give you away and arouse suspicion. The palanquins are generally a part of Vidikan marriage processions. So, we will be mimicking a marriage procession. The soldiers are dressed in these fancy tuxedos to appear like wedding guests and will be accompanying the procession by dancing around the palanquins."

"You better dance well," said Aman with a wink.

"Hu nash tame aper," proclaimed the translator.

The soldier stood mute for a while and then broke into a peal of laughter. The others joined too and the procession reverberated with roaring laughter.

* * *

The melody of blowing trumpets and beating drums filled the air, practically curbing all other sounds that they could have potentially heard. Occasionally, the celebratory music mellowed down, enabling those inside the curtained and flower-studded palanquins to hear the playful yells of children, chatters of adults, footsteps, hammering thuds and dog barks. There was only a thin piece of cloth barring them from indulging their curiosity by taking a quick peep of the city view. The repeated instructions from Rick restrained them from doing so. Tisha sat with Benji on her lap, facing Rick on the opposite seat in one of the three palanquins. Noticing the silence, Tisha said,

"Rick, since you have been here for a while, I wanted to verify some of our discoveries with you."

"Of course. Go ahead."

"While investigating the interiors of the Vidikan palace, we came across evidence suggesting that Queen Loma supported research on enhancing the capabilities of animals for military warfare. There was also quite concrete evidence suggesting the deployment of rabid dogs and stampeding elephants during the battle of Vidika. We also learnt about the incident involving Queen Loma's rescue as a child by her pet dog, which piqued her interest in animal warfare.

Apparently, she had developed a research laboratory inside her palace and leveraged the isolation of this island for further secretive research. Is this true?"

"I am impressed by all this that you have been able to uncover. It is true and we will probably discuss this in more detail inside the palace. You missed a few points though. Queen Loma pioneered this research not only to strengthen her armies but also to improve the lives of her citizens in several aspects."

"In what ways?"

"She sought to utilize this research in the domains of agriculture, textile weaving and irrigation. She chose this island not only for its isolation but also its biodiversity. When Vidikan seafarers came across this pristine island, they noticed how various unique species thrived on this island in the absence of humankind. Many of the discovered species had gone extinct on the mainland and some were altogether new. The scientists interbred the island species with the mainland ones to select for desired attributes. For example, the mainland hornbill's diet comprises of figs. Intruding hornbills continue to ravage the crops of fig-growing farmers till this day, leading to immense losses for them. The scientists noticed that the diet of the island hornbills consisted of specific mushrooms, which were otherwise poisonous to humans. She realized that these traits of the island hornbills would not only save farmer's losses but also prevent the deaths of children who accidentally ate wild mushrooms every year. Her research team started capturing female hornbills from the mainland to transport them to the island so that they could mate with the male island hornbills. After raising a significant number of interbred hornbill adults, she planned to repopulate Vidika with adult hornbills belonging to this new species. However, there was one problem among the male-female dynamics that Vidikan scientists failed to study closely and foresee."

"That the male island hornbills didn't feed the female mainland hornbills during the incubation period. Right?"

"How do you know this?"

"A bejewelled male hornbill that landed in our city ignored the calls for food by the female hornbill from the Western Ghats that we had introduced into its enclosure."

"This was expected. Since the male island hornbills weren't used to feeding the female mainland hornbills, the female mainland hornbills couldn't survive on this island. The hybridization experiment failed. Not to say that there weren't any successes though."

A soldier parted the palanquin curtain and peeped inside. The procession sounds stopped. He said something to Rick and the palanquin was placed on the ground. Rick translated,

"We have reached the foot of the hillock on which the palace is situated. We have to get out and walk over the ascending sloped paths to reach the palace gates."

Both of them stepped out to notice that the others were already out of their palanquins. There were fortress walls spiralling around the grassy hill slope. Soldiers wearing steely armour walked on the paths beyond those walls with spears taller than themselves. The palace atop the hill consisted of a multi storeyed black marble structure with four turrets hoisting a red flag on each of its corners.

A wooden drawbridge stood over a deep moat separating the land where they stood from the sloping path entrance. The moat seemed empty and devoid of any water. Had Tisha not already known about the local's hydrophobia, she would have been surprised.

As she looked up, eagles hovered in circles around the hillock, some of which occasionally flew down to perch on the arms of patrolling soldiers. A four tusked elephant with a mahout could be seen ascending the sloped path. On the other side of the drawbridge, she noticed a middle-aged woman talking to the soldiers. She held a leash tied to a diminutive brown bear with one hand and held a cage of green bee-eaters in the other hand.

Noticing Tisha's confusion, Rick said, "The tiny bear is a result of repeated breeding across generations among a selectively captured cohort of small brown bears in the forests. The trained bear attacks the overgrown dangerous hives on the fortress walls and the bee-eater birds swallow the fleeing bees."

One of the soldiers shouted at the group from the other side of the drawbridge. The colourfully dressed soldiers led the way by crossing the bridge first. The others followed in their footsteps.

"Tread carefully and ignore what you see in the moat," announced Rick. "The elevation is enough to keep you safe."

The wood creaked as they cautiously placed each of their feet onto the drawbridge. As she looked down, Tisha noticed a bulky lion with a thin mane and a pale orange body with fading light brown stripes. There were more ligers resting on the ground below the other side of the drawbridge. One of them raised its head up, causing its yellow eyes to glisten as it met her in the eye. It opened its mouth wide to let out a deafening roar.

CHAPTER 20

GUESTS OF A LIFETIME

It would be unfair to say that months of separation and anxiety for each other's safety didn't trigger any affectionate emotions at all. There were a few sniffles from restrained tears, a brief hug and even statements of mutual reassurance. But it took barely a few hours for the positive feelings to evaporate and the idiosyncratic quarrels, which had provided the fuel for their impending divorce, to return.

"It was outrageously dumb and irresponsible to steer the airplane towards this dangerous island and endanger not only your life but also our son's," shouted Samantha.

"May I remind you that both of us are safe till this date. Even though the hijackers had been eventually overpowered, they had still managed to kill the pilot. Someone had to keep flying the airplane to avoid crashing into the ocean and killing everyone on board. Considering that the passengers were regular civilians like you and me, I had to hover the airplane close to the sea for a long time because everyone took time to overcome their nerves and jump off the airplane with parachutes. Can I even blame them when I noticed that my own son was the last and only remaining person on the edge?"

"How could you ask the poor kid to jump off an airplane? He is scared to even go on the roller coasters at amusement parks."

"Skipping a park ride isn't a matter of life and death. Our situation at that time unfortunately was. The safety jacket would have kept him afloat until the arrival of a rescue plane."

"Anyway, why didn't you fly back to Mumbai?"

"I might have been a pilot but my last flight was a decade back.

I only had a cursory understanding of the controls present in that novel airplane model. I knew how to land it but the knowledge of that is useless when you can't ascertain the direction to move in. I could have flown for miles across the open stretch of ocean, exhausted the fuel and drowned with everyone else in the water. That didn't seem like a wise choice to me. So, I kept flying it slowly at a low altitude until everyone had a chance to get off."

"So, how did you end up here?"

"When I noticed the trembling body of Rick, I didn't have the heart to ask him to dive into the waters. Since I had spent several hours staying in the same area to allow everyone to get off, the fuel had been mostly spent. I proceeded to take the risk of flying the airplane in a single direction while hoping to come across a piece of land for us to land on before the fuel ran out."

"And you landed here. Now that I understand the complete context of your circumstances, I feel that you might have taken the right action. Rick might not be the bravest boy but he is definitely among the most brilliant. How is he doing?"

John smiled and said, "You know that he gets it from his mother."

*　*　*

As the only person, fluent in both Vidikan and English, Rick stood in front of the podium, which was placed at the centre of the royal court. The translator application in Aman's mobile could have been utilized if the inspecting guards hadn't suspiciously seized their mobiles despite multiple reassurances that they weren't weapons. The royal court's seating arrangement resembled that of a multi-tiered indoor stadium.

Dozens of men and women occupied their places in the seats encircling the vacant area where the podium stood. One of those seats stood out from the rest. It wasn't just slightly elevated but also had two outward-facing golden peacock heads with pink ruby eyes carved onto the armrests. Rick whispered to the others to inform them that it was the Ranija's throne.

The Ranija was a tall woman, who looked resplendent in a golden zari-bordered blue sari paired with a contrasting green blouse. She wore a red bindi on her forehead and a slender golden tiara on her head. She bore a stern look as she looked down at the foreigners that had arrived at her court. Sensing that something was amiss, Aman put his hand on his chest and bowed down in front of her. Her face instantly broke into a wide smile and she followed it with a rapturous laugh. She said something which Rick conveniently translated for the others,

"Nobody bows to me. We are all equal on the island of Mos.

I simply oversee broad administrative decisions since the people of this island have entrusted their faith in my ability to do so."

She continued, "Welcome to Mos! I have been told that you finally received the messages that we had been trying to communicate through the bejewelled birds for several months."

Aman asked and Rick translated, "Thank you. We are still not clear about one aspect though. If the people of this island can build such a magnificent city, then why can they not build a massive ship to cross the seas and reach the mainland?"

"The island is surrounded by wide regions, full of hot steaming geysers, on all sides. The high temperature makes it impossible for us to pass through or construct anything near the mirror wall. We tried to build a staircase over the wall but failed. How did you manage to get past those hot geysers?"

Rick translated for Aman, "We flew over them."

"Did you ride a bird?"

Tisha tried her best to suppress her giggle but the Ranija noticed how she had cupped her mouth.

She clarified, "We actually tried that. We had raised and trained the Mos bird not only to fly over the seas and send a message. We also wanted to check if it was possible for someone among us to ride it safely and successfully reach the mainland. Considering that neither Toshi nor the bird returned, we feared the worst. Did you meet him? He is a slim young boy."

* * *

"My grandson's name is Aman Gill. Can you please let me know the room where I can meet him?" asked Maya as her forehead curled with apprehension.

The receptionist nodded and clicked a few keys in front of the computer. She looked up and replied, "Sorry, Madam. Nobody by that name is currently admitted here."

Maya sighed. She was about to pull out her mobile phone from her tote bag when a policeman in khaki uniform entered to intervene. He showed his police certification and whispered to the receptionist. She nodded, looked down at her computer again and whispered back. The policeman faced Maya and said,

"Ms. Maya, please come with me. I will take you to the room. We haven't given Aman's name yet since we haven't been able to verify the person's identity. That's why she didn't recognize the name."

Maya followed the policeman into the lift. They were the only occupants in it. When the lift door closed, there was pin drop silence inside it until the policeman heard a sniffle.

245

"I know that this is a painful phase for you but I can assure you that if an airplane had crashed into the sea, we would have most likely retrieved it by now. I don't think the rescued boy is Aman. Also, the fisherman, who found the floating body, would have found the others too if this boy is Aman."

"I understand, Inspector Singh. I hope that your words are true.

I am still confused why this boy keeps muttering the name of Vidika though."

"He could be a resident of Vidika. Maybe he was crying for help to be transported back to Vidika before he fell unconscious."

"I see. How has a colossal airplane vanished in thin air? We should have been able to trace it by now. It has been more than two days."

"I am afraid that I don't know much of the ongoing investigation on the sea. The navy is heavily patrolling the region where we received the last signal from the airplane. I guess all we can do is to be patient and hope for the best."

The door opened and there was a momentary clicking sound to indicate that they had arrived on the fifteenth floor. They stepped out and hastily walked to Room No. 15 on the left. There were two constables guarding the door, who greeted Inspector Singh when he arrived and made way for the two of them to enter. Maya shook as she moved towards the bed on which the lanky boy lay underneath a white bed sheet. Sweat trickled from her forehead when she bent over to look at the boy's face. After a brief inspection, she announced,

"I am sure this is not Aman. He looks similar enough to confound anyone but I know that Aman has a birthmark on his neck. It isn't present on this boy's neck."

She further added as she stood up, "The wounds on this boy's face seem severe. Let us pray for his well-being."

She had barely clasped her hands in prayer when the boy unconsciously started muttering the words she had been hearing about.

"Vidika…Vidika…Vidika."

This was followed by a distinct repetitive mutter.

"Toshi…Toshi…Toshi."

* * *

When the fluffy pink rabbit, which would have come across as adorable if it wasn't almost as tall as them, emerged for the first time at midnight, there was a state of pandemonium in the hay-filled nest. After frantically shaking John to wake him up from his deep sleep, Samantha dragged his half-awake self to the inside of a bushy mound.

"What is it? Why are we hiding here?" whispered John.

Samantha put her finger to her lips and stared at him with wide eyes. Getting the signal, John hushed up for the next few minutes and looked around for any hints. The answer arrived soon before his eyes. The prominent pink hue of the fur, magenta-shaded raised ears and the glistening red eyes were impossible to miss. The tremor on Samantha's face was only matched by the enthusiasm with which John rushed out from the bush towards the rabbit. Samantha chased him but John had embraced the rabbit in a hug by standing on his feet by then.

"What is going on here?" said Samanth with a puzzled frown.

"He is Mona. He keeps coming and disappearing from here. When I saw him for the first time, I was intimidated by him too. Infact, I almost fainted when I saw him briskly scampering towards me only to feel the affectionate and soft touch of his paw over my sweaty forehead moments later."

"We seem to have an exceptionally close bonding here. Would you care to explain how your buddy gets out of here?"

"I wish I knew. I thought Mona could lead me towards an escape route but it is impossible to keep up with him when you follow him.

He effortlessly leaps over high mounds of soil while I struggle to climb and cross onto the other side with my bare hands. Considering that rabbits are experts in digging burrows, I have a strong hunch that Mona has built one, which enables him to arrive and get out of here whenever he pleases. I just don't know where that is."

"We need to find a way today itself. The water in this tiny pool won't last long and the edible hay has numbed my taste buds. We have no clue what the birds intend to do with us in the next few days and I don't plan to stay to find out."

"Since you are so determined and brilliant, why don't you find a solution that could help the both of us?"

"I already have. If it goes wrong, we will die from dehydration today. If we don't try, we will anyway die of dehydration in the coming days. I like those odds."

She scooped up water between her conjoined palms from the tiny pool, tacitly approached the rabbit and poured it on one of his paws. The rabbit instantly noticed and darted away, rejecting John's affectionate snuggle as he helplessly lay on the ground to see him disappear.

John retorted, "You wasted our water and caused him to flee. What have we exactly achieved here?"

Samantha pointed to the trail of muddy paw prints that Mona had left behind.

CHAPTER 21

BLAST FROM THE PAST

A golden statue of a woman, dressed like the Ranija herself, stood beside the throne. While the others dismissed it as a generic statue of a queen, Tisha found the the statue's long eyes, slender body and slightly round nose oddly familiar. She strained her brain to recollect the cause of her nostalgia. After a few minutes, her wandering mind stopped at the memories of the paintings they had seen inside the palace of Vidika. When the realization struck, she blurted out,

"Why do you have Queen Loma's statue installed in your court? Isn't she responsible for your decades of misfortune?"

She waited for Rick to translate her questions and convey them to the Ranija but instead, he snapped back, "You can't be so blunt. This might offend the feelings of these people. You don't have complete context on this situation yet."

"Then tell me the complete context. We need to know all the details to arrive at a solution to get out of here."

"I will let you know after this meeting. Let us not get into anything too controversial at the moment, which might strain our relationship with these people."

The cat had already been let out of the bag by then though. The Ranija had caught the word 'Loma' being mentioned and enquired in

Vidikan, which translated to,

"What are you saying about Queen Loma?"

Rick froze when he heard the enquiry. He weighed every word before actually saying it. He said, "My friend recognized Queen Loma's statue here. She wanted to know more about her."

The Ranija was silent for a moment, looked down and her stern expression gave way to a smile. She pointed towards Benji, who absolutely stood still besides Tisha and said,

"Your friend has one of the last few remaining descendants of the brilliant dogs genetically engineered by Queen Loma's war scientists. I can understand her curiosity."

She continued, "Queen Loma recognized the potential of dogs in military warfare as a child when she was rescued by one from her treacherous uncle. Considering that dogs hadn't been known to recognize threats to human children and even more surprisingly go on to defend them, the princess wanted to get to the bottom of the dog's mysterious abilities. Her father always encouraged her to interact with courtiers and experts from diverse domains from a very young age so that she could instill the self-confidence and knowledge needed to rule Vidika. She especially knew the Minister for Animal Husbandry very closely and so, didn't hesitate to approach him regarding the matter."

Aman chuckled, "I was such a shy kid. I could never."

Ranija smiled and continued, "The Minister was glad to engage with her and connect her to the procurer of pet dogs, who informed them that the dog had been delivered as a puppy to the royal palace within a month of its birth by a hound dog in the royal kennel. She was further told that the puppy hadn't received any specific training or special treatment within a month of its birth. Being the custodian of the dog since that time herself, the princess knew that she hadn't imparted any special training to her pet either. When she explained her predicament to the procurer, he told her that the specific hound breed was known for its intelligence and sharp sight. He explained how these remarkable traits had led to this breed of dogs being specifically raised in kennels across Vidika to perform all sorts of jobs from hunting to watch keeping.

She became content after understanding the context but still felt dejected that her pet wasn't uniquely proficient but rather just another specimen of a special breed. She moved on until…"

A dozen people, dressed in white robes, entered the court chambers, carrying glasses of jaljeera drinks in silver trays. The Ranija nodded and they diverted in different directions to serve the drink to parched courtiers and the speakers across the hall. The group noticed that the silverware cups were adorned with intricate patterns of flowers when a man approached them with the drinks. The thirsty group gulped their entire drinks within a few seconds. Once everyone returned their empty glasses by keeping them on the trays, the Ranija continued,

"She once took her pet to the kettle to socialize with other dogs. During that time, she came across a hunter with a caged wild hound of the same breed. The hunter claimed to have captured it from the forest. The ferocious barks, untypical of tamed dogs, seemed to affirm his claim. Still partially unconvinced, she hypothesized that if her pet's impressive rescue had been nothing more than an inherent trait in the breed, a wild hound and her pet would react the same way in a given situation. She ordered the establishment of two identical well-dressed scarecrows with firmly placed daggers in their hands. Each of these scarecrows was placed in a long rectangular open yard with high fences to prevent the dogs from leaping out. She stood outside the fence besides the scarecrows to be conspicuous enough for anyone inside. In two separate pilot experiments, each of the dogs was released into the yard. One of the dogs darted towards the scarecrow and shred it to pieces while the other one roamed around indifferently. Can any of you guess which of them was Queen Loma's pet and explain the reason for their divergent behaviours?"

As the most experienced biologist in the room, Neil gladly jumped into the discussion. He said as Rick conveniently followed up with a Vidikan translation,

"The one who reacted was definitely Queen Loma's pet. It is no fluke that it reacted the same way twice. Allow me to explain. By virtue of heredity, we inherit genes from our parents. Think of genes as repositories of information about the traits that our parents have. The traits could be of all sorts - the colour of eyes, mathematical proficiency, social inclinations etc. The experiences that the parents go through in their life can influence how strongly the genes pass on certain traits to their children. For example, a parent who loves playing the guitar and practices regularly can transfer a stronger musical ability to their children."

Neil paused as another jaljeera drink was served to him. He gulped it up and continued,

"So, let me circle back to the context of domesticated trained hounds versus wild ones. The puppy that Queen Loma received as a child was born to domesticated parent hounds from the royal kennel. As the procurer mentioned, the puppy's parents were likely trained for hunting or fetching stuff since their childhoods because of their prized breed. So, even though the puppy itself didn't undergo any such training, it partially inherited these traits from its parents. In contrast, no wild hounds or their ancestors were ever given such specialized training. So, these instinctive abilities didn't develop as strongly in the wild hound generations."

It was evident that Dr Neil's explanation was correct and already known to the wide audience of courtiers, owing to the loud and overwhelming applause that he received from them. The Ranija stood up to clap and join the applause before sitting back on her throne.

She said, "You have provided a brilliant explanation indeed. We don't use the exact terms that you mention but the philosophy of Queen Loma's research was on the same principles. After noticing the aberrant behaviour, she ordered a more thorough investigation of the circumstances of her pet dog's birth. This led her to come across the fact that the dog's mother had been deployed by the police to track down suspicious activity across Vidika. The mother had especially received training in detecting shiny knives or daggers in public areas. Vidikan law prohibited civilians from carrying arms in public and the dog aided the police in tracking down such law-breakers with its sharp eyes. The pet dog's father was a watchdog for a residential area, which had been specifically trained to attack robbers in the night and pin them to the ground until its barking alerted the security guards to arrive on the scene. So, as you can infer, Queen Loma's puppy hadn't received any specialized training but indirectly inherited the skills acquired through specialized training from its parents. Anyone can see that it would be impossible to efficiently train a single dog for diverse and multifold operations, each of which requires distinct physical and mental capabilities to be developed. Queen Loma realized the potential of developing a hyper intelligent and powerful dog by repeatedly cross-breeding dogs working in various domains - guard dogs, hunting dogs, vigilante dogs. In this way, all the traits could eventually be passed onto a single novel breed after several generations.

Over the years, she raised a significant number of military dogs belonging to this engineered breed. These powerful dogs would prove to be one of her biggest assets in the battle of Vidika against a numerically superior adversary. While she decisively won that battle, there was an unexpected side effect that had gone unnoticed prior to the battle."

She stopped and said something to Rick. Rick informed his friends that she was offering them lunch if they were hungry and apologizing for not asking earlier. Their stomachs were growling from the long journey and their craving tongues had been hoping against hope for delicious, cooked food since they had arrived on the island. The offer was a tempting one but their piqued curiosity couldn't let them wait to hear the rest of the narrative. After a disgruntled and half-hearted consensus, they agreed to listen to it first. Once the message was conveyed to the Ranija, she continued,

"As you all might know, dogs can harbour a fatal disease, which not only harms them but also whoever they bite. Most of such dogs either die from the disease on their own or are killed by their fearful owners for public safety. However, a minuscule minority of such dogs possess immunity against the disease, which allows them to carry on with life as usual with little to no symptoms. Some of such dogs made their way into Queen Loma's cross-breeding program, causing the newly-developed dog breed to exhibit a heightened immunity against this disease."

Aman whispered 'rabies' to clarify but the other keen listeners had already understood the reference and hushed him up for interrupting.

"This fact was virtually undetected since the dogs didn't display the idiosyncratic aggression typical of this disease.

It came to light only during the battle of Vidika when the furiously biting military dogs unleashed a wave of this disease among the enemy soldiers. Fear of water was a prominent symptom of this disease and the panicking soldiers could neither flee towards the raging sea nor rush towards the battalion of trampling elephants. They perished from the disease, heightened fear, human weapons or elephant tramples. The remaining survivors, including our ancestors, were captured by Queen Loma's soldiers and put in dungeons. While wars led to massive loss of lives every time, Queen Loma felt guilty for paving the way for a disease to sustain itself and wreak havoc in such a gory way.

The survivors also painfully reeled from the effects of the disease and Queen Loma felt that it was her ethical responsibility to cure them. She sent all of them on a ship expedition across the sea to be treated at the secret research facility on this island. She also sent away her entire military contingent of dogs here so that they didn't pose a risk to civilians in Vidika by secretly hosting the carriers of that disease."

Aman remarked, "Turns out that she wasn't as Machiavellian as I had assumed."

"The scientists realized that the species of bats residing on this island were completely free from this disease due to a certain chemical substance in their blood, which generated a highly specific and strong immunity. This chemical substance was noticeably missing in the bats on the mainland, which transmitted the disease to both humans and dogs every year by biting them. The research team was able to isolate this chemical substance successfully. They administered it to a few of the war prisoners infected with the disease on a trial basis."

"And it cured them, right?" asked Karan.

"Not completely. But it prevented them from dying and significantly lessened the severity of their fear of water. Earlier, they had to be serendipitously given water by a care staff while they were sleeping or deliberately rendered unconscious. After this treatment, they were able to sip water from a glass while closing their eyes. Coupling this chemical treatment with a form of mental therapy proved to be even more effective. The mental therapy involved training the people to gradually get over their fear of water through gradual exposure techniques like travelling on short boating trips or seeing water bodies from afar etc. Sadly, the fear of water got passed onto the next generations of descendants too but practicing this dual treatment has made it possible for us to live comfortably with minor symptoms. Babies generally start with a strong fear of water but can overcome it to a great extent by the time they become adolescents through early childhood treatments. You can still see families picnicking on the lake shore while maintaining a safe distance from the copious water. Or atleast used to be able to before the bird attacks. Travelling over vast stretches of water across the sea is much more challenging though. We can't even figure out a way to get past the geysers and the towering walls. The older generations have learned to cope with these limitations and are content with the lifestyle. However, the enthusiastic and curious young generations are keen to explore the world beyond the island and find a more perfect cure for the disease. That's why we sent out messages to the mainland through those bejewelled birds. The last message that we sent through the giant bird finally reached you but it has come at the cost of us not being able to get out of the city much due to attacks from infuriated birds."

She paused to clear up her throat. Her eyes reflected a renewed yet carefully risen hope as she nervously asked,

"Now that you all are here, can you think of a way for us to travel beyond this island? You all must be looking forward to going back to your homes too."

Preeti said, "We understand your concerns and are sorry for the issues that you had to face. We will be more than happy to help you get out of here but the mode of transport through which we arrived here got destroyed in an elephant attack. If there was a way to send a message to the mainland, we could definitely get a rescue team to reach this island and help us."

"I am still curious. How did you manage to fly over the geysers while arriving on this island?"

"We have a transportation vehicle designed to carry large numbers of people across the sky over long distances."

The entire assembly gasped at the revelation. Chatters and murmurs reverberated throughout the court hall. Barring a few daring locals like Toshi, who had dared to ride on a gigantic bird to take to the skies, most of them were alien to the pursuit of flight. Flying through a human-made vehicle sounded totally unimaginable yet exciting. The Ranija asked everyone to hush up so that the discussion could proceed.

Aman asked, "I am confused. How did your ancestors travel to Mosika on ships from Vidika if the entire island is surrounded by these steaming geysers?"

"I wish I knew," said the Ranija with a sigh. "That remains a mystery for us too till this day. We have been searching for any secret route, which could have potentially facilitated safe movement beyond the island coasts, for several years but without any success."

Tisha said, "Didn't your ancestors or the resident scientists notice how they arrived here?"

"There is a common folklore about a beach with sand as dazzling as gold. Apparently, some of them claimed that they had seen such a beach when they travelled to the island. We have never come across such a beach or rather any beach ever though. It could have been an exaggerated or a false tale for all we know."

Tisha recollected the image of the beach that they had seen in the lighthouse mirror. It was certainly present on the island albeit without the glamorous sand. She wasn't sure if this was the right moment to convey this critical information to the Ranija. She decided to stay mum until they had discussed the issue among themselves. Instead, she proceeded to ask,

"What happened to the Vidikan ministers or officials who accompanied you to the island? Didn't your ancestors get in touch with them?"

"They had briefly discussed the terms of their repatriation to the mainland with the Chief Minister before his last visit to the island. He had promised them that he would arrange ships for them to move back to the mainland on his next visit. Before departing, he mentioned how a group of violent and powerful species of monkeys that Queen Loma's scientists had developed for her military had backfired on Vidika's civilians. He had been urgently called back to Vidika to resolve the crisis. Unfortunately, he never returned. There was no visit or even a message from the mainland ever since he left."

* * *

The man, formally dressed in a navy blue uniform, pressed his fingerprint against the securely locked door. This was the last of several security checks that he had to pass through to get inside the conference room filled with a highly selective and elite group of experts across domains. He quietly seated himself on the seat number assigned to him and watched the stage and big screen in front of him. The silver letters on the screen read - 'Welcome to NTFHO'.

Within a few minutes, the entire room went dark barring the lit up stage and the bright screen. A lady arrived on the podium and announced, "As you would know, we have finally managed to piece together some of the monkey bones that we found underneath the kitchen laboratory at the Vidikan palace. Without any further delay, we will be presenting the skeleton shortly along with an approximate image of how it might have looked based on our simulation."

A wooden platform rolling on wheels was pushed onto the stage. Atop the platform, an assembled skeleton of a monkey stood with its head perched at a height almost enough to touch the ceiling. The most noticeable part of the head was the couple of sharp fangs that projected from the monkey's jawline. The audience's gasps only grew louder when the screen displayed a potential depiction of the monkey's actual appearance.

The monkey looked unusually tall. The bright yellow eyes were wider than usual. The fangs were as long as elephant tusks. The innocuous grey and black langur monkey, which the people were accustomed to seeing, looked ferocious enough to change their perception.

The lady announced, "Next on stage, we have an esteemed historian among us, Dr Kaju. He has not just successfully excavated the literature written by a traveller from the 1750s but also deciphered the most relevant chapter in that book.

Remember that this book was written around a decade after the last date of any excavated artifact in Vidika or in simpler words, the abrupt disappearance of the kingdom from public view. I invite Dr Kaju to read his decipherment of the text in that book chapter."

Dr Kaju slowly made his way with a walking stick in his hand. He didn't bother to introduce himself. Wisened or perhaps jaded with age, he knew nobody cared about his awards and where he graduated from. He started reading the text as soon as he reached the podium,

"Contrary to the horror stories narrated by people regarding abnormally large and blood-thirsty gray langur monkeys, I witnessed only calm in that decaying city. Most of the people were dead and the very few surviving residents had fled to other kingdoms. There was an atmosphere of death and sickness in the air. The few remaining monkeys were fairly gigantic - almost twice as tall as me. But they were violent and powerful no more. Their frail and aged bodies lousily dragged themselves from one place to the other. The brown eyes, which would have triggered fear at one time, now only expressed helplessness and evoked sympathy. When a monkey came rushing towards me, I was taken aback for a moment but as soon as it came near me, it collapsed onto the ground and never rose again. There was a terrible stench in the air from the decaying corpses of such dead monkeys everywhere. They were all old male monkeys, which explained why no young monkeys were around to displace them. The sun had set on the first glorious empire of monkeys, making it their last one too."

CHAPTER 22

BATTLE IN THE SKIES

When the bale of hay around the last muddy paw print was painstakingly removed, the space revealed a dark hole in the wall. Samantha and John jumped with joy at the prospect of an escape. The excitement was short-lived once they realized the extreme darkness inside the burrow. The unpredictability of what lay inside soon began to haunt their thoughts.

"What if there are snakes slithering inside?" said Samantha.

"What if we can't make our way out in the complex network of tunnels and get trapped while gasping for breath?" said John.

"On the other hand, what if the Pelagornis bird feeds us to its chicks, who tear us to shreds?"

"Don't worry. I just remembered. These birds can't eat humans. We are somehow toxic for their digestive systems."

"How do you know that?"

"I came to know through an incident that the locals told me about. An old islander was against going to the mainland because he preferred his peaceful life here and didn't want to adapt to a new world. So, he dug up human corpses and mixed human bones in the water to kill the giant bird that these islanders were raising near the lake to send a message to the mainland. Thankfully, he was caught in time and the bones were scooped up from the lake before the bird could consume them.."

"Unfortunately not. The bird that arrived in Mumbai died shortly after and human bones were found in its body. It must have drunk the water by then. Or maybe some bones were accidentally left in the lake water."

"Atleast, it died after completing its mission."

"I don't understand one aspect though. Why has the bird captured us if they can't feed on us?"

"They use us as live bait by dropping us into the sea to entice sharks onto the surface. Then, they swoop in to catch the sharks for their meal."

"Why am I not excited about this alternative option? We don't have the luxury of choices here. I am getting in. Follow me."

She stepped forward to jump into the burrow when two bright red eyes emerged from the dark tunnel interior. She would have almost fallen back if the approaching red eyes hadn't revealed Mona's adorable face. The pink rabbit looked at her benignly for a moment with its innocuous eyes and then began to lick her hands with its huge tongue.

"He likes you too," shouted John with a smile on his face.

He stepped forward and hugged Mona.

"Let us follow Mona and get out of here. Your reunion can wait."

John stepped away from the rabbit and shot back,

"You realize that you don't have to be so mean every time. We are stuck in this horrifying situation together."

"Maybe I wouldn't be so mean if you hadn't tried to clip my wings earlier. You wouldn't support my dreams of getting into historical research or becoming a university professor. Had I not gathered the courage to pursue my dreams after your disappearance, I would have never truly understood the extent of my potential."

"I understand but I didn't want to adversely impact Rick's childhood. Kids of his age require parental attention."

"Exactly. They need 'parental attention'. This includes both parents. Both should step up to be for their children. Am I the only one who can teach him after school? Am I the only one who can drive him around? Am I the only one who can cook his favourite meals? No, I am not. You can't shrug off your share of responsibilities and expect me to sacrifice my career for it."

"I get it. I am sorry for…"

"Mona is running away. We need to chase her to find our way out of here. Run as fast as you can."

John turned back to see a pair of scampering paws retreating into the darkness. He fled after Mona while trying his best to avoid the random tree root projecting out from the soil. After a brief athletic spurt, they spotted Mona resting on the floor.

"She is speedier than a cheetah. We will never be able to follow her out if she continuously keeps running. There's only one way."

John took a deep breath and leaped onto the rabbit's back. Mona budged for a moment but didn't seem to mind his presence. John affectionately patted the rabbit's lowered ears. He nudged Samantha to join him. He held out his hand as she nervously made her way onto the rabbit's back. As someone who had been reluctant to ride a tamed horse on their trip to the Himalayan mountains, the experience was novel and terrifying. The strong jolt that Mona gave them when she stood up on her legs didn't help. Had they not held each other's hands, they would have fallen off and landed at the rabbit's feet. They firmly held the rabbit's fluffy pink fur as it trudged up and down along the burrow. The pitch darkness prevented them from seeing each other for prolonged periods. At one point, Samantha asked,

"John. You are there, right?"

"Yes, I am. Will we ever see the light of day again?"

Their patience paid off when they finally saw light at the end of the tunnel in a both literal and metaphoric sense. When the first rays of sunlight streamed in through the open end of the tunnel, their eyes squinted while trying to adjust to the brightness after being in absolute darkness for hours. Their cramped legs also took their time when they finally landed on a solid surface. The muddy forest floor was devoid of the fallen leaves that they were accustomed to seeing. Not even a single green leaf grew on any of the giant oak trees. An eerie silence prevailed in the forest only to be broken by a hushed remark from John.

"There is a reason they call it the forbidden forest."

"I can't even hear a chirp. Where are all the birds?"

* * *

In a village on the outskirts of Mosika, a teenage boy and his father were plucking apples from the trees on their farm. It was a proud moment for the teenager who was finally tall enough for the exercise. The chaos began when his father abruptly cupped his mouth and pulled him under the apple tree's shade. The boy looked around for a clue. When he ran out of directions to look on the ground, a shrill cry from the sky quenched his curiosity. Witnessing the long black wings of the Pelagornis bird, flapping directly over them, caused him to tremble but he kept his quiet. A cloud of dust blew up in the air, smearing their faces completely as they closed their eyes. Within a few minutes, the dust settled and silence prevailed. The boy set himself free and rushed towards the horse-driven carriage stationed outside the farm. He ignored the shouts by his father to come back.

"Where are you going?" yelled his father.

"The bird was heading towards Mosika. Mom is working in the city library today. I need to take her to a safe place before the bird wreaks havoc in the city. You should stay in the cellar underneath the hut on this field until I come back to fetch you."

His father hesitatingly nodded, knowing the unstoppable determination of his son. He watched on with concern as the horse cart sped away on the road. The boy's hands shook with fear and the carriage's rapid movement. He still managed to write a legible note on a piece of paper. He pulled out a white dove from a cage kept inside the carriage, put the note in its beak and released it. The dove fluttered away ahead of them.

"Hope it reaches Mom on time," he whispered to himself.

He didn't need to see the city walls to realize when he was close. The loud shrieks informed him. They were accompanied by the idiosyncratic shrill sound of the Pelagornis bird. He froze in his seat when he witnessed three overhead birds descending swiftly towards the carriage. A hand jerked him from the carriage seat, causing him to tumble sideways towards the edge of the road. The horses whinnied and darted away as they were set free from the carriage, which had been smashed to smithereens. Within a few miles from the site of the accident, the boy asked his mother, who was tightly holding his hand, "Why didn't you hide in a cellar as I had asked you?"

"Because I am a mother," came the terse reply.

* * *

The defence minister, Vir, raised an alarm,

"Even our highest walls will not stop these birds from flying over. Our defences have been rendered practically useless and it is only a matter of time till they destroy the entire city and reach the fortress. We need to act fast. There is not one but dozens of them."

The Ranija was more composed. She calmly said, "This war shall be fought in the air. Send a regiment of our finest archers and gunmen to the city. These birds are too physically strong to be taken down in a one-to-one fight. Ask them to break up into small squads and surreptitiously attack these birds using guerilla tactics. If they can't comprehend the source of the attacks, they will begin to contemplate an attack from every quarter. The ensuing panic should be enough to scare them off."

"Aren't we compromising the safety of the fortress if we send them away?" said Vir.

Their eyes turned towards a shrill cry that they heard from the palace balcony. Amidst the white afternoon clouds, a couple of Pelagornis birds could be seen flying across the sky in the distance. The ensuing moments saw the black wings in the sky multiply at a rate that the blue sky almost got shrouded.

The Ranija said, "Don't worry about the palace. The fortress is surrounded by cannons on every side. We don't have the time to drag these heavy cannons into the city. We will charge flaming balls at these raging birds from here while the archers and gunmen save the people in the city. Our foot soldiers are also partially trained as archers. They can reinforce the defences to an extent and buy us time to evacuate people or come up with a better plan."

The first cannonball barely flew past a shrieking bird and exploded on the ground with tall flames leaping into the air. The bird recognized the source of the attack and swooped towards the cannon with its terrifying yellow eyes. The archers were quick to take notice and showered a barrage of arrows in its direction. The sharp tip of these arrows was embroidered with wool sheared from island sheep. The prickly wool was a natural defence mechanism for the Mos Island sheep. The wool was sharp enough to pierce attacking predators and injected a fluid into their skin, which rendered them unconscious. While most of the arrows missed the target, the high numbers ensured that at least a few luckily pierced the belly of the bird. The impact was almost instantaneous as the bird fell to the ground with a thud. A part of its wing landed in the moat, causing a loud uproar among the ligers who later pounced on it.

Meanwhile, Karan ran across the winding corridors in the palace to look for elderly people and children. As soon as he found someone, he gestured them to accompany him to a basement entrance with descending stairs. Preeti patiently waited for them there and escorted them to the bottom of the dark stairs. Aman stood in the basement with a flaming machete in his hands and assisted the soldiers in organizing the huge, assembled crowd. Despite the team's best efforts, some children kept on sobbing with the darkness and parental separation haunting them.

The basement was connected to an escape tunnel, where Rick, Neil and Tisha were hurrying out people in batches to avoid a stampede.

Neil's expressionless face indicated that he was deep in thought. Tisha noticed it and asked, "What are you thinking?"

"Something happened to the Pelagornis bird in Mumbai. The incident seemed like a minor issue back then but it might be the key to ending this war."

* * *

The guns proved to be futile as the rudimentary bullets couldn't hit the birds at such a high altitude. However, the regiment of skilled archers didn't take much time in controlling the situation in the city. The numerous huts and business complexes provided ample space for them to hide, launch coordinated and effectively-targeted attacks and hide again. When the last bird fell to the ground, they still had some arrows left in their quivers.

Their relatively untrained peers on the fortress weren't achieving the same level of success though. Owing to their lack of archery practice, it took them a much higher number of arrows and bullets per bird to effectively strike them down. When they noticed themselves running out of ammunition, they reduced their attacks to be more careful. This empowered the birds to launch more attacks on the soldiers by whipping up wind storms and chasing them on the high walls. The slowly moving cannons weren't of much help either as they failed to target the swiftly moving birds and simply belched smoke all around the fortress by exploding on the ground. When the birds redirected the flow of smoke towards the palace itself by fluttering their wings, it made matters even worse. Noticing the issues, the commander eventually ordered the cannons to halt firing.

The birds grew more aggressive as their shrills grew louder, the swooping attacks more frequent and the gusts of wind emanating from their wings stronger. The coordination among the palace archers almost broke down as they struggled to prevent themselves from falling off the edge by withstanding the stormy wind streams. Some of the birds flew down to perch on the boundary walls so swiftly that the soldiers got almost no time to react. As they fled their positions, they gave way for the perching birds to displace them.

The Ranija looked down with despair on the soldiers regrouping within the inner walls on higher elevations. Some of the birds flew in circles around them while the others perched on the outer wall situated at a lower elevation along the hill slope.

With a hand placed on her forehead, she said, "We can't let them win. We finally have some hope to escape this island. These birds have grown furious and cynical about our motives since we stole their egg to raise their chick. They will make it impossible for us to live on this island any longer. This makes our migration to the mainland even more important."

There was some respite as the delegation, which had been sent to relieve the city, returned after a successful campaign.

They circled around the foot of the hill and began to bombard the birds perched on the fortress walls with arrows. Taken by surprise, some of them succumbed, causing their heavy bodies to tumble and roll down along the hill slope. The ligers roared with their heads raised upward as they anticipated the arrival of delicacies into their moat. Faced with attacks from two sides, the birds struggled to find a direction to escape amidst the chaos. Realizing that the best immediate course of action would be to fly into the high skies, they flapped their wings and soared into the sky.

The arrows couldn't scale those heights to chase them and so, they disappeared above the white clouds. The weary soldiers heaved a sigh of relief.

"The battle has been thankfully won for today," said the Ranija. "We will still need to prepare ourselves for future attacks. They might have gone away for now but their hatred for us hasn't. They will return soon."

As the terror ended, the relieved people began to leave the basement where they were hiding. The palace windows were soon filled with spectators, curious to witness the rosy aftermath of a dark phase. The rosiness wasn't purely metaphorical. The ascending soldiers on their horses blushed as rose petals were showered upon them from the palace windows.

The pleasure of victory was short-lived though. The birds, which had seemingly fled away, re-emerged from the clouds as they swooped down towards the scattered regiment on the hill slopes. The horses neighed in terror and started galloping in all directions. Some of the horse riders fell onto the ground. Bereft of the opportunity to regroup and coordinate, the scattered soldiers were left to fend on their own. Some chose to fire ineffective isolated shots while the others tried to make their way towards the palace. The children watching the scenes from the palace windows began to scream at the sight of flying birds with people gripped in their talons.

Neil made his way through the crowd and reached Rick. He whispered something in his ears. Rick nodded and ran towards the Ranija. He said something to her and she nodded with delight. Soon, soldiers could be seen carrying numerous boxes and leaving them on the palace windows. The people were asked to step back.

At the count of three, the lids on all the boxes were simultaneously removed. Buzzing sounds filled the air as a swarm of bees escaped from the boxes. After a moment of haphazard wandering, they began to jet upwards in a uniform direction. The discipline with which they moved together had an almost military-like aura. They headed towards the flying birds and clung all over their feathers. The birds tried to shrug them off by furiously flapping their wings. The bees were unrelenting though as their constant bites continued to irritate the birds. The shrill shrieks of the birds reverberated through the air. It was only a matter of time before they flapped their wings and fled away from the fortress.

"How did you know this?" asked Preeti.

"I remembered how a bee had made its way into the bird's enclosure one day," said Neil. "The bird kept shrieking until the solitary bee was removed. This was enough to convince me of their adversarial relationship."

His smile betrayed a feeling of self-pride.

"The apiary has lost an entire year's worth of honey," sighed the Ranija. "I suppose we will have to find a new home remedy for our sore throats."

She chuckled at her last remark. Years of life experience had taught her that laughing at situations was sometimes all one could do.

CHAPTER 23

A NIGHT GLIMMERING WITH HOPE

"If there's one lesson that I have learnt from movies, it is not to endlessly walk around in circles when you are lost," declared Samantha. "I would feel so dumb if we came across a place that we had already passed. Let us strictly keep walking in the same direction and we will hopefully get out of this forest."

Darkness had descended over the skies and John could only see a faint apparition of her. The stars shimmered with a peculiarly high brightness, unseen in the hazy skies of Mumbai. In Mumbai, the stars faced intense competition from the artificial lights emanating from endless skyscrapers, malls and street lamps. Contrarily, on an almost pristine island, the stars were their only guides.

"Can we hold hands? We would feel even more foolish if we got separated in the dark," said John with a smirk that tried hard to hide his fear.

Samantha quietly held out her hand towards John. Their clasp was firm but their shaky minds grappled with the unknown.

"Which direction do we even walk in?" sighed Samantha.

"Considering that there's no way to know any better, let us just walk ahead and hope for the best," suggested John.

The events of the night had been tiring enough but they knew that time was valuable. They couldn't afford to waste it and let their captor birds return before their escape. They dragged themselves through the soil while huffing and panting. Their newfound companion, Mona, preferred another approach. The rabbit took turns between lying on the ground and rapidly leaping to make up for the lost distance.

John kept wondering if Mona was lost to the darkness. Yet, the agile rabbit kept dispelling his doubt every time he turned back. He could always see a pair of red eyes darting towards him.

They walked for miles in the company of the myriad sounds of the forest's inhabitants. They couldn't see anything but the distant hisses, whistles and meows informed them that they weren't alone. However, none of these sounds were loud enough to startle them until they heard a strong cluck. They froze in their tracks to listen again. There was silence for a while and then, they heard the distinct cluck more clearly again. Before they could discuss their next steps, the clouds began to rage and a spark of lightning shone across the sky.

The momentary brightening of the forest floor allowed them a peek at the source of the clucking sounds. A bowl-shaped straw nest stood a few feet ahead of them. It housed a chick, almost as tall as them, which was popping its black head out from the nest. Its wide-open vibrating beak faced the sky. It looked like a miniature version of an adult Pelagornis Sandersi bird, barring its undeveloped tiny wings.

"The poor chick seems to have been abandoned," said John. "This might be its way of asking for food. Can we feed it one of the plums we picked on the way?"

"We should. It will probably starve to death without any aid. It looks quite feeble and young. We should just fling the plum towards the nest from a distance and run away though. I don't want to put ourselves in danger by drawing attention."

As John nodded and began to pull out the plum from his tight pocket, Samantha said, "Do you not find the position of the nest a bit strange?

Most nests are built on trees."

"Yes, I agree. Why would a parent leave its chicks on the ground, where they are vulnerable to predators?"

"I doubt that these birds have any predators. Which animal can dare to attack them with their terrific size?"

She had barely finished speaking when a shriek was heard from the sky. The flapping of wings was heard, accompanied by a strong gust of wind.

"I think we have realized by now what that means," whispered John.

"The Mom is back. Or Dad. Who cares? Run!"

They circuited around the huge nest that stood in their path and sped away to disappear among the shady trees. Mona followed and raced even ahead of them. The loud shriek obscured the buzzes of innumerous bees on the tree branches over the nest. Even the mightiest had their nemesis.

* * *

"When are we going to rescue my parents?" said Rick.

"They are in more danger than ever with those birds retreating back to their abode."

"We are still reeling from the trail of destruction that the birds have left behind," said the Ranija. "Our entire staff is engaged in mobilising efforts to treat the injured people. They are rebuilding destroyed homes for those who have been rendered homeless overnight. We can only spare one person for now. His name is Mido. He led a contingent to steal the Pelagornis bird's egg earlier. He knows his way around the nooks and paths in the forbidden forest."

Making no attempt to hide his anger, Rick retorted, "A single person will take ages to find them in the whole forest. Who knows what the birds will do to them by then?"

"I know that this is difficult for you to understand but this is an unprecedented crisis. Unfortunately, we have no choice. We can't abandon our people."

"You are ungrateful," shouted Rick. "Had it not been for our ingenious idea, your army would have never managed to defeat and ward off the attacking birds. Your people owe us."

Unused to such brash criticism at the highest levels of authority, the Ranija was taken aback by the outburst and silently stared at the young boy. Tisha ran towards Rick to calm him down. Karan also rushed to the scene upon hearing the outraged yell and tried to make amends.

"I apologize for his behaviour. He is clearly upset by the separation from his parents. Any kid would be."

After finally winning the trust of the locals, Aman's translator had finally been handed back.

The Ranija listened intently to the translation and replied,

"To be honest, he just spoke the truth. We are indebted to Neil for his effective solution. Without his advice, the entire city would have been reduced to rubble. I suppose that I will dispatch a team of ten soldiers. In return, you all will have to pitch in by helping the townsfolk while the soldiers are gone."

"I would like to accompany them," said Karan. "I happen to have experience in military investigation."

"If you are going, I will join this expedition too," said Preeti as she approached them. "How far is it? Hopefully we can reach there on time."

The Ranija replied, "The forbidden forest is on the opposite end of this island. You won't be travelling on a slow horse carriage though. You will be drifting across the fast-flowing River of the Blue Hippos in a houseboat."

"How will your soldiers ride a houseboat? Aren't they scared of water?"

"One of our men, Mido, is blessed with a complete lack of hydrophobia. We don't know why but his ability makes him a huge asset for us. He often steers the boat, allowing his companions to stay inside their cabins during river journeys."

* * *

The Ranija decided to accompany the contingent to the river shore. She rode in a horse carriage along with Tisha, Rick and Neil while the contingent rode in another. After a teary-eyed farewell, Karan and Preeti proceeded to board a wooden houseboat, embellished with dyed floral patterns. The turbulent river stirred up white foam and shook the boat, repeatedly banging it against the harbour fence. Before they could board, the Ranija ran towards them and said in a hushed voice,

"None of us, who had ever stepped foot there, had returned alive to tell the story until Mido successfully stole an egg from one of the nests there. Although most of the forest is still unexplored, Mido understands the ways of the forest better than any of us. Stay close to him."

* * *

"What is this tall tower-like structure?" said John, pointing to the dark apparition standing out in the backdrop of the grey
    pre-sunrise sky.

As they crept closer, they noticed that it was a multi-storeyed treehouse towering over the oak trees surrounding it. The enormous amount of moss growing on its walls rendered the structure a distinct light green colour. A high brick walled fence could be seen behind the tree house. It stretched on both sides as far as the eye could see.

"I wonder if this tall fence marks the edge of the forest," said Samantha. "Do you think that anybody lives in this tree house?

"I highly doubt that. The way in which the moss has completely taken over implies that it has been in a state of constant decay for a while."

"Intelligent observation. Plus, why would anyone even choose to inhabit a tree house far away from any civilization in this remote forest?"

"Then, what are we waiting for? Let us climb these ascending stairs and allow the bird's eye view to guide us out. Maybe the escape route lies beyond this high fence."

"Our friend has already taken the lead."

Mona had hopped onto the first floor of the tree house and was staring down at them with its big red eyes. Following its lead, the duo huffed as they tried to keep up with the rabbit's flawless ascending hops over broken gaps in the creaking stairs. The slipperiness caused by the overgrown moss and the oak branches along the stairs created further impediments but they persistently continued their climb. On their way, a disturbed squirrel leapt onto John's shoulder and furiously started biting his half-torn shirt.

As Samantha frantically tried to shoo away the squirrel, she yelled, "This violent creature is changing my perception of the adorable squirrels that I am used to seeing in my terrace garden back home."

What her relentless attempts failed to achieve, the roar did. It wasn't only the squirrel which fled. The roar reverberated throughout the forest with such an intensity that flocks of tiny birds could be seen collectively emerging from the treetops as they fluttered towards the sky.

Samantha looked down to inspect the source. Her eyes met the yellow and flashy ones of a bulky tiger, which bared its sharp canines to let out another roar upon seeing her. Despite the significant elevation separating her from the bottom of the tree, the sight and sound of the tiger shook her to the core.

"Come on up quickly," muttered John. "Tigers are excellent tree-climbers. It won't take long to climb this tree. Assuming it doesn't simply use the stairs."

Not wishing to waste a moment during a matter of life and death, she blindly followed his advice. She didn't even turn back to check if the tiger was following them upstairs. Ignoring the intermittent spine-chilling roars, she refused to stop until she reached the rooftop. John was waiting and wiping off the sweat from his face when Samantha finally caught up with him.

"Is it climbing?" asked Samantha.

"Surprisingly not. It is simply walking around the base of the tree house in circles. I can't figure out what it is up to."

At that very moment, the tree house trembled, causing both of them to grip the fragile railing tightly. Struggling to bear their combined weight, the shaky fence broke free from the floor, hurtling toward the ground. It would have taken them with it if not for Mona's quick thinking. He leaped to the other side, tilting the floor just enough for the duo to slide back to safety. John, lying on his back, inched his way to the edge and peered down, but there was no solace in sight. The tiger stood almost upright, pounding its massive paws against the tree house's base.

"This rusty tree house will crash into the ground," said John with tears rolling down his cheeks. "I don't want to be a tiger's gourmet meal."

"I think you are giving yourself too much credit with the gourmet part."

"This is no time to make jokes!"

Yet, silly humour was one of the few ways that Samantha used to keep her from going insane in difficult situations.

The tree house offered them a bird's eye view of what lay beyond the fence behind the tree house. They saw a dense canopy of palm trees stretching beyond the horizon. The lush green colour had evaded their eyes since they had landed in the forbidden forest. They noticed a taut rope tied to a hook on the floor. It descended into the canopy by sliding over the fence. A metal chamber, housing half-broken seats, dangled from the rope.

"This is a kind of cable car," said Samantha. "Let us take these seats and slide down along the rope."

"What do we know about creatures awaiting us down there?" said John.

There was another thud.

"I can only wish that we had the luxury of options," said Samantha.

She pulled John towards him and occupied the seats within the chamber. Mona hopped onto the chamber to join them.

"We need to push this to allow it to slide," said Samantha. "Give it whatever you got else we die."

"A box cannot be moved by pushing it from inside. That's basic physics. It needs an external push from outside."

"I am not a teacher of physics so…"

The external push was provided by the tiger itself. The tree house's vibration gave the chamber a forward thrust. It slid smoothly over the rope but its rapid descent led to loud screams from the duo. They landed with a thud on the forest floor.

They were left with aching backs after the fall. Yet, they summoned every nerve to crawl out of the chamber and looked up. The dense canopy made sunlight almost impregnable. They didn't need to see though. The violent crashing sounds and loosened rope informed them that the tree house had been smashed to smithereens.

"Do you also hear the thundering sound?" said Samantha.

John wrapped his hand in a coil-like fashion around his ear and tried to hear clearly. He remarked,

"It is more than thunder. I can also hear the pitter-patter sound of drops and a gurgling sound."

"Is it raining? If so, why are we not drenched yet? Is the canopy shielding us from the torrential rain?"

"It is not the sound of rain. It resembles the sound of sea waves crashing against a beach."

"If that's true, these palm trees would make a lot of sense. But where is the beach?"

They heard a squeak and turned around to see Mona nibbling away at the leaves of a bush. The feeding was so voracious that the bushes were completely stripped of their leaves within a few moments. Mona sniffed around and then proceeded to make its way through the entangled network of branches to disappear into the other side.

"I think the sound of water is also coming from that direction. Let us follow Mona," said John.

Samantha nodded and they leapt over the bush. They navigated through the spaces between the palm trees and followed Mona as it speedily scampered across the forest floor. They noticed that the soil grew less firm and their feet sunk deeper as they covered more distance.

The sound of the hypothetical sea waves also became louder and clearer. While Mona finally halted on seeing a fallen coconut to sip water from, the peculiar view ahead beckoned Samantha and John to continue marching forward. It looked as if the fantasy world painted by an artist had come to life.

Beyond the palm trees, they were greeted by a vast stretch of golden sand that softly shone in the moonlight. Samantha scooped up some of the sand and allowed it to slip out through her fingers.

"It has a rough and prickly texture. It isn't soft like regular beach sand. Could it be gold?" she exclaimed.

"Who knows? But if it is, we could become filthy rich."

As he said that, he lay down on the beach and started waving his hands over the sand to feel it. Unable to bear the extreme brightness, Samantha shielded her eyes and stood up. She said,

"The concept of wealth makes sense only on the mainland. If we can't get out of here, this supposed gold is as worthless as stone. Let us inspect the sound of the sea waves. We could find a potential route for all of us to escape."

John balanced himself on the uneven sand while Samantha aided him in getting back on his feet. They realized that they didn't have to walk much further. The faint sunlight at dawn allowed them to see things hidden by the darkness. Seashells. Dead crabs. Most importantly, a towering black wall barricading the beach. The source of the roaring sounds seemed very close but there was nothing in sight to claim it.

"I still can't see it," said John with a frown.

Samantha pressed her ear to the wall and smiled. She said,

"You won't be able to. The sea lies beyond the boundary wall."

CHAPTER 24

A SPECTACLE SPARED BY TOURISTS

As the morning sun fully rose to bathe the sand with its copious rays, it evaporated John's dreams along with the dew drops on the palm leaves. The sand, which glowed like gold in the darkness of the night, lost its lustre and adopted the austere appearance they were used to seeing. John lamented,

"It is simply regular sand which somehow glows in the dark. My aspirations have been flushed down the drain."

"I am surprised that you are even concerned about anything beyond basic survival on this dangerous island," sighed Samantha.

They sat on the beach and heard the crashing of waves. John dozed off but Samantha's faint recollection couldn't let her sleep. When her eyes eventually fell on the dusty mirror projecting out from the sand, she recalled where she had seen this place before. It was one of the views that she had witnessed in the lighthouse mirrors of Vidika. Once the realization struck, she immediately stood up on her feet and ran towards it.

The screen was hazy because of the settled dust but Samantha spared no effort in scrubbing the persistent layers off. As she peeped inside, her eyes met the wide counterparts of a moustached man, whose gaping mouth signalled his surprise. Once he recovered from his shock, his moving mouth showed that he was trying to speak. Unfortunately, words were no use because mirrors don't transmit sounds. Fearful of losing her possibly last chance at communication, she showed him her raised single index finger.

This was generally how she nonverbally requested anyone to wait for a minute patiently. It worked. The man didn't budge.

Samantha tried to tilt the mirror case towards the sand. She possessed neither a pen nor paper but the smooth sand was her whiteboard, where she could draw with her hands. The mirror was heavy though and her strongest attempts failed to tilt it to any degree. She pulled back her long hair and looked at John. She had barely opened her mouth to call him when their furry friend came to the rescue. Mona leapt on top of the chamber holding the mirror. Under his heavy weight, the mirror case began shifting its focus towards the sand.

Grabbing the opportunity, she looked up and illustrated the sentence - 'Fly over the wall from the east' on the sand with her fingers. The sun partially rising over the wall had informed her about the direction. When she was done, she looked up towards the mirror to check the reaction of the man in the lighthouse. He wasn't opening his mouth or nodding his head but simply staring at the illustration. Samantha wondered if he understood her message. Before she could validate that, a wave of water swept over her illustration and completely blurred it. Aghast, she looked aside to notice low-lying waves of seawater trickling through a wide gate in the wall. The gate soared upwards, allowing greater amounts of water to gush out onto the beach. Within a matter of minutes, the vast sea was visible through the opening.

"What did you do?" screeched John.

"I just tilted the mirror here," said Samantha with despair.

"It seems to have triggered some sort of a switch to open this massive gate."

John tugged at her hand and started dashing towards the grove of palm trees.

"What's holding you back? Keep running," said John.

She stared at the furious waves lashing against the mirror case.

It struggled to stay above the water for a while but eventually got submerged underneath the rising sea levels. The yellow tinge omnipresent on the vast stretch of sand became history under the blue foaming water. The raging and unforgiving waves seemed destined to destroy everything in their path and were headed towards them.

"Our last chance of communication is destroyed," sighed Samantha.

"I don't understand what that means but let us plan to live for another day. We need to climb one of these palm trees."

Without any side branches, the palm trees weren't prepared to allow an easy climb though. Whenever they managed to ascend a few feet, they lost their balance and fell back onto the ground with a thud. With excessive sweat trickling from their foreheads, they gathered their courage and kept trying. The nervousness stemming from the imminent threat didn't help.

On the verge of giving up hope, they heard a series of squeaks. They swerved their heads to see long rows of pink rabbits lining the beach. They came in all sizes but their activity was the same. They were digging up sand from the beach and pulling it away from the raging sea. The tall mounds of sand that gathered behind them within seconds testified to their remarkable deftness and coherence. The deep and long pit that they dug up allowed the water to flow inside and stemmed its rise. Mona leapt and darted towards the herd of pink rabbits. Seeing Mona, another adult pink rabbit followed by two tiny bunnies ran towards it. The adult rabbits licked each other's ears as the bunnies danced in circles around them.

"Atleast someone is back home," smiled John.

"And reunited with their family," added Samantha.

* * *

Karan and Preeti bid farewell to their companions inside the houseboat to head out to the balcony. They were curious to get a closer look at the fishes in the clear blue river water. The hydrophobia of their companions made them uncomfortable when they stayed close to water for extended periods of time.

So, they preferred to stay away from the open and roofless section of the boat. Schools of multicoloured and shiny fishes could be seen swimming underneath the surface. The snakes wading through the water were mostly slender and tiny but one of them stood out with its long body wrapped in a coil at the bottom of the river. Not a single creature could be seen close to its black striped body. Both stepped back in fear for a while but the boat peacefully drifted above it.

"Once we find Samantha and John, we will still need to find a way out of this island. Have you thought of a plan?" said Preeti.

"I am worried about the same too. The Ranija mentioned a beach with golden sand which acts as an entry and exit point for the island. The locals haven't been able to find it for several centuries though. Might be just a myth."

"They might have missed some parts of the island though. Didn't they say that they rarely ventured into the forbidden forest?"

Their attention was diverted by a red flag waving with the wind on the grassy river shore.

"I wonder why that red flag has been hoisted there," said Preeti.

"Should we go and ask the captain driving the boat?"

"Why don't you ask him? I will wait for you on the deck."

Karan nodded and rushed inside the chamber as the boat drifted past the flag. Preeti apprehensively watched the swirls building up inside the water barely a few moments after they had crossed the flag. The calm river turned choppy and the boat began to pick up speed like an athlete on the last leg of a marathon.

When Karan approached the captain's seat, he noticed that the captain was dozing with his head tilted sideways and mouth wide open. Karan tapped him on the shoulder and he woke up with his eyes almost popping out. Considering the language barrier, they carried a wooden board with a charcoal stick to draw. Karan picked up the stick and began to rub it against the board, sprinkling the black dust in the form of a flag on the board. As soon as the captain saw the illustration, he pulled a trigger beside him, screeching the boat to a halt. The quietened sound of the wobbling boat allowed them to hear a series of growling noises from all directions.

The dark blue hemispheres projecting out of the water began to come closer to the still boat. Preeti shrieked as she witnessed the hippopotamus heads popping out one after the other as they heaved themselves against the rocking boat.

* * *

"We have achieved something truly remarkable today," said John. "The locals told me that they haven't been able to find a safe escape route for centuries. The island has been cordoned off from the rest of the world by sky-high mirrored walls. The only way even to approach these walls is lined with steam-exhaling geysers. The boiling steam essentially blocks every escape route across the island's borders…"

"Except the one here?" asked Samantha.

"Exactly. They probably missed checking out this part because those terrifying birds forbid any sort of exploration."

"Makes sense. In fact, now that I think about this place, the tree house could have served as a lighthouse to guide the incoming ship."

"If that's true, that was one feeble lighthouse."

Both laughed and looked at the adorable rabbits. "I was scared out of my wits when I saw the tons of water rushing in. We would have been swept away if these brilliant rabbits hadn't engineered that solution."

"We are safe for now but how long will we persist on this island?

I hope that the man inside the Vidika lighthouse was able to read my message before it got erased. He showed no reaction though."

Even though the island's mystique was an intriguing subject for conversation, the weariness of the journey was too strong to resist. They dozed off on the beach sand, causing their loud snores to scare off a couple of bunnies.

The deserved slumber was both fortunately and unfortunately cut short by a whirring sound accompanied by the squeaks of terrified rabbits running helter-skelter. John and Samantha rubbed their eyes as their frowns betrayed their displeasure. It didn't take long however for their half-awake brains to come back to their senses. They raised their eyebrows with sparkles in their eyes. While they couldn't spot the source initially, the sound drew their attention towards the wall.

"It is coming from the other side of that wall," said Samantha.

Validating her statement, the cockpit and rotating blades of a grey helicopter became partially visible over the wall. John and Samantha rushed across the sand to frantically wave at the incoming helicopter. They couldn't see anyone through the black-tinted glass of the cockpit but their gestures coincided with a gradual lowering of the helicopter towards the ground. The beach had surprisingly become clear of all the frolicking pink rabbits by the time the helicopter landed. The door opened and the duo watched with bated breath. Maya stepped out in a jungle-print green-brown uniform with her matted grey hair tied in a bun. She was followed by a similarly dressed man holding a gun. Samantha ran forward to hug Maya.

"Fair to assume you got my message," chuckled Samantha.

"Yes. A tourist in the lighthouse informed the police upon seeing your message. I requested the rescue team to let me accompany them."

Even though Maya was chatting with Samantha, her wandering eyes didn't escape the notice of Samantha.

Samantha said, "I know that you are searching for Aman. In a weird turn of events, we got separated from him but we will find him somewhere on the island."

"You understand motherly instincts. Is he safe?"

"We hope so. It's a long story. Why don't we get inside the helicopter and travel around the island to search for him? I will narrate what happened along the way."

Maya nodded. The helicopter's whirring sound dominated the atmosphere again as it began to gradually lift off the ground with its rotating blades picking up speed. The evening sky lit up with the pink hue of sunset and the clear seawater partially reflected the shade. John's eyes were closely scanning the horizon when he noticed that the rabbits had cleverly camouflaged themselves underneath a small pool of seawater close to the beach.

"This is probably a common tactic to hide from predators," commented Samantha when she witnessed the spectacle of slightly prominent moving pink dots in the pink-ish water.

John didn't think much. He assumed Mona to be one of the countless rabbits hopping around in that water and bid the rabbit a farewell as tears welled up in his eyes.

** * **

It wasn't only the rabbits. The blue hippopotamuses also blended well with the blue river water, making it easy for them to launch surprise attacks. The shrieking boat riders bore the cost of that effective camouflage.

CHAPTER 25

LIFE ISN'T A STRAIGHT PATH

The massive hippopotamuses relentlessly slammed their bodies against the trembling boat, even after the last man had made a desperate leap from the deck. With a resounding splash, he swam toward the distant shore, struggling to regain his balance upon reaching the muddy riverbed. He observed the eerie calmness of the boat, realizing the ferocious beasts had shifted their attention elsewhere. Reluctantly parting with his sticky slippers, he joined his companions in a frantic sprint across the grassy plains. The loud thuds of pursuing hippo legs reverberated behind him, but he dared not glance back. Fearful that facing his fears would hinder his escape, he maintained unwavering focus. The strategy seemed effective as the intensity of the thuds gradually waned.

His unwavering attention on the path ahead quickened his pace but blinded him to potential obstacles lurking ahead. Suddenly, a rock struck his foot, causing him to stumble and crash to the ground. He desperately tried to stand, but his twisted ankle stubbornly refused to cooperate. He closed his eyes as he anticipated the incoming danger.

When he fearfully reopened his eyes, he was surprised to not see a bunch of raging beasts. Instead, Preeti and Karan were looking down at him. He heard a few whispers and in the next moment, he was being lifted by the duo as they darted across the plains. The absence of trees removed all obstacles for the hippopotamuses during their marathonic chase. A chill went down his spine as he witnessed the long teeth of an approaching hippo as it bared open its jaw. Ahead of them, Preeti and Karan could see a dense forest into which their companions had headed into or were heading towards. The trees could provide refuge on their high branches and the narrow spaces would impede the hippopotamuses' speedy unchallenged run. The only challenge was the lack of time as they came to realize with the grunts louder than ever.

The grunts were soon to be overpowered by a unique whirring sound that the locals had never heard. They ran their eyes across the ground for an answer only to realize the source was in the sky. Whizzing through the white clouds drifting overhead, a helicopter arrived on the scene as the onlookers on the trees watched it with wide-eyed fascination. When Karan and Preeti looked up to witness it, their reawakened hope mixed with the dismay from the stomping noises behind them. The helicopter was lowering towards the grassy plains and approaching them. But so were the furious hippopotamuses. When she realised that their rescue help might come too late, Samantha popped her head out of the window and yelled,

"Run in a zigzag fashion. The hippopotamuses can run quickly in one direction but their heavy bodies aren't agile enough to constantly change directions."

Karan recognised the familiar voice even though the face was blurry from that height. Karan and Preeti didn't know how to translate that message for their local companion. They grabbed his hand impulsively and swerved towards the left. The trio ran for a while and then changed their direction towards the right. The perplexed hippos paused at each rerouting and as predicted; the constant change of directions slowed them down as they took time to adjust repeatedly. The intensity of stomps began to grow milder again. The sounds finally stopped when the trio reached the summit of a tree and managed to climb one of its high branches. The hippopotamuses circled the tree and brushed their heavy bodies violently against the trunk.

"Why can't they just let it go?" screamed a visibly frustrated Preeti.

The respite came when the helicopter began approaching the branches. Their companion looked at the contraption with a puzzled expression. Samantha and John held out and lowered their hands. After an intense struggle, the three of them managed to hop onto the helicopter. On receiving the nod from Maya, the pilot steered the helicopter towards the blue cloudy sky. The anger and dismay of their companions left to fend for themselves on the trees was palpable from their raised eyes and curled up foreheads.

"What about them?" sighed Karan.

As the helicopter flew higher, Karan saw blue dots on the green plains retreating towards the river. He sighed with relief and peacefully dozed off with a clear conscience.

* * *

A gold bust of a crowned man, almost as tall as the ceiling itself, awaited them as the entry gates parted to reveal the contents of the treasury room. Mountainous heaps of gold and silver coins could be seen scattered across the room. In the valleys created by these namesake mountains, one could see silver pots and pans; gem-studded miniature sculptures of women and men and occasionally, a gold bust like the one at the entrance. The blinding glitter caused them to squint their eyes.

As Rick promptly explained, the Ranija offered,

"Half of these riches will be yours if you take our people to a safe place and provide them with the necessary resources to settle on the mainland."

Samantha, who stood close to her son as she constant hugged him, said, "We would have definitely helped your people even without this incentive. You welcomed my son into your home, fed him and protected him for months without expecting anything in return. I cannot thank you enough for your generosity."

John frowned at the suggestion of leaving the riches but Samantha's disapproving stare mellowed his expression.

Maya said, "Unfortunately, our vehicle over the skies has limited capacity. We will not be able to transport all the residents of Mos this time. We can accommodate one person though, who can support us in understanding the logistical operations required to evacuate the others from here. Would you like to accompany us, Ranija?"

"I would love to but the people need strong leadership to manage such a drastic transitional phase in their lives. Our Chief Minister has been engaged in public service for decades and will be able to effectively convey the needs of our people. He will greatly help you in organizing the logistics. Please consider taking him along."

* * *

The usually bustling markets in the city of Mos stood largely empty. Their customers had deserted them to enthusiastically assemble outside the palace gates. Nobody wanted to miss out on the once-in-a-lifetime spectacle. The murmurs turned to ecstatic shouts when the helicopter lifted itself from the roof of the hilltop palace. The Ranija, dressed in a gold-laced red sari for the occasion, waved adieu to the passengers as she looked up from the roof. Even though the samosas, considerately brought by Maya, were quite tempting to gorge on, Aman patiently kept them aside to focus on the last views of the island. Having grown a strong connection with it over the days, he quietly observed the grassy plains, dense forests, herds of diverse animals and the sparkling blue lakes.

Even though she had been yearning to reunite with her family for a long time, Samantha reflected on her newfound identity that her attempts at achieving that reunion had brought to the surface. If she could derive willpower from motives beyond rescuing her family, she realized that her intelligence could help her unearth many more such historical secrets. John's increased recognition of these facts was the reason for the hand placed on his forehead. Regretting his rash plan to divorce her, he worried how a return to normal life would look like for him and how he would react to questions which would confront him once again.

Having found charging points finally, Neil and Tisha's mobile phones sprung back to life. They carefully inspected every photograph that they had managed to click on the island. They smiled as they imagined the shocked faces of their fellows in the scientific community. Benji slept blissfully in Tisha's lap as he dreamt about going back to his pampered urban lifestyle that his ancestors in the royal army could only dream of.

Aman had learned more within a few days than he would ever learn in classrooms over his entire engineering program. The learning wasn't just limited to academics. The art of effective collaboration with unique individuals, which had ensured their survival, would stay with him forever.

Rick couldn't forget the shine in the children's eyes outside the palace, reflecting their dreams. Being the fuel that had kept him alive in a completely unforeseen complex situation, he recognized the power of hope. He prayed that those children wouldn't be let down.

Having found someone as brave as themselves after searching for one throughout their lives, Karan and Preeti spoke few words and let their eyes speak for themselves.

The collective dream of a better future was duly captured by the symbolic Queen's Necklace, consisting of Mumbai's iconic skyline, beginning to appear on the sea's horizon. The City of Dreams was awaiting the return of some of its countless dreamers, who dared to think big everyday against all odds.

* * *

The policeman interrupted the long and winding queue at the zoo entrance, which spilled over to the street and had been blocking the traffic for an hour. After making his way through the chaotic crowd, he talked to the person at the counter. After a brief conversation, another ticket counter opened and the queue split into almost two equal shorter halves, which freed up the road for vehicle movement. Inside the zoo, huge crowds thronged the numerous viewing areas, hosting odd species they had never witnessed before. A herd of quaggas, brought back from extinction, peacefully grazed the hay scattered all over their open enclosure. A liger rested atop a tree inside a much more shielded shelter with see-through glass walls. Some of the parents struggled to make their children see the well-camouflaged blue hippos resting in the pools right in front of them. While the crowds were everywhere, the rush towards the zoo's star attraction could put the busiest streets of Mumbai to shame. Several gasps mixed with the crying sounds of babies when the Pelagornis bird flapped its huge wings to briefly fly in the air.

As the tickets were handed out, a dashboard in a pharmaceutical office prominently updated its fund collection figure. After a successful three-phased trial, a drug to completely treat the unique rabies disease afflicting Mos Island residents had received approval. However, a specialized manufacturing facility was economically unviable to set up for a small number of people. That was where a large portion of the zoo revenue stepped in. The remaining funds were leveraged for rehabilitating the residents on the mainland by arranging accommodation, food and reskilling camps to train them for new careers.

After a few weeks of relaxation to get over the trip fatigue, Samantha was back at the Sanjay Gandhi National Park, determinedly making her way to the Kanheri caves. The renewed stamina from the endless climbs and walks across Mos ensured that she had little reason to make an en route stop this time. She persevered past gigantic rocks, intimidatingly tall trees and menacing monkeys to finally complete her unaccomplished ascent to the summit. The orange sun rose behind the austere walls of the Kanheri caves as she approached the entrance. Mesmerized by the tantalizing view, she took a step back to get a full glimpse. She was lost in the tranquility of the weekday dawn until someone tapped her on the shoulder. She shook and looked back to face a young boy holding up an identity card.

"Ma'am, is that yours?"

Samantha nodded with relief, thanked the boy and held the card in her hands. It mentioned her name followed by the designation - "PhD student, Department of Archaeology, University of Delhi". After teaching history to uninterested students for several years, she had forgotten the reason she had picked teaching as a career option in the first place. She wanted to impart the joy of learning to others but had forgotten it herself in the process. Her like-minded PhD classmates, who kept suppressing their yawns on that early morning, reminded her of that joy once again.

While John's repertoire of romantic gifts hadn't extended much beyond flowers earlier, he stood in the bookstore to carefully inspect each shelf that day. He knew he would have to reinvent himself as a supportive partner if he wanted to win back Samantha. The choice of a thoughtful gift for their upcoming anniversary was the first of many such steps towards getting there.

As Rick stood outside the school gate waiting for his father to pick him up, he heard a familiar voice. It wasn't John's. Maya had popped her head out of her car window to gesture to him.

"Do you want me to drop you at your house? I am going to meet Aman at IIT Bombay. It will be on the way."

Rick smiled at the familiar face of a person, who had not only rescued him and his family from a dangerous island but also delivered a stellar speech as a guest speaker at the school's annual function that day. Being one of the female pioneers in her field, her talk on challenging societal expectations had received a standing ovation and several encomiums from Rick's classmates.

A few miles away, Aman walked on the regular trail from his hostel to the lecture hall. Realizing that giving up his current academic program meant wasting his technical prowess, he had abandoned his decision to drop out. There wasn't a complete reversal though. His arms merrily waved not only because of the pleasant weather. The elective class that he was heading to as a part of his history minor could explain a big part of his glee.

Karan blushed when he heard the pilot announcement inside the passenger airplane headed to Auckland -

"Hello, I am the pilot, Preeti Kaur, who will be flying you to Auckland. I wish you a happy journey."

The endless spa sessions and binge-watching had soothed their frayed nerves but they missed the thrill and sense of purpose. Knowing that Preeti would get to stay in New Zealand for a week because of her scheduled flight, they had planned a short trip to Queenstown, an adventure tourism hotspot. Even though the adventure wasn't organic, a few days of rafting, hiking and sky diving would be enough for them to get their mojo back and prepare for bigger adventures ahead.

A few miles away from Mumbai, a ship sailed past the open section of a towering wall, which blended perfectly into the darkness with its mirror reflections. The glittering beach sand welcomed its first visitors through the gate in centuries. Loud squeals and thuds filled the air as the resident pink rabbits fled in large numbers to disappear among the coconut trees. When Neil and Tisha stepped on the beach that night, they wanted to closely study the newly discovered and undiscovered species on the Island of Mos. John had no such motivation as was evident from his chase of the fleeing rabbits. Struggling to spot anyone in the vast wilderness with his small torch, he sighed and slumped to the ground. He pressed his hands against the ground to lift himself up after his patience gave way to disappointment. Suddenly, he felt the familiar snuggle of a furry coat against his leg. He turned his face to see Mona's glistening red eyes staring at him.

WORD FROM THE AUTHOR

Thank you for reading The Bird That Ruled Bombay! It has been an honor to share this story with you, and I am endlessly grateful to everyone who decided to embark on this adventure.

Born in Mumbai and raised near Delhi, I was always fascinated by the idea of countless untold stories hidden in the centuries-old palaces and forts that I visited as a child.

While studying data science, I imagined how fun it would be to apply it to decipher extinct languages or unravel historical mysteries (instead of the mundane conventional applications they teach you in school).

Growing up, I always noticed an intense rivalry between the sciences and the arts. I wanted to imagine another world where this rivalry gave way to a powerful collaboration. That's why the characters in the book combine their knowledge across disciplines to solve the mysteries together. I truly believe that when people with unique strengths decide to join forces, it can lead to wonders.

If possible, I hope you would consider leaving a review wherever you purchased the book from and on Goodreads. I love to hear thoughts about the book from my readers.

Feel free to follow me on social media platforms to join my writing journey and for some amazing book recommendations. You can also check out my website arnavbooks.com to join my mailing list and stay updated on the latest releases and offers.

Instagram - @arnav_author

Facebook - @Arnav_author

www.ingramcontent.com/pod-product-compliance
Lightning Source LLC
Chambersburg PA
CBHW060656190726
48289CB00002B/427